MAGGIE ANN MARTIN

THE BIG F DISCARD

Swoon READS

NEW YORK

For Mom, Dad, and Abbie
(and Scooter, too!).

Also to my Grandma Kathleen.
She would have thought this
was the coolest thing ever.

A SWOON READS BOOK

An imprint of Feiwel and Friends, a part of Macmillan Publishing Group, LLC.
175 Fifth Avenue, New York, NY 10010.

Our books may be purchased in bulk for promotional, educational, or business use. Please contact your local bookseller or the Macmillan Corporate
and Premium Sales Department at (800) 221-7945 ext. 5442 or by e-mail at
MacmillanSpecialMarkets@macmillan.com.

Library of Congress Cataloging-in-Publication Data is available.

ISBN 978-1-250-12321-3 (trade paperback) / ISBN 978-1-250-12322-0
(ebook)

Book design by Carol Ly

First Edition—2017

1 3 5 7 9 10 8 6 4 2

swoonreads.com

<u>FAILURE</u>:

somebody or something that
is unsuccessful.

LIFE CAN BE A LITTLE WEIRD WHEN YOUR MOM IS A PSYCHIC IN OHIO. And not the witchy, crystal-ball-reading psychic—a college psychic, helping budding students find their perfect school. Call it hokey, but kids come from all over the Great Plains states to get an hour with my mom. It's pretty ironic, then, that I managed to earn a rejection letter from the school I was destined to attend.

The second letter revoking my admission to Ohio State in the fall sat tucked under my mattress, the prime hiding spot for my every teenage secret. I failed my senior English course, of all things. After a series of unfortunate events, including a complete misunderstanding of my final assignment and an unforgiving teacher, I didn't pass the class—the one class that

1

Ohio State required for my major in "New Media and Technology," whatever that meant.

"Ohio State is a perfect fit for you, Danielle," my mom had said. "I've been able to observe you your whole life; my reading for you is going to be spot-on."

I trusted her. She did know me better than I knew myself sometimes. She could sense when I was upset, when I needed guidance, when I preferred to be left alone. Luckily for me, her senses had been consumed with new clients for the past month, and she hadn't questioned me about the perpetual and clichéd storm cloud over my head.

My mom's readings come in two phases. First, she has a one-on-one session with students where she asks them some basic questions about what they're interested in, where they think they want to go to school, what they think they want to do. Then she gets into the nitty-gritty of what students actually like, seeking out deep and repressed vibes. Like a kid who had been bred her whole life to be a doctor but dreamed of being a museum curator and should actually pursue art history. Those parents are always the worst when they hear that their pride and joy is not who they expected. Nine times out of ten, I see students walk out of our home with relief on their faces. Even if my mom really isn't a psychic—if she's just really good at reading people and knows a lot about colleges—it's comforting to know that someone can validate your future.

Slipping on my fuzzy socks, I headed downstairs to find my mom leading a group out the front door. The family was all smiles, so this must have been a very nonconfrontational session. I slinked into the kitchen and stayed out of sight. There were pictures of us hanging from every angle of the house, but when Mom had clients over, we were to stay invisible. Staying invisible was easier for me than it was for my dad and brother, who liked to watch early morning cartoons at full volume. You'd think that since Noah was fourteen now they would have shaken that habit, but when I opened the door to the kitchen, the sound of the Road Runner accosted me.

They barely looked up as I walked in. I went over and kissed my dad on the side of his head and reached to refill his coffee mug. This one said "Greetings from Oahu!" with chipped palm trees winding up the handle. My grandparents were huge travelers, and the X marking their current vacation spot was a cheap mug in the mail. I grabbed a mug that said "Someone from Paris Loves Me," remembering the year that my grandparents lived in France. It was the longest they stayed in one place my entire life, and the memories of one summer there when I was fourteen grounded me in my desire to travel.

"Mom's working, you know," I told them both.

"It was an emergency session; she's done now," Dad said.

"Emergency session" was code for a kid who had waited until the last minute to apply anywhere. On top of Mom's knowledge of colleges, she also held a bit of clout when it came to admissions. She could usually work some magic to get admissions to take another look at an application and knew the right things for kids to write in their appeal letters. After she was a student at Ohio State (go figure) she worked in their admissions office for a few years before hopping around to other colleges. She made so many connections from moving around that she started to realize that she could recommend schools based on all the experience she had. She started out with the neighborhood gang of soon-to-be college students when I was the ripe old age of twelve, and the rest is history.

"It's all hands on deck for dinner tonight," Dad said. "Aunt Rachel and Claire are coming."

My aunt and her angelic daughter only came by the house for one of two reasons: they had something they wanted to brag about or something they needed sympathy for. More often than not, Claire came for her bragging rights. We had dinner when Claire was voted homecoming princess, when she got her swanky internship at *Teen Gleam Magazine*, and when she got into Northwestern—the school that my mom had so perfectly helped her find.

"And you're all staying to eat?" I asked.

"No way," Noah responded, finally looking up from the TV. "Dad's taking me to acting class tonight."

"I can drive you to acting class," I said. "I'll get us ice cream and a puppy after."

"Nice try," Dad said, turning off the TV. "Your cousin will be happy to see you. She's only back in Denton for the weekend."

"I don't think she's ever particularly happy to see me," I said.

"I don't think she's ever happy to see anyone," Noah said. I sent him a mental fist bump of sibling solidarity.

"Who are we talking about?" Mom asked as she made her way into the kitchen.

"Oh, you know, the Queen of England," I said. "I've heard she's kind of a diva."

"The queen?" Mom raised her eyebrows.

"That's what the rumor mill is churning out these days, Mom; you should really tap into pop culture more often," I said. She could see through my BS but chose not to say anything. "How was the emergency session? They seemed smiley."

"Just a run-of-the-mill late application. Very minor work on my end," she said. "The good news is, now we have more time to get ready for dinner. Danielle . . . I know you and Claire have your problems—"

"Dad already warned me. I'm mentally preparing myself. Though I would be really okay with taking Noah to his class tonight if that makes things easier for everyone."

She crossed her arms. "Can't you ever do something nice for me without complaining or trying to get out of it?"

"I'm kidding, I promise," I said, holding up my hands.

Dad and Noah sat in tense silence trying to find their way out of the room and the awkwardness.

"Why don't you and Noah go to the store and grab a few things for me?" she asked. The family took a collective breath as the tension lifted.

"Sure," I said. "Make me a list and check it twice!"

She wasn't amused. Noah left the room to change out of his pajamas, and I took his exit as my cue to leave as well. I closed my bedroom door behind me and sank against the door. The lie of my rejection was bubbling inside me, and I felt like the truth would explode out of me. It could quite possibly kill my mom. Sure, she'd probably have an emergency plan in place, but it seemed pretty hopeless. My room was already stacked to the brim with Ohio State–embellished dorm room merchandise, including a rather comfortable toilet seat cover. I flopped onto my bed, my hand reaching to that space in between the bedframe and the mattress where my shame hid. I opened it up one more time, thinking that the words from the dean of admissions would magically change by positive thinking.

Dear Ms. Cavanaugh,

It is with great regret that I inform you that we will not be accepting your application to Ohio State University this fall. After a thorough review of your final transcript by our admissions board, your final grades did not match the stipulated grades for our competitive New Media and Communication Technology program.

If you wish to retake the classes in which the competency levels were not reached, you may apply again for admission in the spring. More than 10 percent of our students join classes in the spring semester and are still able to complete their degree within the four-year time span.

Thank you for your interest in Ohio State University, and we hope to see your amended application in the spring.

Dr. Caroline Bates

Dr. Caroline Bates

Dean of Admissions

Ohio State University

Over the past month, I'd come up with elaborate schemes to get rid of the letter. I could burn it, feed it to the neighbor's dog, turn it into confetti in the paper shredder—but nothing seemed to resonate. One of my favorite units in elementary school was this "Crafts Around the World" program, where we worked on a project that was inspired by a different country each week. The best week was Japan, when our class made paper crane strings that wound around the ceiling of our classroom for the rest of the year. The colors always stayed in my mind, and even now I sometimes make paper cranes when I feel stressed out or in need of focus. I tore off the bottom of the letter, leaving the paper in the perfect square shape to start creating the crane. Memory wasn't normally my strong suit, but the folding technique of the crane came back to me instantly.

When I finished, it seemed much smaller than I thought it

would be. I couldn't read the words that haunted me anymore. They jumbled together into nonsense that looked sort of beautiful.

"Shall we start shopping for the dinner of doom?" Noah asked, popping his head into my room. I quickly placed the paper crane on my bedside table and hopped off my bed.

"Let me throw a sweater on, and then we'll roll," I told him.

He nodded and left, and I took the crane back into my hand. I could have sent it flying out my window and watched it float away, but I placed it on the top of my bookshelf instead. Even though it was probably around eighty degrees outside, there was something comforting about wearing a sweater. Also, I think my blood circulation is shoddy—I'm always freezing. If it were socially acceptable to carry a blanket around in public, I probably would.

The door to Mom's office was closed when I came back downstairs, but her grocery list was on the counter alongside the keys for our family minivan. Driving the minivan was a special treat. It should have gone into retirement years ago, but my dad refused to get rid of it. I call it the Jankmobile for numerous reasons, one of which is the gross kick of exhaust it puffs out each time you turn the car on.

I wasn't super disappointed about having to go to the store because it meant I had an excuse to see my best friend, Zoe. She started working at Freeman's Market when she was probably too young, and she was promoted to shift manager two years ago. Being shift manager meant she could sneak her best friend and her best friend's little brother reject donuts if they asked nicely for them.

"What's on the list, Noah Man?" I asked.

"Chicken breasts—the nice kind behind the counter—peppers, onions, mushrooms, and spinach noodles," he said.

"Spinach noodles?" I asked.

"Apparently Claire is gluten-free," he said.

"Of course she is."

Freeman's Market wasn't terribly crowded, but I figured we'd see at least ten people we knew just walking in. Denton wasn't a Podunk, everyone-knows-everyone type of town, but it was one of the smaller suburbs of Cleveland. You were bound to see a familiar face wherever you went. I squirted some hand sanitizer on the handle of our cheap basket before picking it up and heading straight for the bakery.

Zoe hated wearing her uniform while she was working in the bakery. They had a mandatory hairnet rule (for good reason), and the all-white uniform clashed with every overly colorful outfit Zoe picked out for the day. I spotted her working meticulously on frosting cupcakes, a job that only she had the patience for. Zoe was happiest when she was being creative. Her hands had permanent damage from many a hot-glue-gun burn. Crafting was her favorite destressing activity.

"I would like to place a complaint with the shift manager," I told one of the young workers at the front of the bakery. The look of horror on her face confirmed that she did not recognize me or appreciate my sense of humor. The poor girl flitted back to Zoe, who wiped her hands on her apron and smiled my way when she saw me.

"I'm taking a break, Claudia. Don't let anything burn down," she told the girl. Zoe flung her apron off and ducked under the bakery counter to join us. She turned around and grabbed two donuts with smudged frosting that were misshapen and handed them to Noah and me.

"To what do I owe this pleasure?" she asked.

"We're on food duty for a Claire dinner tonight," I said.

She cringed appropriately. "I made an awesome pear cake this morning if you would like to offer it as a sign of peace?"

"Not even your baking can offer the peace we need to have a civil dinner," I said. "The little brother over here has managed to get out of it, twerp."

"Hey, I just got lucky that my acting class was at the same time," he said.

"But who will make faces with me when Claire makes a backhanded comment?" I asked.

"I'm sure you can manage for one night," he said.

"So, pear cake, yea or nay?" Zoe asked.

"I mean, what can it hurt at this point," I said. She ducked back under the counter and emerged with a simple cake that hadn't been frosted yet. Quickly she spread some sort of white icing all over the cake, spinning it on one of those cake wheels that you see in reality TV baking shows. She placed the cake in a box and put a big discount mark on the top for us to use when we checked out.

"You're an angel," I told her. I put Noah on cake-carrying

duty as a tiny punishment for leaving me alone for the impending dinner of doom.

Something clanged loudly from the back of the bakery, and Claudia yelped.

"That's my cue," Zoe said, ducking back under the counter. "My shift ends at six. Call me if you want to vent about it afterward over a basket of Moe's fries."

I saluted her. "You can probably count on it. Thanks again for the cake."

She waved at us before rushing back to help Claudia, who seemed to be trapped under a fallen drying rack.

Noah and I cruised through the store, only having to ask for some help when it came to the spinach noodles. Apparently Freeman's Market has an entire organic and health food section that I didn't even know existed. I prefer my food chock-full of gluten and inorganic materials.

When we made it home, the fancy tablecloth covered our beaten wooden table and Mom was in the process of pulling out the nice dishes from the cabinet above the fridge that no one can ever reach. Was Claire winning Miss America? Noah made a quick exit with my father to head off to acting class, and he gave me one final thumbs-up before he left.

"Can you grab the plates and set them on the table?" Mom asked, blowing off a layer of dust bunnies from the top plate.

"Sure; how many?" I asked. It was usually a toss-up if Uncle Brad would join us. I think Uncle Brad has enough Aunt Rachel time at home without involving her obnoxious extended family.

"Five, please," she said, a little smile creeping onto her face.

"So Uncle Brad is braving it today, huh?"

"Not quite," she said, her smile getting bigger. "Your cousin is bringing someone to dinner! Isn't that exciting?"

Or horrible. "Who is it?"

"I think it's that boyfriend of hers from Northwestern. They're getting pretty serious, according to Rachel."

"Oh!" I said, with more inflection than I think Mom expected. Actually, this development wasn't horrible. It was really to my benefit—if the focus was on Claire and her serious boyfriend, then my failure might go unannounced. Perhaps the "Danielle Is Going to Ohio State" dinner was being renamed the "Claire Tricked a Boy into Liking Her" dinner, and for once I was completely okay with that.

"He's studying to be a doctor," she said.

Of course he was. Only Claire would be able to find herself madly in love with a doctor-to-be. After I set the table, I helped Mom with the spinach noodles and threw all the salad fixings into a bowl. We were a pretty good team as long as I didn't have to do any major cooking. I have a bit of a bad track record with the stove. Somehow my hands or forearms always end up burned one way or another. Mom only trusted me with salad prongs.

In the middle of my superb tossing, the doorbell rang. Part of me wanted to open the door and be the first to see Dr. Charming, but Mom was too excited for me to take that away from her. She skipped to the door in a way she only does when Noah gets a new acting job. Noah's first shining, skip-worthy moment was being an extra in a toothpaste commercial. He was labeled as Cavity Kid #2 and had to smile with a mouthful of gauze in the back of the dentist's office. We were pretty proud.

"Oh hello! Come in, come in!" Mom said from the door, her voice reaching new octaves in her excitement.

"Thank you," said a deep voice I assumed to be the boyfriend's, unless Aunt Rachel had started anabolic steroids. I joined Mom by the front door.

"Hi, Dani, you look cute," Claire said, giving me a hug. How could she make "cute" sound bad? She had a gift.

"Thanks," I said.

She smiled and straightened out her pink sundress before wrapping her arm around Dr. Charming's waist. He towered over her by almost an extra foot, and he looked like he probably shared Claire's spray tan package at Tan-a-Palooza. They even shared the same dark-brown hair and eyes. He was obviously older than she was, probably by four or five years, and extremely good-looking. Almost too good-looking. Zoe and I have always agreed that it's never a good idea to have a boyfriend who's prettier than you are.

"This is Marcus," she said.

He held out his massive hand, and I took it with the firmest shake I could manage.

"Danielle, I've heard so much about you," he said. Just glorious things, I presume. I nodded and smiled politely as he shook Mom's hand. She and Aunt Rachel sent each other girly batting-of-lashes looks, and I pretended not to notice.

"Whatever my sister has cooked up for us tonight smells

delicious," Aunt Rachel said, motioning toward the kitchen. "Shall we?"

We all filed into our small pea-green kitchen. Mom instructed each of us to get our plates from the table, and she dished out the chicken and gross spinach noodles. Marcus kept up a casual conversation with Mom, reiterating how lovely her home was and how much he missed home-cooked meals from his mom. He actually seemed genuine, and I once again wondered what sort of hypnotizing power Claire held over everyone but me.

Claire could get away with anything with a flip of her hair and a quick smile. Her mom was locked under her thumb, always believing Claire's side of every story. Our feud started the moment I was brought into this world and Claire suddenly had someone to compete with for attention. The pinnacle of the Claire–Danielle feud came in my third-grade year, her fourth. We were both auditioning for the part of featured angel in our church Christmas pageant, and Claire knew how badly I wanted it. Before we auditioned for the part, Claire challenged me to a fizzy soda drinking contest. Being the girl who is always up for a good dare, I decided to take her up on it. Little did I know that every time I looked away from Claire, she was spitting out the soda. Long story short, I made a public, pee-filled spectacle of myself in front of all the kids auditioning. That year we watched Claire perform as the featured angel during Christmas Eve mass.

Once we were all seated around our white tablecloth with a still-visible cranberry sauce stain from Thanksgiving and with our good napkins tucked neatly on our laps, the conversation began with innocent pleasantries.

"Claire, I'm so glad you've brought Marcus here tonight," Mom said. Claire took Marcus's hand and smiled at him.

"I'm glad he could finally meet you, Aunt Karen," she said. "It's just so hard to find a time when we aren't caught up in all our work and can make it back to Ohio, but I'm so glad we made it tonight. His family lives here too—isn't that a wonderful coincidence?"

"How lovely! Makes traveling easier for both of you," my mom said. "How is *Teen Gleam* going?"

"So well! My boss is trying to get a new slew of mobile journalists in the Chicago area, so she's promoting me from an intern to reporter," she said. Marcus squeezed her hand.

"She hardly takes a break," he said.

"How exciting!" Mom said. She looked at me as if to say "tell her how amazing that is," but once again, I could only nod and smile. The crippling and suffocating feeling of my own failure took too much out of me in that moment. The little anxious voice in my head was starting to warn me that I should go to the bathroom or something to get away, but of course I did not listen.

"Marcus and Claire have had a lot of excitement lately," Aunt Rachel said with a devilish grin. I looked up from my plate then and saw Claire turn a little red.

"Mom," Claire said. "You know I'm keeping that a secret for a while!"

"Sorry!" Aunt Rachel grinned.

"Anyway," Claire started, "is there anything new with you, Dani?"

I shrugged and mumbled a quick "nothing" while trying not to give in to Claire's fishing for questions about her big secret. I'd played this game a few too many times—I saw right through her.

"You can't leave us hanging like that, Claire," Mom said. Claire made a big show of sighing and being bashful.

"I wanted to wait until Uncle Peter and Noah were here, but I guess we could tell you all now," she said.

I stopped chewing. Was she pregnant? No, Aunt Rachel wouldn't condone that and be jumping to tell Mom and me. If she wasn't pregnant, there could only be one thing going on. Claire fiddled with her purse hanging off the side of the chair, grabbed something inside it, and came back up.

"Marcus and I are engaged," she squealed, holding her left hand out for all to inspect. Mom hopped up from the table to hug Aunt Rachel, and they did a little happy dance together. I sat there awkwardly, to the side of all the action, not sure how I should respond. I didn't know what I felt in that moment. The feeling wasn't jealousy, but it was nowhere near happiness. I mean, Claire was only nineteen. We'd grown up together our whole lives, and while I felt like I was just starting mine, she was ready to settle down with one guy forever and already had the job of her dreams. I couldn't even pass my contemporary literature class.

"That is so wonderful, Claire!" Mom said. She gave me that same look, demanding me to join in.

"Congratulations," I said.

After the jumping and screaming ended, we sat back down to finish the bits of spinach noodles we'd all pushed to the side of our plates to make it look as if we were eating them. Marcus and Claire kept smiling at each other, and Claire's eyes would slide to mine every once in a while, to make sure I was watching them.

"Aunt Karen, this chicken is delicious," Claire said. "But I do know that you only make it for special occasions. Did Mom spill the beans before we came?"

"Of course she didn't! The dinner was meant for our guest. Well, for him and for Danielle. She'll be leaving for her freshman year at Ohio State at the end of the summer, and I wanted to celebrate her graduation and success. Cheers, Danielle!" Mom said, holding up her glass. "And cheers to Claire and Marcus on their engagement."

I kept shoving more into my mouth, hoping that the excess food would soak up my guilt. Claire looked at me again, and I knew she could see it. She can taste fear, smell weakness, and hear my heart pounding with every lie. Her let's-get-Danielle mentality was still intact, even if she brought her shiny new fiancé to dinner as a buffer. She hadn't seen the rejection letter, but she didn't have to. She knew something was up.

"Actually, my younger brother is going to be a freshman at Ohio State next year too," Marcus said. "Do you know where you're living? Maybe you're in the same dorm."

"Um," I said, "I haven't gotten my letter yet."

"Oh, I thought Bryan got his a couple weeks ago," he said,

shaking his head. Claire stared me down again, spotting the weakness.

"I heard there's actually a dorm shortage up there now," Claire said. "Aunt Karen, I hope she didn't get waitlisted for a dorm room!"

"I hadn't heard about that yet," Mom said. "Danielle, did you get an e-mail about this? I want to call and ask them what the holdup is."

My armpit sweat was seriously soaking through my shirt, and my hands started to shake. The lie that I had bottled up so perfectly was bubbling and bursting inside me, and I felt like I could throw up. I'm a terrible liar, and now the one lie that had eaten me up for the past month was going to explode in front of my perfect cousin and her sexy new fiancé.

"Mom, I think I accidentally threw the letter away," I said, the lie somehow still able to come out even though my stomach crawled as the words left my mouth.

"You should have a university account with all the info on it," Claire said, handing me her smartphone. "Just log on and check."

The phone shook in my hands. "I don't remember my log-in info now; I'll just do it after—"

"Just put in your e-mail and reset your password," Claire said with more force.

"Claire," Aunt Rachel warned.

I messed with the phone for a few seconds and then tried to hand it back to Claire. "Really, we'll just do it later when—"

"I won't be able to sleep if I don't know you have a room next year, Dani. Please, find it," she said in her voice that was the subtlest mix of sweet and evil. Her eyes were hard, staring at me in the way that showed her premature victory. It wasn't enough for her to come engaged and with a new job, she had to humiliate me too.

"I-I don't have a log-in," I said.

"But every student does," she said.

"I haven't gotten mine yet," I said.

"That's interesting, Dani, everyone else has theirs," she said, her voice finally reaching its normal tone. Maybe it would do some good to have Dr. Charming see her at her finest moment of devilry.

"Sometimes these things take time and—"

"No, not really." She smiled.

"Claire!" Aunt Rachel hissed again. Marcus had started to put his arm around her to get her to stop, but she kept plowing ahead.

"You never got accepted, did you, Dani?" she asked, that same horrible smirk on her face.

"Claire, honey, sit down," Marcus said.

"What kind of accusation are you making, Claire? Of course she got accepted. I saw the letter last fall, and we've had it hanging on the fridge ever since," Mom said. "I wanted to make a great dinner for you and your fiancé, and you come here and accuse your own cousin of something horrible—"

"Mom," I said.

"She doesn't lie," Mom continued. "You know better than to think twice about Danielle's character—"

"Mom," I tried again.

"I would appreciate it if you would apologize to your cousin right—"

"Stop!" I yelled. Everyone turned to me at once. Claire still had her arms crossed, and her face was bright red. Mom's mouth stayed open as she looked at me, and Marcus looked like a bewildered puppy.

"She's right," I whispered.

"What?" Mom asked. No one moved, and the silence that hung in the air stung my ears.

"I didn't pass English, and Ohio State revoked my acceptance," I said.

Nothing can describe the feeling of your mother's disappointment and your cousin's vehement hatred rolling over you all at once. The tears were already falling down my face, and I knew that if I didn't leave soon my sadness and embarrassment would explode all over the dining room, leaving no survivors in its wake. I took another look around the table before I ran upstairs.

All the air seemed to seep out of my room, so to breathe again, I climbed out my window and onto the roof. I curled my arms around my legs, allowing myself to cry. Everything had finally fallen apart. Mom knew, Claire knew, and now I finally had to admit it to myself. I couldn't pretend that it would work out or put off the discussion for another day. My failure was here, in my face, and ready to punch me in the gut repeatedly. I pulled out my phone and called the one person who can solve any crisis.

"Zoe? Come pick me up? It's an emergency."

She was on her way before I finished my sentence.

<u>FATE</u>:

the force or principle believed
to predetermine events.

"WOULD IT MAKE YOU FEEL BETTER IF WE DOOR-DINGED HIS BEEMER?" Zoe asked as we pulled out of my driveway. Though it was tempting, I knew I couldn't punish Marcus for the horrid nature of my cousin. Surprisingly, the family stayed after our little battle royale to help Mom clean up. I watched them through the kitchen window after I shimmied my way down the front of the house. I actually have never had to sneak out of the house, but I've always known that my room would be epic for it, with the low roof and the rain gutter underneath my window. Up until now, I also never failed classes, but not having a future was making me a rebel, I suppose.

"I don't care what we do, I just want to get out of here," I said.

Zoe complied, speeding out of my cul-de-sac and onto the highway. As she drove, she subconsciously sucked on the tip of her thumb, probably nursing a new blister from her hot glue gun or another hole from a stapling incident. She has a bit of an addiction to crafting when she's stressed out or fighting with her mom, and I knew it couldn't be good when I saw her backseat. It looked like she stole the contents of Martha Stewart's house and threw it in the car in time to make a quick getaway. Thankfully, for both our sakes, we didn't press much out of each other until we pulled into the parking lot of our favorite diner: Moe's.

Moe's wasn't your average diner in the grimy, greasy way that is usually associated with diners. Moe's tried its hand at sophistication with black leather booths and beige walls, making for a very minimalist-with-a-touch-of-quaint restaurant. Denton, Ohio, didn't really scream cuisine capital, but the few places that we did have were nice. Denton's marketability expanded with new restaurants and stores after the community college was built.

We ordered a pot of coffee and an endless basket of fries to split from one of our favorite waitresses. When Moe's was really slow, Laurie would join us, but people crowded the diner on this Friday night. Even though school wasn't in session, the Denton Community College kids that either lived with their parents or worked in Denton over the summer partied hard together every Friday night. Moe's was just a pit stop.

"So what did the wicked witch do this time?" Zoe asked, popping a fry into her mouth.

I sighed. "She found out that I'd been lying about something. No, nothing you know about."

"A secret withheld from your best friend? This better be pretty damn good," she said.

"It's not that I didn't want to tell you, it's just . . . I didn't really want to admit it to myself yet," I said, looking down.

"Are you pregnant?" she asked.

I laughed. "Oh yeah, with all my sexual partners, I could feasibly be pregnant."

"Just saying, you're being really shady about it," she said. "What the heck happened?"

I paused again, pouring myself some more coffee. "My acceptance to Ohio State was revoked after my final transcripts were sent in."

Her eyebrows furrowed. "What? How?"

"I failed Franco's AP lit class," I said.

Zoe's face was still contorted. "Everyone and their dog was in that class. How did you fail?"

"I didn't turn in my most stellar work, okay? I couldn't think of anything to write about for the final paper; everything came out like jumbled mess, and it barely even made it in on time. You know how I'm terrible at working under pressure. I didn't think Franco would *fail* me for one paper, but he said that I showed a 'distinct lack of progress' throughout the class 'without asking for help,'" I said, air quotes included.

"How did you graduate high school without that credit?" she asked.

"It was AP—an extra class to get me directly into the program at Ohio State. My mom thought it would be this great way to get me ahead of the game, but it just screwed me over.

The grade made my GPA plummet, so they couldn't accept me on merit either," I said.

"And you didn't think to ask me for any help? Or your mom? She gets paid to help kids write letters, Dan," she said.

The same suffocating, air-compressing-in-my-lungs feeling started again, and I tried to focus on the salt and pepper shakers across the table from me. Breathe in four seconds, breathe out five. Hands flat on the table. Breathe in four, out five.

"Hey," she said, reaching over to take my hand. "I didn't mean to stress you out. I'm just a little shocked that your mom wouldn't have pulled some strings for you to get back in already."

I just shook my head, my voice falling down my throat and lodging itself in my chest. If I tried to talk now, everything would come out in a sloppy and incoherent sob.

Zoe tapped my foot under the table, urging me to look up from the salt and pepper and at her. "You could have told me about this, you know."

I nodded, keeping up with my breathing regimen throughout.

"What are you going to do?" she asked.

I hadn't given much thought to what I'd do. I could always take the semester off, get a job in town, maybe at Moe's, and apply for the spring semester later. Or I could curl up in my bedroom and watch Netflix for the rest of my life while Noah made me PB&Js until I died. Either option sounded okay with me.

"I don't know," I said.

A loud group of Denton Community College partiers flowed in through the door behind us, a few of the girls singing a horrible radio pop song in about three different keys. Zoe poured more coffee while I people-watched. At the back of the group was a tall guy walking by himself. He looked familiar, but I hadn't had a chance to see his face yet. He played with his phone idly and looked at the group lazily, responding to his friends every once in a while.

"Danielle, you're hard-core staring," she said, snapping my focus back to our conversation.

"Sorry, I thought I recognized him," I said. Zoe turned around with the subtlety of a five-year-old, and the boy decided to take that moment to turn his head our way. His eyes were the first thing I noticed. They were a color of blue that you couldn't possibly forget. His face had changed, lost some baby fat, but Luke Upton was the same eleven-year-old boy who hid toads in my backyard playhouse and devastated me when he moved away.

She smiled at him foolishly, and I let my frizzy bangs fall in front of my eyes. When she turned around, her smile was even bigger. "Well, now I don't blame you for being a stalker."

"I'm not a stalker," I hissed. Even though it was loud in Moe's I felt the need to whisper, in case Luke could hear us somehow. "That's Luke Upton, my old neighbor. I didn't know he had friends here still."

Zoe turned around to look at him again, and I kicked her shin under the table. She cursed at me and faced me once more.

"He's wearing a DCC T-shirt. Are you sure he doesn't go here?"

I scoffed. "That's impossible—his mom would have called my mom if they were back."

"Maybe it's just him," she said.

"Maybe," I said, still staring. I reached for the coffeepot but paused as his eyes met mine for an actual length of time. He gave me the look, like he knew who I was but couldn't quite place me. All I could do was smile back as casually as I could manage.

His last friend got his food, and the group started to pack up. My face probably resembled a tomato. We kept our intense gaze as he left, and he stopped near our table. I almost thought he was going to say something—that he'd realized how he knew me—but he followed his band of party animals outside.

"A little unresolved neighborly business there, Dan?" Zoe asked once he left.

"No more than the average neighbor," I said. At least I hadn't thought so. The name Luke Upton hadn't even crossed my mind in over seven years.

"Whatever," she said. She smiled her wicked grin again and took a sip of coffee. "But I do have an idea for you that is completely unrelated to your ex-neighbor-boyfriend-hot-guy. Come with me to DCC this semester."

"What?" I asked.

"Come be my community college buddy. I need moral support, and I don't feel quite as selfish asking now," she said.

"Do you think they'll let me in—"

"Danielle, DCC will let you make up missing AP credits, so you could totally go to Ohio State in the spring if you finish the English class here. And then we can be freshmen together and save each other from the freshmen fifteen or be designated drivers—"

"Because we went to so many parties in high school," I interjected. Zoe scowled.

"College is going to be different, Danielle, I can feel it. Can you imagine being at the same school again? That would be so much fun!" she said. Zoe and I did have a ridiculous amount of fun together, and though I'd never thought to consider DCC as an option since I'd been born and bred an OSU fan, I warmed up to the idea more as we discussed it.

"I guess it would be, but my parents were so set on Ohio State. It's the Reevis-Cavanaugh legacy to go to OSU. I mean, my mom probably has an emergency plan in place. I'm sure she's making calls right now to try and get me an appeal interview," I said. "I have no idea how I'm going to tell my dad."

"Well lucky for you, your bee-otch of a cousin already did the job for you. Now comes the asking for forgiveness and crying," she said. "Maybe they'll look at it like my mom does—it's a character-building school that teaches you about responsibility. I've already taught Alyssa that there's no use slacking off in school. If you want to leave Denton in our family, you have to get a scholarship. God, I wish I figured that out sooner."

Zoe's mom took care of Zoe and her little sister, Alyssa, by herself, and had done so for as long as I'd known them. While Sara Cabot rocked the whole single mom gig, money was always tight with them. Zoe had worked at Freeman's Market for her entire high school career to pay for her car and anything else she wanted outside her mom's budget (which included her enormous amounts of crafting supplies). Denton Community College opened doors for Zoe without piling on heaps of debt. Zoe has gotten over the fact that she couldn't feasibly afford even in-state colleges, but the fact that Zoe, who was destined to be a fashion/home décor designer, couldn't go to the school of her dreams wasn't fair.

"Is everything okay? Your car is a bit of a craft tornado," I said, recalling the explosion in her backseat.

"Oh yeah, just the same old stuff with Alyssa," she said. Alyssa had reached the same age as Noah, but where Noah channeled his fourteen-year-old angst into acting, Alyssa channeled hers onto Zoe and Sara. Her latest display of angst involved ruining one of Zoe's newly crafted tables and calling her a loser.

"What happened?" I asked.

"Nothing. I don't want to talk about it," she said. Zoe downed the last of her coffee in a large gulp and slammed the mug onto the table. "Let's do something fun, Danielle! I need a distraction, pronto."

My mind drifted back to Luke Upton and the group of pre-buzzed, hormone-filled college students undoubtedly heading to a party. The thought of going home right now made me want to disappear. Heck, we both wanted to avoid home right now. A small part of my brain started chanting "party, party!" and the usually rational part of my brain agreed. Luke Upton aside, Zoe and I were going to have fun tonight against the odds.

"Did you see where Luke and his friends were going?" I asked.

"And the rebel is here to stay." Zoe smiled.

It didn't take much driving to find the mass of cars in front of an older house tucked into a tree-filled neighborhood. Zoe drove down the block and parked by the curb. We sat in her car for a minute, gathering our wits and deciding if the party was really in our best interest. Both of us were obviously past the point of wanting what was best for us. And, while that seemed like force enough to send us home, we both hopped out of the car and headed to the house party overflowing with kids.

We walked in the door and the crowd engulfed us. No one really danced like in movies; they all just stood around laughing and passing around cups. We'd been slammed into by passing people at least a dozen times, and Zoe screamed as beer splattered her feet. A kid in the room next to us yelled something and cranked up the music, inciting some casual head-bobbing.

"Ladies, no drink in hand? Everyone has a fun time at my party." A skinny, gawky guy shoved cans into our hands and moved quickly on to his next victims. Zoe threw her head back and took a sip while I held mine more for show. If Zoe planned on going all-out on her first night of rebellion, I needed to keep my can full. Zoe pulled her headband out of her hair and threw it into her purse, shaking out her curly mess of dark hair. She smiled at me again and grabbed my hand.

"Let's go dance!" she said. Out on the patio and into the backyard of the house were the dancers. The bass of club-type songs beat loudly, and I wondered how their neighbors kept from calling the cops for noise disturbances. She pulled me onto the grassy area where sweaty bodies pressed up against each other, and I gagged as my arm wiped past a few of them. Zoe's empty can hit the grass so she could dance, and when I matched her idea, mine splattered over my pants and on the couple behind us. The guy yelled, and I apologized profusely. Zoe just laughed.

"Don't worry about that! Just dance!" she said. Where Zoe possessed the ability to dance in a semi-cool fashion, I did not. My go-to "robot in a grocery store" dance routine was not as big of a crowd pleaser as anticipated. To make matters more awkward, a guy came up and started to dance with Zoe, and I was left to third wheel it up with them.

"I'm going to get another drink!" I yelled at her. She waved her hand to tell me to go, and she turned around to face the guy.

I wove my way back out of the bodies and into the house, where things had cleared out even more. I found the kitchen and looked around for cups but couldn't find any. Seeing no other solution, I grabbed a beer can and started to dump its contents down the sink. After it was emptied, I swished water in it before filling it up again with water and taking a drink. When I turned around I almost spit out all the water in my mouth.

"I think the point is to drink what's already *inside* the can," Luke Upton said.

I laughed a little. "Haven't you heard? All the cool kids dig watered-down poison now."

He actually laughed at that, making his face crinkle around those blue eyes. After his laughter subsided, he gave me the I-should-know-you look again. I weighed my options in this moment. Option 1: I could let him out of his misery and tell him who I was. This could lead to an outcome of either excitement or disappointment. In an effort to avoid his possible disappointment in realizing I was the eleven-year-old neighbor who had had a horribly obvious crush on him throughout our childhood, I went with Option 2: Pretend that I don't recognize him either.

"Obviously," he said. "And to think I was drinking mine like this all the time."

I shifted, leaning up against the sink. "So do you go to DCC?" I asked.

"Starting this semester," he said. "You?"

"Considering it," I said. "Though I don't know if this is quite extreme enough for me."

"Oh don't worry, I've heard Cody's been known to throw some extreme sober parties too," Luke said.

I took a sip of beer-water. "Really?"

"Nah. I've only lived here for a month, and I already know

the words 'Cody' and 'sober' don't ever belong together," he said.

It was my turn to laugh as he ran a nervous hand through his wavy white-blond hair. His muscle flashed as the sleeve of his DCC shirt fell down a bit, and I suddenly felt self-conscious about my outfit choice. His confused look persisted for another second before I changed the subject again.

"Since you're the first person at DCC I've met so far, give me five reasons to come next year," I said.

Luke whistled. "You're putting me on the spot here!"

"I need a high dedication level if I'm really considering it," I said, crossing my arms.

"Well . . . the classes are good, I guess," he said, laughing. "Sorry, sorry, that was weak, I know. The kids are pretty cool. Um . . . the parties are awesome. The food's decent, and of course, *I* go here."

"Of course." I smiled. "But you forgot to mention that Moe's is a block away."

He stared at me again. "I saw you there tonight."

"Oh yeah," I said, shrugging. "What a coincidence."

"Yeah," he repeated. We stared at each other for a long time before I was interrupted by the thought of drunken Zoe by herself outside.

"Thanks for the advice," I said, walking away.

"Wait," he said, grabbing my arm. "What's your name?"

"I think you already know who I am," I said, winking. "See you later, Luke."

As I turned my back I let out the largest breath of my life.

Had I actually been flirty and mysterious with a guy? An extremely hot guy? Maybe DCC gave me a new sort of power over my helplessly awkward fumbling. Or perhaps the fates had shown me the good that my failure could bring. I never thought I'd say it, but Denton Community College seemed perfect.

FINAL:

conclusive and allowing no
further discussion.

**GETTING BACK INTO THE HOUSE WAS GOING TO BE
NOWHERE NEAR AS FUN AS SNEAKING OUT.** I dropped a
mildly intoxicated Zoe off at her house and drove her car back
to mine as slowly as possible. I circled my cul-de-sac at least
five times before pulling up just outside my driveway. A small
light flickered in my kitchen window, warning me that my
parents were watching TV in the living room. They'd waited
up for me. I took a deep breath, unlocked the car doors, and
walked toward my angry parental fate.

The quiet house creaked under my feet, and I cursed. They
would hear me. As if on cue, footsteps grew louder from the
kitchen. Mom and Dad emerged from around the corner, both
in their pajamas, both fairly expressionless. They motioned
for me to sit on the couch in the living room. Dad turned off the

TV and stayed standing in front of me. It was subtle, but standing up was a way to show more power over me. He crossed his arms and turned to Mom before he spoke.

"I think it goes without saying that sneaking out is unacceptable," Dad said. "Where have you been?"

"I was at Zoe's," I said, picking at my nails. Trying to distract myself with anything to keep from looking at them.

"You smell like a brewery," Mom said. "I know Sara would not let you drink like that at her house."

"We started at her house and went to someone else's. I swear, I'm not drunk. Someone spilled his drink on me," I said.

"Is this supposed to excuse everything that's happened tonight?" Mom asked.

"No, I'm just clarifying one thing so I'm not charged for it later in my sentencing," I said. As soon as it left my mouth I regretted it. I saw my mom's hands ball up into frustrated fists. She breathed in deeply through her nose and out her mouth, looking at Dad to take over the conversation.

"I guess we're a little confused, Danielle," Dad said. "You've always been honest with us. We taught you to be honest with us."

"It's not that I didn't want to be honest," I said. He held up his hand.

"You let your mother buy all your dorm things, we bought student tickets for you already—how could you let it go this far?" he asked.

"We will have to get started on damage control tomorrow. It's going to be challenging, but I can call in to Ohio State in the morning and see about a delayed appeal process. We can change your major, fit the requirements a bit better. I'm sure there's—"

"Stop trying to fix things for me," I said. "I messed up, and I'm going to fix it."

"Danielle, my job is to help students get into college. I can't have my daughter setting an example of failure for the rest of my business."

"Karen—" my dad interjected.

"You realize how serious this is, don't you, Danielle? This needs to be remedied immediately, and I will see to it that it happens," she said.

"No," I said, shaking my head again.

"No?" she asked, crossing her arms.

"I'm going to retake the class at DCC this semester, and I'm going to get a job to make up for the lost money," I said.

"You would go to DCC just to prove that you don't need my help?" she asked.

"I want to fix it on my own. I messed up, and I should do something about it," I said, my voice rising to a new pitch.

She stared at me for a long time, and I sensed her mind turning, looking for the best and most cutting comeback. Instead, she looked at my dad and said, "I'll be in our room," and turned to leave without looking back. My dad and I sat perfectly still in the living room, waiting to hear her door slam. Once it did, I breathed out a shaking breath and felt tears start to sting my eyes.

"Are you sure this is what you want to do, kid?" Dad asked.

I nodded but felt more unsure than ever. Was I making the right decision? Should I have let my mom work some of her college psychic magic and get me in through the back door?

"I know you probably already guessed, but you're very much grounded. And on Noah-driving duties for the fore-seeable future," he said. "I like that you have a plan and that you're finally taking some responsibility. I just wish you would have told us. It would have saved your mother and me a lot of heartache."

He slinked up to their bedroom as I sat staring at our family picture hanging over the mantel. I wished I could write "this is a lie" underneath all our smiling faces. She kept it there for show, to give some semblance of normalcy throughout her unconventional job. I remembered a time, it had to be almost five years ago, when my mom was being featured on the local news for her success and they had come to interview the family. She told us to keep smiling and let her do the talking. If they asked us a question, we needed to be positive about the business. We couldn't talk about being banished to our rooms when people were over or being woken up by late-night emergency calls from desperate parents. I hated it most of the time. She started this job to be at home while Noah and I were still in school, but I see less of her than I do of my best friend, who lives fifteen minutes across town.

The tears I'd managed to hold back for the majority of the night were finally catching up to me. I let them fall into my hands, my legs curled up underneath me on the couch.

"Dani?" I heard from the top of the stairs. Noah tiptoed

down and joined me. He held out an arm for me to rest my head on his shoulder. Even though Noah was only fourteen, he sometimes felt like he was forty. He always knew the right things to say to cheer me up and had this wisdom that I had no clue where it came from.

"Did Mom tell you about me tarnishing the family name?" I asked.

"I heard bits and pieces," he said.

"I've felt so sick about it for so long, Noah. And it makes it one hundred times worse that Claire was the one to call me out on it," I said.

He hugged my shoulders tighter. "You're not the first person to keep secrets from her parents. They'll get over it. You'll get over it. It's not the end of the world."

"I don't think Mom will ever get over it," I said, another sob rolling through my body.

"She will. You're both so stubborn that it might take a while, but she will," he said. "Besides, it sounds like you have a plan. Mom is always game for a thought-out plan."

He leaned down to make me look him in the eyes. "You know it will be okay, right?"

"I guess," I said.

He smiled wide and let his arm fall from around my shoulders.

"Wait." I grabbed his chin and pulled his face back to eye level. "Smile again. You have a spinach noodle stuck in your front teeth. Did you even brush your teeth tonight?"

"I must have forgotten," he said, picking it out.

"You are so foul," I said, smacking his arm.

"Want a kiss?" he asked.

"No," I yelled, running up the stairs. "Get away from me!"

===

It wasn't that I was embarrassed about driving the minivan, but our old Jankmobile was always tricky to start. I sat in our driveway for a good three minutes trying to get our POS car a movin' until the engine came to life. I could barely see out the back from the piles of dorm necessities I was returning.

Today I decided to get the ball rolling on all my Denton Community College plans. I was going to sign up for classes and apply for whatever jobs they had left. Mom and Dad didn't even ask me to find a job, but if I was going to be forced to live at home for another semester, I would do whatever it took to stay away for as much time as possible. As I pulled into the department store parking lot, my phone buzzed in my pocket. It was Zoe.

> **ZOE:** You better have my car.
> **ME:** I'll drive it over later. Go back to bed, Sleeping Beauty.

When I left her at home last night she passed out easily on her bed. Her mom would be in for a very un-Zoe-like reception this morning. At the time of the party it didn't seem like Zoe drank much, but she's a tiny person—like barely five feet tall. I'm pretty sure even a couple ounces of alcohol could put her over. I wondered if I even consumed close to an ounce with my watered-down concoction. I tried to make it completely water, but the beery residue still sloshed around in there, making it probably even more disgusting than straight beer. Luke had laughed at me about my improvisation.

Luke. Did he know who I was by now? Or did I make a complete fool of myself for assuming that he'd finally gotten it? It wasn't like I hadn't made a fool out of myself in front of Luke before. When we used to be neighbors, his little sister, Olivia, and I were best friends. We played dolls in her backyard for as long as I could remember—until it wasn't cool anymore. Luke had been twelve at the time and really into scaring us girls. One afternoon when I went over to visit Olivia, he'd been in the backyard by himself.

"Is Liv here?" I asked.

He shook his head. "Nope. But I'm glad you're here. Let me show you something."

My heart skipped a beat, and I tried to hide my blush. Luke wanted to show me something without Olivia around. The only time we talked without her was when Olivia would walk inside to get Popsicles or go to the bathroom while we played together. The girls at my school declared him the dreamiest boy in the sixth grade, and we all agreed that whoever kissed him first would have eternal bragging rights. Now was as good a chance as any.

He tromped through the tall grass lining the fence, and I followed dutifully. We crouched around a pile of rocks at the far end of the backyard, and I looked for what he wanted to show me.

"What is it?" I asked.

He pointed to the middle of the rocks. "Can't you see it? I trapped a toad."

"Ew!" I shrieked.

His face turned up into a side smirk. "What, you don't like toads, Danielle?"

"Dani," I hissed. My face turned red, and I spun on my heel away from him. I hated my full name back then, and he knew it. I heard him giggling, and I stomped back toward my house.

"Dani, wait," he said, running up to my side. My stomach flip-flopped again, and I faced him, feeling tears stinging my eyes. "Are you crying?"

"No."

"I didn't mean to make you mad—"

"You didn't," I said, and turned around again. I couldn't stay here anymore, not if the dreamiest boy in the sixth grade saw me cry. No reputation could rebound from that.

"Liv went with my dad to go look at new houses," he said. I stopped dead in my tracks, and my heart dropped. "We have to move soon."

Real tears started to roll down my cheeks, and I knew that sounds were about to come with them. I needed to run away and not let Luke see me upset. His face scrunched up a little bit, and I could tell that he was sad too. He'd lived here his whole life, even before my family moved in. Luke awkwardly patted my shoulder, and a tiny sob escaped my lips.

"We'll come back to visit a lot," he said.

I stared straight into his eyes, not caring anymore that a combination of snot and tears ran down my face. "You promise?"

"I promise," he said.

And they kept that promise for a while. For two years after the big move Olivia and Luke visited the neighborhood during the summer. One summer Liv came back by herself, since Luke was starting football practice and couldn't leave home for that long. After that summer they both became busy with high school and activities and never made it back to Denton to their barn-red house with the Toad Motel still built in the far corner of the backyard.

As I piled my rejected dorm accessories into two carts, I felt the judgment of other shoppers coming my way. First, they would judge me for the sheer number of things that were embellished with the Ohio State logo, next for the rainbow colors of everything else that clashed terribly. But the final thing they would judge me for would be bringing it all back. I should have made copies of my rejection letter to hand out to bystanders to explain my situation. It would probably save some confusion on their part and some sanity on mine.

The teenager at the return desk was less than pleased. She smacked her gum and sighed when she saw my two carts.

"You probably won't get a full refund on this" was the first thing she said to me. Like that would change my mind and make me pack the two cartloads back into the Jankmobile. I nodded, and she slowly checked out every item, gradually putting the Ohio State furniture fortune back onto Mom's credit card.

At least this would save them money in the long run. The teenager picked up an OSU-embellished toilet seat cover I'd become rather attached to, and I reached out to grab it.

"Actually, I still want that," I said.

She raised her eyebrows and said, "Okaaay," in the most disturbed way. What? A girl can't get sentimental about toilet seat covers?

As she scanned the last of my Ohio State mugs, she printed out the receipt and blew a giant bubble with her gum. "Thank you for shopping with us."

"Oh, it was truly a pleasure," I said. The teenager rolled her eyes as I left the store.

I flung the toilet seat cover into the back of the Jankmobile, and the car started without much of a problem. Now that the barrier between my Ohio State past and my future was gone, I felt ready to conquer whatever Denton Community College had to offer me. I researched a bit about classes and signing up for DCC and found out that I only had to go into the school's admissions office to sign up with all my information. I didn't have to be accepted through a process—I was a student if I showed interest. This kind of empowered me, knowing that I was the one who dictated my future, not an unforgiving English teacher or a hundred-and-fifty-word rejection letter.

The parking lot to the DCC admissions building was pretty bare. Only a few cars dotted the edges of the lot, most likely the secretary and the counselors here to help. I reached for my transcript and diploma and headed inside. The bricks of the building looked worn down from the heavy snow during the wintertime. Ohio usually had the most brutal of weather changes, ranging from hot and humid in the summer to bitter cold and snowing in the winter. Thankfully the campus size wouldn't be much to tackle in the horrible weather when walking from class to class.

A woman with a tight blond bun on the top of her head waited at the front desk. She was engrossed in a cheesy romance novel with Fabio on the cover. His hair blew in the wind while his arm muscles flexed, holding a half-naked woman in a dramatic dip. At least she was enjoying herself. It took a small cough from me to get the woman's eyes peeled away from the book and onto mine. She blushed and dog-eared the page of her book.

"I'm so sorry," she said. "Can I help you?"

"Yeah, actually," I said, handing her my paperwork. "I'm interested in registering."

"Of course." She took my papers and clicked a few buttons on the computer before reaching for the phone. "Mr. Ollenburg? I have a student out here who would like to register. Are you available?"

She put down the phone and handed my paperwork back to me. "Just go down this hall, and his office is the second on the left."

Walking down the stark white hallway depressed me a bit. The outside looked so old but had character, while the inside had been completely redone with plain white walls and little decoration. I turned to the second room on the left and saw the first evidence of personalization on the outside of Mr. Ollenburg's office—a wire star that hung off his doorknob. The glass window on the door was blocked with dark paper that had glow-in-the-dark stars glued on. I knocked on the glass window and waited in silence until the door swung open quickly.

"Oh my God!" I yelped in surprise.

Mr. Ollenburg laughed. "Sorry, didn't mean to frighten you there. Come in! Come in!"

The inside was nothing like I expected. He had the planets in orbit on his ceiling with every type of *Star Wars* and *Star Trek* paraphernalia scattered around the office. More of the plastic stars were stuck haphazardly around the room—I'm talking everywhere. Even the pictures of his family had the little plastic stars on the frames.

"My name is Mr. Ollenburg, but you can call me Jeff," he said, holding out his hand.

"Danielle Cavanaugh," I replied. He motioned for me to sit down.

"So, a last-minute registration, Danielle?" he asked.

"Time just sort of got away from me," I said. I didn't want or need to delve into my reasoning behind the late registration, I just needed to get registered.

"All right then. Do you have your transcript?" I handed my paperwork over to him, and he eyed my grades. He set them down and started to type things into the computer, much like the receptionist had. "What's your area of interest?"

"I want to major in communications," I said. He nodded and typed some more. "But I also have to make up an AP English class from high school. Also, I might as well get some math out of the way while I'm here."

He studied my transcript for a few seconds before looking back up at me.

"AP Literature? Well, we don't have that specific class, but we have one that's close and would probably count for the same credit. It's called Literature Theory. This semester it has a focus on American literature. A lot of freshmen take the class," he said. "Are you planning on transferring the credits?"

"Yeah," I replied. "Eventually to Ohio State."

"Wonderful, wonderful!" he said. "I love a student with a plan."

If only he knew that the plan had been concocted less than twenty-four hours ago. Mr. Ollenburg shuffled around in a file drawer and pulled out a sheet of paper, filling out the same information that he typed into the computer. I took the time to gaze back up at the solar system on his ceiling. I had to admit it was pretty impressive.

"Are you a fan of space?" he asked. I tore my eyes away from the ceiling.

"Do star signs and horoscopes count?" I asked.

"I suppose so. Space has always fascinated me. Something that can exist billions of years before you and will exist for billions after you—that's just incredible. It can make you seem pretty insignificant," he said. "But it also makes you want to leave something to be remembered for as long as the planets will be, you know?"

I nodded. Because I did. Isn't that what all humans wanted? To be remembered for something? To believe that the cosmos or God or something greater than ourselves has a plan for us? When I was little I really wanted to write comic books. Noah and I would sit in the living room together while I wrote the pages and he illustrated them. I thought that my comic books would be my big accomplishment, but as I got older, things became harder. Our comic books were rough, to say the least. Now Noah was off becoming an actor, Claire was off living her dream as a writer for *Teen Gleam*—they were leaving their mark. How was I supposed to leave my mark if I lived in Denton, Ohio, for the rest of my life?

"Well, Danielle, I have you signed up for two computer science courses, a calculus course, and the Lit Theory course. Is there anything else you were interested in?"

"A job," I blurted. "Do you offer any work-study programs?"

Mr. Ollenburg nodded and clicked the mouse again. "Most kids already applied months ago for campus-based jobs, but I can see if there's anything left."

At this point I would take working as a lunch lady or cleaning the bathrooms during my off period. I needed the excuse to leave the house . . . and to help my parents pay, of course. His eyebrows rose, and a small smile crept onto his face.

"There's actually an opening at the Denton Bookstore. Someone must have quit this week—those spots always fill up quickly," he said. He scribbled something on a scrap of paper and handed it to me. "Either try going over there now or call later to see if you can apply for the job. They'll need the help as soon as possible when students start getting their books next week before classes."

I grabbed the piece of paper with the bookstore's phone number on it and thanked Mr. Ollenburg again for everything. He had also written down my DCC online information so I could print off my schedule and so I could send in tuition. The bookstore was just down the street from the admissions building, and I could walk there easily. No need to start up the Jankmobile twice before going home. The Denton Bookstore was in the strip mall that still had all the original building intact without a refurbished inside. Walking into the shop almost smelled like walking into an antique store with the musty smell of old books and moldy water stains dotting the ceiling. A bell chimed as I entered the relatively empty bookstore, aside from the middle-aged woman restocking shelves in the back. She popped up from the ladder she sat on and came to the front when she heard me enter.

"Hi there!" she said. Her sweaty hair was pulled back into a ponytail, and I didn't blame her—the lack of air-conditioning really made me sweat. There was an oscillating fan propped up on the front desk, but it hardly did anything. August in Ohio was unforgiving. "How can I help ya?"

"My counselor told me that there was a job opening?"

"Oh right," she said, coming back around to the outside of the counter. "Let's walk and talk. I really have to get these books finished back here."

I followed her to the back bookshelves as she filled out inventory sheets and restocked shelves. I would occasionally hand her the books out of boxes when she asked me as we talked.

"My name's Misty, by the way," she said over her shoulder.

"Danielle Cavanaugh," I replied. I'd been saying it so many times today I should have been wearing a name tag.

"You a freshman?" Misty asked. I replied with an all-too-teenager-y "Um-hmm!"

She asked for more books, and I handed them to her quickly. "I'm going to be straight with you, Danielle. We really need the help, and I'm no good at interviews. You can come back tomorrow at noon, and I'll show you the ropes. Mostly you'll just work inventory so my old back doesn't wear out doing it by myself."

"Really?" I smiled. "Thank you so much!"

"No problem," she said. The bell chimed again, and Misty hopped down from the ladder. She made her way to the front of the store as I glanced around at the stacks of boxes.

"Oh good, you're here," Misty said to the person who walked in. They both headed back. A guy my age, maybe a little older, with a dramatic T-shirt featuring a band I didn't recognize, stood next to Misty. His hair seemed to be perfectly messy, and he had eyelashes that were longer than mine. We looked each other up and down. "Porter, this is Danielle. She's taking Freddie's spot. Damn kid quit yesterday."

"Porter Kohl," he said, holding his hand out. I took it as firmly as I could manage and waited for either of them to say something else.

"I'm teaching Danielle inventory tomorrow, so I'll need you on the register," Misty said.

"Sounds great," he said. His sarcasm kind of impressed me. It actually sounded sincere—only the kings and queens of cynical could pick up on it. The doorbell rang again, and Misty left us standing alone.

Porter and I stared at each other. "So, are you from around here?" I asked. He seemed vaguely familiar, but I couldn't place where I'd seen him before.

"I'm from Valley View," he replied. So about thirty minutes away. I must have recognized him from one of the sporting events I had been dragged along to, with dates who thought I enjoyed watching my classmates tackle each other. He wiped his palms on his pants, and I silently willed Misty to come back here and relieve us from our mutual awkwardness.

"Cool," I replied. I figured cool was the most uncool thing to say in this moment and regretted it. My goal was to make my coworkers believe I wasn't a socially awkward shut-in, but I was epically failing to prove that now.

"So, are you a student?" he asked.

"Yes!" I said. "Actually just enrolled about twenty minutes ago."

"Cool," he replied, smirking at his use of my phrase.

"Ah, okay, I'd better go," I said, scrambling for the bag I'd left near the bookshelf. "It was nice to meet you, and I'm sure I'll see you around."

To say I hightailed it out of there is an understatement. I saw the door ahead of me, beckoning me to the freedom of the

Jankmobile, but he called after me just before my fingers touched the handle.

"Wait, Danielle," he said. I turned around, red-faced, and he came up to my side with my transcripts in hand. "You forgot these."

I swiped my report with the big F in the middle of the page and blushed deeper. "Thanks."

"Don't mention it, Freddie 2.0," he said, putting his hands in his pockets. "See you tomorrow."

<u>FRIENDSHIP</u>:

a relationship between two or
more people who are friends.

SOME OF THE BOOKS I RESHELVED WERE OLDER THAN MY PARENTS AND SMELLED LIKE THEY'D ROLLED AROUND IN DISGUSTING AMOUNTS OF SODA AND TOBACCO OVER THEIR LIFETIME. They also wore the classy names of the previous owners, like "Mike Hawk" or "Ben Dover." I didn't quite know whether to find comfort in the low maturity of my college classmates or feel ashamed. For the sake of my sanity I decided to laugh. Pretty timeless jokes there.

Inventory proved to be as fun as I'd imagined. Misty's scattered set of records and last-minute restocking of last year's books made it more challenging to complete the monotonous task. But hey, I could be scooping out lunch to my fellow classmates or scrubbing their toilets, so I'll take monotony any day.

"Sweating yet, Danielle?" Misty asked. She reappeared from the back room with two bottles of water in hand. I gladly gulped the bottle until only half of it remained. My hair had stayed down for a grand total of five minutes before being thrown into a ponytail, and I could feel the humidity soaking in, bound to turn my hair into a giant frizzball. Thankfully, jeans and a T-shirt were acceptable in their dress code. I'd perfected the art of hiding sweat stains in this outfit. The key was dark colors and, if things got really dire, extra sticks of deodorant or body spray at an arm's reach.

"Seriously, what's the deal with the air?" I asked.

"I've been promised that it will be fixed before our big sale day," Misty said. "At this point, I'm about ready to find a tutorial on DIY air-conditioning repairs online."

"Let me know if you need any help when or if it gets to that point," I said, sipping the water again.

"Darlin', I've known you for all of two days and have witnessed your clumsiness. DIY might not be your God-given talent. Maybe you can be my navigator, reading me the step-by-step instructions," she said.

"That's fair," I said.

Misty peeked at a book I had propped open on a stool behind us. I'd taken a picture of the book with "I. P. Freely" and "Dixie Normous" written in it and sent it to Zoe and Noah. Misty laughed.

"I see you've found some of the treasures in the piles," she said.

"Who knew there were so many unfortunately named DCC students," I said.

"Who knew." Misty smiled. She and I worked in a concentrated silence. It wasn't awkward—we were a pretty good team. I'd hand her the books and cross them off the inventory list while she'd shelve. The pen I used ran out, and I headed back up to the counter to get a new one. Toward the front of the store were the "real books." Like, the ones people actually wanted to purchase. I saw the blaring Fabio cover that the woman at the front desk had been reading and picked it up. This time I noticed the broken ship in the distance and the fire on the sandy beach at their feet. *Love Castaway*, it was called. I shuddered. It looked terrible.

A million school notebooks and sticky notes lined the racks by the "real books," along with some computer software and other miscellaneous supplies. Tomorrow would most likely be the Black Friday of textbook sales for the store—classes started in a week and the books were all 25 percent off. Misty said that there would probably be about five workers tomorrow and for the rest of the week, rotating out. Since I was the newbie, I'd most likely be retrieving books or doing more of my favorite task, inventory.

With pen in hand, I headed back to Misty. She looked from her watch and back to me. "I have to pick my daughter up from swimming lessons," she said. "Porter's supposed to be in to work the register, but I can see that he's late. You ready for a crash course?"

I nodded and followed her up to the front. The register was fairly easy—it was old-fashioned with an actual key that I was told to guard with my life. Misty said a quick thanks and headed out the door, after writing down the instructions on one of the notebooks from the rack.

I jumped as the bell on the door rang and Porter walked in. He sauntered in, dropped off a bag in the back room, and joined me at the cash register. He'd barely nodded at me as he walked in, and for some reason it really bothered me that he didn't greet me. Granted, I hadn't returned the favor, but still. I was going to make a point to show him I was the bigger person. I grabbed a random book off the shelf and walked to the front of the room where Porter scribbled in the notebook that contained the cash register instructions. His eyes stayed trained on the notebook as I tried to casually get his attention. I probably looked like a broken toy car circling around the front of the bookstore, but no matter what subtle thing I tried, he would not look up.

"Uh, Misty left me in charge for a bit, that's why the notebook has directions in it," I said. He peered up from the page and nodded before writing in the notebook again.

I breathed out like a deflated balloon. I put the book on the completely wrong shelf and came by the counter.

"So what are you writing?" I asked.

Now he smiled. "Observations."

"Like, of the store?" I asked.

He nodded. "More or less."

"Make sure you get the part about the hideous Fabio book over there. Who buys that junk?" I asked.

He scribbled some more, and I peeked at the notebook.

"Did you just write that I'm nosy?" I asked.

"Only a nosy person would be looking," he said, that little smirk creeping the corner of his mouth up.

I crossed my arms. "Well, I'm going to go back to inventory. Have fun writing in your little judgey notebook."

"Will do," he said. I scowled again and for the thousandth time headed to the textbook section of the store. I almost turned back with about twenty snarky remarks, but I kept walking.

=====

The apocalypse of book sales days had finally come. The store braced for the massive crowds of textbook-hungry students. Misty worked her way around the store in repetitive circles, bringing up miscellaneous things from the back room that she deemed necessary. This time she came back with five candy bars in hand and passed them around to the four other workers and me.

"You're going to need this later. Save it for break," she instructed.

I nodded, hiding it in the back pocket of my jeans. I'd have to be extra careful not to sit down on it. A brown candy bar stain on the back of my pants definitely wouldn't look good. There was another girl that I hadn't met before named Megan who was on running duty with me, along with Porter at the front, and two guys named Jason and Chris in charge of circulating and helping to find the books. It was a surprisingly well-planned attack, considering Misty didn't seem to be one for organization.

For the first hour it was similar to what I believed hell might be like. The air-conditioning still hadn't turned on, even after Misty's daily pestering about it, and I constantly stayed on my feet, running to the back room to get books in stock or helping people find them on the shelves. I heard customers complain about the heat, and I wanted to hit them all over the head with one of their precious textbooks. None of the workers really talked to one another—we all had specific missions that we were on and none of us wanted to be bothered. Every once in a while I would eye Porter at the register and see him smiling—actually smiling—at customers as they left. He was capable of being decent to everyone but me, apparently.

When it reached about noon, my stomach growled loudly. I had eaten the melted candy bar at least an hour and a half before then. Thankfully Misty came over to Megan and me and ordered me to go on a thirty-minute lunch break. I thanked her profusely and raced to the back room. I snatched the crinkled brown sack with my name scribbled on it and sat at an old table in the corner of the stock room. Microwave soup never sounded so delicious. As the microwave heated up the concoction of broccoli and cheese, someone shuffled into the break room.

Porter pulled out his water bottle and sat at the table silently. I joined him with my soup, and we sat for a while without saying anything.

"How's it going out there?" I asked. I can't help myself. If there is an awkward silence, I must fill it.

"Fine, thanks," he said, taking another gulp.

"Good." I nodded. Was he just really bad at small talk or did he hate me for no reason?

"So have you been writing more in that notebook?" I asked.

"You mean more about you?" he asked, with that little smirk we'll just call "the Smirk" from here on out.

I blushed. "No, just in general. I mean, there's a lot to observe today with all these people."

"A few things, I guess," he said. He finished off the rest of the bottle and stood up. "I'm going back out."

"You're a brave man," I said.

He forced a little smile before leaving, and I had visions of drowning in my broccoli cheddar soup.

Things started to settle down around three, and Misty came back to where Megan and I were shelving more books and clapped her hands.

"All right, Megan, you can go on home," she said.

Megan let out a huge sigh of relief, and I waited for Misty to tell me the same. Unfortunately, per my luck, she had a different idea.

"You don't mind closing up, do ya, Danielle?" she asked.

I gritted my teeth. "Sure, that's fine."

"Great! Porter's still got the register, and I told him you had the shelving handled back here," she said. I nodded and waited for her to leave me to cry a little. I had told Zoe that we could go out later to Moe's, but it seemed like it would be a tiny bit later than anticipated. Zoe'd been busy lately keeping up with her job and helping her mom out with her sister, and tonight was finally going to be our girls' night.

I watched as the last customer took his glorious time in finding just the right textbook with the least amount of wear and tear and waved at him as he left. I turned around to sigh at Porter, but he was already scribbling away at his notebook again. I internally rolled my eyes and flipped the door sign to "Closed." Just as I was about to walk away, car lights shined through the front door as a new car pulled into the parking lot.

"You've got to be kidding me," I said under my breath. I opened the door. "We're closing up."

By some cosmic power I'm still trying to fathom, Luke Upton in all of his glory, large pizza in hand, stared at me from the sidewalk. A small smile crept onto his face.

"Of course you work here," he said.

"Did Porter order pizza?" I asked.

This made him laugh. "I guess you could say that. Porter's my roommate. He was complaining that he was hungry and had to lock up, so I played the good roomie and brought him food."

My eyes widened. "Roommates?"

Porter opened the door, and we both jumped as the bell rang. "I see you two have met. Danielle, Luke; Luke, Danielle."

"Dani Cavanaugh?" he asked. When Luke finally said my name, a shiver went up and down my spine. He looked at me like he'd just found his lost teddy bear, and I couldn't help but smile. We both had so many questions that we didn't realize how prolonged the silence was.

"Hello? An answer would be nice," Porter said.

"What?" I asked, shaking out of my daze.

"I asked if you two knew each other," Porter said, turning to Luke.

"Yeah, we do," Luke said. "We used to be neighbors when I lived here."

Our eye contact never faltered as Luke talked to Porter, almost like he was trying to figure out how he never realized who I was before. Granted, my sixth-grade school picture would probably scare small children, but I didn't think I had changed that much since the last time we saw each other. Maybe I just wasn't one to leave much of an impression. My face fell a bit, and Porter coughed—probably a side effect of the uncomfortable air that was spreading between us.

Porter looked at his watch and then back at me. "I actually have somewhere to be. Luke, thanks for bringing the pizza, but I'm meeting Emilie at Moe's in ten."

"Oh," Luke said. "Yeah, no problem, man."

"Don't let the pizza go to waste," Porter said. "Why don't you two have a little neighbor reunion? It's cute, really."

"Yeah, yeah," Luke said, hitting his arm. "Tell Emilie hi."

"Surely," Porter said, nodding at me. "If you're not moving around too much, the motion-sensor lights will turn off, just fair warning. Keys are in the back. Close up when you're done."

"Uh—" I started.

"You two behave," Porter said, wiggling his eyebrows.

"*Good-bye,* man," Luke said, pushing a laughing Porter off the edge of the sidewalk. We watched as Porter's Jeep backed out at a frightening speed and flew around the corner. Once he was safely out to the street, Luke turned back to me. He shook his head, laughing silently at either Porter or the situation that he had gotten himself into. Probably both. He drummed the pizza box with his fingers for a few seconds before deciding to fill the silence.

"So, do you like sausage?" he asked.

I giggled. "The pizza topping? Yes."

"Oh jeez." He laughed. "I'm normally more on top of avoiding sexual innuendoes on the first date."

"Date?" I asked.

I anticipated a blush, but the ever-charming Luke held out his hand to me. "I figured a date would make up for me being an asshole at that party. I knew that I remembered you, and I should have recognized you right away."

"Am I supposed to grab your hand?" I laughed.

"Yes," he said, taking mine. "I'm leading you into the date. The date place? The place of the date."

"Ah," I replied. "I guess I've been doing the whole date thing wrong all this time."

He pushed the door open with his back and pulled me in before him. I brushed against his leg as I passed, and in my distraction I bumped into the pizza box. Hard. I sucked in a sharp breath and inspected the monster scratch that now bled on my forearm.

"Oh no," he said. "Are you okay?"

"Just incredibly klutzy," I said. "I think we have Band-Aids somewhere. I'll be right back."

I scrambled to the back room, digging through shelves trying to find the first aid kit that Misty described to me on my first day of training. The scratch was more of a gouge now that I looked at it up close. I imagined my obituary—death by pizza box and faulty blood platelets. I managed to find some paper towels on the break table to hold up to my arm and stop the bleeding, but they were getting soaked through pretty quickly. How was I bleeding this badly? Maybe my hormones were pumping my blood faster than normal. Or I had an autoimmune disorder. I reached for another wad of paper towels as my phone rang.

"Oh my God, Zoe," I said, answering the phone.

"You are beyond late," she replied.

"I am so sorry," I said. "I meant to text you earlier that I was closing up, and I'm bleeding, and I'm sort of on a date right now—"

"Wait, what? Why are you bleeding? A *date*?" she almost screamed.

"I cut myself on a pizza box," I said. "Luke Upton's pizza box."

This time she really screamed. "You're on a date with Luke? This is a crucial best friend update. I'm so hurt!"

"It just happened like ten minutes ago. Please don't disown me. I will call you later tonight and give you all the details. Aha!" I yelled as I found the first aid kit. "Zo, I've really got to go. I promise, promise, promise I'll call later."

"Whatever, I'm too proud of you to be mad," she squealed. "I can't believe our stalking paid off!"

"Good-bye, Zoe." I laughed.

"Use protection!" she yelled before I hung up on her. I found a large Band-Aid to wrap around my arm and could feel the bleeding starting to subside. Thank God. I put the kit back and took a quick look in the mirror by the door before leaving. Well, Luke had picked the perfect moment to have this date. I'd been sweating all day, and my hair resembled a messy, fake-blond perm from all the humidity. The latest color Zoe experimented with on my hair was a far cry from my naturally muted brown hair, but I was assured it made my eyes pop. I licked my fingers and tried to smooth out some of the curls around my face, but it was pretty useless at this point. A lot of my makeup had also smeared over the day so I had the drowned-raccoon look going for me as well.

"Sorry I took so long," I said, rounding the corner. Luke had set out the pizza on the floor in front of the textbooks in the back, pulling two boxes full of books next to each other to make seats. He had a stack of printer paper by the pizza box and was smiling shamelessly.

"I couldn't find plates, so I stole some printer paper to use," he said. "How's your arm?"

I sat on the box across from him and held out my battle wound. "On the mend."

"Good," he said. He opened the box and handed me a piece with three pieces of paper stacked underneath it. I could already feel the grease soaking through the paper so I grabbed three more to make a sturdier plate. The pizza hit the spot, even though I had been craving Moe's onion rings all day. Pizza in the bookstore may be my new favorite tradition.

"So," I said. "The one thing I've been trying to figure out this whole week is why you came back here. Aren't there plenty of schools closer to Cincinnati you could have gone to?"

He swallowed his bite of pizza and looked up at me. "There are, but surprisingly, Denton's one of the only community colleges in Ohio with a decent football program. And since I was injured in my senior year, they are letting me come here on scholarship and train with the team. They are the only ones who still wanted some damaged goods."

"I'm sure they're so lucky to have you," I said. "What's it like being back in your hometown after all this time?"

"It's definitely weird being here and not living at the house, for sure," he said. "I sort of applied as a joke, but they ended up giving me the best deal. Plus, I've heard that the DCC girls are wild in bed."

"That's why I applied too," I said.

He laughed. "I don't remember you being so funny."

"That's because every time I was around you I could barely

talk!" I said. "You really didn't know the effect you had on eleven-year-old neighbor girls."

"Are you saying I don't have the same effect now?"

"I've learned how to manage it," I said, taking a huge bite out of my pizza. "How is Olivia doing? I haven't heard from her in years."

"She's about to start her senior year of high school. You know how that goes," he said.

I nodded. "Is she still involved in every activity humanly possible?"

"President of her class," he replied, shaking his head. "Everyone loves Liv."

"That's how I remember it. It's sad how we can practically live with someone for years and then completely lose touch with them. God, I mean Liv and I had our weddings planned out when I was ten and pinky swore to be each other's maids of honor," I said. I think we buried our wedding scrapbook out back by the Toad Motel. I'd have to save that embarrassing revelation for later.

"It was tough leaving here," he said, looking around. "It was hard on her."

"But eventually everyone adjusts," I said, thinking back to how difficult it was to connect with another friend. Zoe was my first best friend after Olivia—and that was a year after she left. I sort of floated between friend groups in that time, which was challenging starting middle school. I missed having a best friend that I could share all my secrets with and her mom being my second mom. I could tell Carrie Upton more than I could tell my own mom.

From above us we heard a small click as the room went black. Darn those motion-sensor lights! I hopped up and started waving my arms around like one of those inflatable tube men outside of car dealerships. As they turned back on, Luke started cackling, actually *cackling*, at how ridiculous I looked.

"These are some of my best moves," I said.

"Remind me to never take you dancing," he said, his cackle dying down.

"Trust me, that won't be an issue," I said. I sat back down and let the embarrassment of the moment roll off me. Was it hot in here? It was definitely hot in here.

"How about you?" he asked. "Why did you come to DCC?"

I sighed. I wasn't sure how honest I wanted to be with him. If I told him the truth, undoubtedly he'd think I was a loser incapable of planning out my future. I could lie and say that I wanted to take all my general education courses for cheaper than at a state school. Or that I wanted to stay home with my aging parents and see my brother's acting career blossom in front of my eyes. But if Luke remembered anything from my past, it was that I felt disconnected from my family and spent most of my free time at the Uptons' consequently. He'd never believe that.

"I'm still trying to figure myself out," I replied. "And I'm cutting down on my future student loans in the process."

"Fair enough," he said. We sat in silence again for a long moment, letting the smell of the old textbooks and greasy pizza sink into our pores. I'm sure I smelled awful with the combination of the musty book perfume and the sweat that still clung to my clothes. Luke wasn't wearing anything special either, thank God. Just normal basketball shorts and a Clemons High Cougars shirt. "How's your arm?"

"Better," I said, looking down on it. The blood had stopped seeping through the bandage and it barely stung anymore. I grabbed another piece of pizza from the box and replaced my soaked papers with new ones. I hadn't had the heart to tell him that we had paper towels in the back that we could have used. He was so proud of his printer paper.

"So how did you end up meeting Porter?" I asked.

"Random roommate," he replied. "He seems like a decent enough guy—funny as hell. A little moody, which you probably already know."

"Oh yes," I said. I almost brought up a few examples of how moody he'd been in the few days I'd known him when Luke cut in.

"We've been talking about me for too long. What have you been up to since we left?" he asked.

I was terribly uninteresting. I'd basically made my way through middle school and high school floating under the radar with a few core friends. I joined the design club junior year and helped make T-shirts for different school groups. I watched reality TV with Zoe on the weekends. I fought with my cousin-slash-enemy about twice a month and sometimes helped cook dinner with my mom. Also, I became a chauffeur to my brother and helped him with his math homework.

"Nothing too exciting," I replied. "You know, school, family—pretty normal."

"How old is Noah now?" he asked.

"Fourteen. He'll be starting his freshman year of high school. I can't believe how fast he's growing up."

"And he's been healthy?" he asked.

Noah used to be sick all the time as a little kid. Eventually they figured out that he needed to get his tonsils taken out and have some major inner-ear surgery to fix everything. Mom kind of treats him as her miracle child now that he's been healthy for so long. She acts like he had cancer or something.

"Yeah, he's been great. He's actually been starring in a few commercials for businesses around town." I smiled.

"No way! That's actually pretty cool," Luke said.

"And a little weird." I laughed. "Mom's really into all of it, though. It's nice to see her excited about something."

"I bet they're happy that you're staying close to home," he said.

I sighed. "More than close. I'm still living at the house."

"Well, that way you don't have to pay for rent. It really takes a huge chunk out of your pizza budget," he said. "If you ever need a place to hide out for a while you can always come to our place. We live in the complex on Hillis."

I blushed a little. "That's really nice. I might take you up on that."

"I'm really glad that I saw you at that party the other night," he said. My stomach did that fluttering thing, and I could feel my face reaching a new shade of red. I hadn't realized how close we were to each other now, leaning forward on our book boxes, only inches away.

"Me too." We stared at each other for all too long before I coughed and we both backed away. I looked down at my phone to see the time, and I squealed a little bit. "Oh man, I should have been home like an hour ago."

"Darn that curfew," he said. I could have sworn he winked.

"This was so fun," I said. He stood up from his box and held out his hand for mine to help me stand up.

"I had a good time too," he said. We stood in that awkward limbo between a hug and a kiss, and I couldn't read what he wanted from me. I stuck out my hand and firmly shook his, kicking myself on the inside for being so shy.

"Thanks for the pizza," I said, turning away. "I've gotta go."

My face got bright red, and I started to shuffle my way to the front of the store. "Wait! Don't you have to lock up?" he yelled after me.

"Shit," I whispered. "Yep, yes I do."

He pushed the boxes to the side of the room and picked up the leftover pizza to take with him. I scrounged for the keys in the back room and thankfully found them in under a minute. We didn't talk as I led him to the front of the store and eventually out the door. He waited patiently with the pizza in hand as I locked the door and turned around to him.

"Can I have your phone number?" he asked. "You know, in case I'm ever in need of some help with a pizza?"

"Um, yeah, of course." I blushed. He held out his phone,

and I nervously typed in my number as quickly as possible. "Should I be Dani or Danielle?"

"Danielle," he replied. "Remember, Dani is afraid to talk to me."

"Good point." I handed him his phone back, and we stood there again, without knowing how to proceed.

"Good night, Danielle," he said.

"'Night, Luke," I replied. "Drive safe."

"Always do."

<u>FLUKE</u>:

something surprising or
unexpected that happens
by accident.

I WOKE UP TO THE FEELING OF SOMETHING STICKING TO MY FOREHEAD. I swatted at it only to find that a sticky note had been plastered to my head. Reaching up to rub the sleep out of my eyes, I tried to make out what it said.

Good luck on your first day, loser.

One of Noah's favorite pastimes was leaving things on my face while I slept. I envisioned Mom asking him to set it on my nightstand or to post it on my bathroom mirror, but the face was his signature. The most disturbing item-to-face interaction occurred when he was five years old and decided to sling-shot my training bra onto my forehead in my sleep. I slept with a pillow over my head for weeks after that.

Voices filtered up to my room located above Mom's office.

She was starting early today. The end of summer was her busiest time—parents tried to get their seniors in before they went back to high school. These moments were the only times I heard my mom's voice. Otherwise she ignored me. Last week I had tried to have a conversation with her about everything—about how I'd gotten my life together—but she just stared blankly at me.

I knocked my phone off my nightstand and had to get out of the comfort of my bed to pick it up. At least a thousand messages from a very persistent Zoe flashed across the screen, but no text from Luke. Not that I'd expected one. Maybe a little part of me did. This was the part that I hated most about a new romantic prospect—waiting to see if he felt the same way without being overly clingy. If Zoe were a person I was romantically interested in, she would be completely failing in that respect.

Sorry about being MIA. Come over for some breakfast?

Within seconds, Zoe responded. Be there in 20.

Twenty minutes gave me just enough time to throw some clothes on and attempt to manage the tangled mess on top of my head. But if my senior year of high school was any indication, my physical appearance at school had become less and less important. Most DCC students opted for sweatpants and T-shirts during the school day, waiting to become presentable at night or at parties. That was a system I could be down with.

I brushed my teeth and rolled on deodorant before changing into running shorts and a tank top. My hair refused to cooperate so it stayed in a messy bun on the top of my head, chunks of my shorter layers sticking out in all directions. I practically crawled down the stairs and into the kitchen to inspect the food that we had left in the pantry. There were three almost-empty cereal boxes along with a variety of granola bars. In the fridge we had expired eggs, soy milk, and leftover Chinese food my family must have gotten last night. Maybe if I added a side of syrup to the lo mein noodles we could pass it off as breakfast.

Where my family lacked food, we made up for it in coffee. A fresh pot sat in the coffeemaker and it smelled like my mom's favorite cinnamon-bun kind. It was so delicious that it didn't need any of the sweeteners or milk—even though Zoe would probably end up adding some anyway. Her coffee ends up becoming as white as those expired eggshells after she's put all her creamers into it.

My DCC schedule sat on the kitchen counter. Today I had my first calculus class and my literature theory class. Literature theory brought a nervous feeling to the pit of my stomach that was tinged with anger. If it wasn't for this class, I'd be off at Ohio State. I'd be out of the house and finally out of my parents' hair. I'd make them happy. They would be proud of me.

The doorbell rang, and I almost skipped as I went to answer it. Zoe flew through the front door and wrapped me in a large and unexpected hug. "Oh my God, tell me everything!" she said. She pulled me back into the kitchen and I laughed. She sat down on one of the stools and placed her elbows on the counter, face resting in her hands.

"So, get this. My coworker Porter and Luke are room-mates," I said.

"Shut up," Zoe said.

"It gets better," I said. "So Luke pulls up to the bookstore right after we closed, pizza in hand, and I really embarrass-ingly go out and ask him if he's delivering. And then he says that he's bringing pizza for his hungry roommate, Porter!"

"That's some freaky fate," she said.

"Right?" I said. "And then Porter says that he has a date or whatever and that we should finish the pizza together. Luke was super charming and embarrassed that he didn't remem-ber who I was, and we had a pizza date in the middle of the bookstore."

"That is too perfect," she said. She dramatically sank her head down to the top of the counter and let out a fake cry. "Of course this would happen the moment you decided to go to DCC. You're so lucky."

"I consider this a fluke," I said. "There's no way that I should have this much luck out of my own careless mistake. This was never my plan."

"What do they say about doors opening and closing?" she asked.

"When God closes one door he opens a window?" I asked.

"Yeah, but you're not very into the whole God thing. Let's just say that the stars have smiled on you this year." She looked up to the ceiling and lifted her arms into the air. "If you could send me some of her good mojo that would be greatly appre-ciated."

"Trust me, the mojo won't last long," I said. I grabbed the three boxes of cereal out from the pantry and set them in front of her. "How do you feel about a mix of random cereal this morning?"

"As long as none of them are high in fiber. That stuff messes with me," she said.

"You, Zoe Cabot, are eternally classy," I said.

"I try, I try." She smiled.

We ate the cereal at extreme speed and sipped the milk from the bottom of the bowls before we left in Zoe's car. One of the many perks of being best friends with Zoe Cabot was her own car. Where I had to borrow my parents' cars to get around, Zoe had sole control over her vehicle since she'd paid for it herself. She barely even let her mom drive it. The little gray compact car weathered many a rough time while living on Zoe's street, including three separate times that her neighbor backed into it. By the third time, Mrs. Carlson decided that she was too old to be behind the wheel anyway.

"So are you two a thing now?" Zoe asked.

"As in dating? No," I said, smiling a little. "Not yet, at least."

"I hope we run into him today," she said. "I haven't officially met him. Apparently you've already met his best friend, and I feel like I deserve an introduction."

"I wouldn't want to scare him off," I said.

"Ouch! That really hurts, Danielle. After I helped you find the party where you eventually reconnected, you should be indebted to me," she said.

I smacked her arm. "You better not tell him that's what happened that night. I have a lot worse on you."

"Blackmail is unattractive, Dan," she said. "And of course I wouldn't. I'm not completely inept."

"Just making sure," I said, leaning back in my seat. The campus came into view and more cars filled the parking lot that had been so empty just over a week ago. We found a spot fairly close to the front door, and we each took our time grabbing our backpacks. As many times as I'd passed Denton Community College, I'd never guess that I would be attending school here. Growing up, my parents drilled into my brain that I would be a legacy at *the* Ohio State (strange emphasis on the *"the"*) and I, not knowing any better, thought that was where I belonged. Everyone told me it was my destiny—that I'd follow in my parents' footsteps. When it's your mom's job to place kids in the college best suited for them, you tend to believe her.

Zoe's first class was in the east portion of the building, while mine was west. We parted ways with a quick hug and wished each other good luck. My first class of the day was literature. My stomach had churned all night over this class. I had a very detailed plan worked out in my head: I would come early and meet the professor. I'd ask about office hours and how I could be the best student possible. I would not let the Franco fiasco of last semester repeat itself. No matter how much I hated it, I would ask for as much help as it took for me to pass this class.

The classroom was empty when I walked in, with the exception of the professor, who sat with his feet up on the desk, reading the paper and sipping from a plastic coffee mug. His hair barely poked over the top of the newspaper, and his face wasn't visible to me. I looked down at the schedule that I had in my hand and read the name: Finn Harrisburg.

"Uh, Professor Harrisburg?" I asked.

The newspaper moved down slowly until his eyes found mine. I anticipated him at least saying "hello" or "yep, that's me," but he continued to stare at me with a lazy look.

"I'm Danielle Cavanaugh. I'm in your literature theory class," I said.

He shifted in his chair, setting the paper down and taking a look at his watch. "You mean the class that doesn't start for another twenty minutes?"

"You know what they say, early is on time," I said, laughing nervously and throwing in a jovial arm hook like a sailor.

"And who are 'they'?" he asked. His almost beady brown eyes kept staring at me over the top of his glasses, and his eyebrows furrowed deeper as he waited for my reply.

"That was a bad joke," I said. My phone started sliding from my palms with all the nervous sweat I had accumulated, and I cringed as it clanged on the floor. I bent down to pick it up and noticed the glass had shattered in the corner and erupted into a spiderweb of cracks across the screen. Professor Harrisburg had to notice the horror on my face after seeing my phone. That would be the last time I let myself get a cheap plastic case from the mall. "Sorry about that. I just wanted to introduce myself before class started. I, well, I'll just sit here until it starts."

He watched me sit down in the second seat in the front row and pull out a book from my backpack. The only thing I brought was a nineteenth-century anthology that the class required, and the first page I turned to was a Walt Whitman poem where he spouted off about grass and nature in ways that made zero sense to me. The words all seemed to jumble in front of me, and I silently hoped for one of my classmates to join us ASAP.

"We're looking at Hawthorne today, if you really want to get ahead," he said from behind the paper.

"Yes, great, thank you," I replied.

As I read about a man's trip into the forest and his visit with the devil, more students started filing into the room. I recognized some of them from high school and wondered if they also failed Franco's class. The clock ticked down until it reached 10:00. Someone coughed, and Finn Harrisburg looked up from the newspaper and back to the clock before grunting. He folded the paper and placed it inside his desk. He scribbled "Mr. Harrisburg" onto the chalkboard and then turned around to face the class.

"So I know how today is supposed to work," he started. "You're supposed to sit back absentmindedly while I read through a sheet of paper you'll never read again. Why don't we skip over that pretense and get right to the heart of the class. I know that most of you took this class out of general education requirements. Some of you despise the thought of reading and writing. Tell me what you hate most about English. What makes your blood boil when you think about it? You, with the broken phone."

It took me a moment to realize that he was referring to my phone that just shattered all over his classroom floor. I blushed a bit before answering. "I don't have much to complain about."

"Come on, there has to be something you hate," he said.

"Um, poetry?" I said.

"Be more specific," he said.

"I don't know," I said, blushing deeper. Though I was über tempted to point to the Walt Whitman poem I'd been looking at earlier.

"There has to be something about poetry that makes you hate it. Think about it. Think back to that teacher who first made you read poetry. What flipped your switch to hatred?"

I thought back to Franco assigning us huge poetry books every night to analyze and never understanding a word of what they said and then having Franco breathe down my neck, waiting for an answer, telling me to think. "I guess the poets taking the most difficult and roundabout way to explain what they mean, that only a few people can understand."

He nodded. "All right. Danielle, right?"

"Yes. Danielle Cavanaugh."

"Danielle Cavanaugh, who is your idol? Someone you know who has the dream job and lifestyle that you aspire to."

"Uh . . ." I tried to think.

"I don't want you to strain yourself," he said, a few students snickering. "When you get someone in mind, I want you to imagine them doing whatever they do best. Can you do that for me?"

I thought of the conservationist that I'd job shadowed when I was in ninth grade for a school project. Her name was Nancy Earl, and I was so convinced after spending a day analyzing pollen and bee communities with her that I was going to save the planet one tree at a time.

"Now, have they ever tried to explain to you what they do?" he asked.

I nodded, remembering how in awe I was when she explained everything that she did. I thought she was the coolest human being ever when she showed me all her equipment and explained to me how I could be on the same path as she was.

"Did they water it down for you?" he asked.

More kids laughed, and I felt my blush becoming even deeper. "I guess so."

"Then they were doing you a disservice," he said, pulling up a chair in front of my desk. "You see, when things are watered down for you, you lose large pieces of the meaning. It's only when you have to research and think for yourself that meanings have a deeper resonance."

We stared eye to eye for a solid ten seconds before Finn Harrisburg stood up and pushed his chair back to his desk, letting it scrape across the ground loudly. My blood was boiling now, not because of poetry or even Franco. Mr. Franco may have been a hard-ass, but calling me out in front of the class? Never happened. Finn Harrisburg scanned his eyes across the room again and landed on me for a second before smiling.

"Who's next?"

<hr>

I came home to the sound of my mother sternly calling an admissions officer. I threw my backpack on the counter and grabbed one of the granola bars out of the pantry. Its expiration date was a bit questionable, but I was so hungry that I ate it anyway. I was still fuming from my lit professor and had promptly complained to Zoe about his general doucheness for the entire ride home. He had proceeded to ask the class different questions about English while coming back with a snide remark about how we were looking at it all wrong. At one point he blamed all our past experiences for making us narrow-minded. I don't know how you can get any more offensive. Mr. Harrisburg managed to alienate the entire class so much that I wondered who would be back on Wednesday.

I slouched onto the couch, flipping through my calendar on my phone to check when my next shift at the bookstore would be. Porter and I were scheduled to work tomorrow and my stomach flip-flopped. What would he say about Luke and me? I'm sure he would tease me for how awkward it had been while we reconnected in Porter's presence.

The door to Mom's office opened, and we were alone in a room together for the first time in over a week. She'd become skilled in the art of avoiding me, not that I'd been hoping to run into her either. Realizing it would be unmotherly to completely ignore me, she stood beside me at the couch.

"How was your first day?" she asked.

"It was fine," I said. "My English professor is a little tough, but I'm hoping it will be a good class."

Her phone buzzed, and she peeked down at it. Of course.

"I have to take this," she said. "We'll talk more at dinner."

"Duty calls," I replied. She walked back into her office, and my heart sank.

<u>FUN</u>:

a time or feeling of
enjoyment or amusement.

NOW THAT CLASSES HAD OFFICIALLY BEEN IN SESSION FOR A WEEK, THE BOOKSTORE BUSY-NESS DIED DOWN. A few students would trickle in to get last-minute textbooks, but for the most part, we all were on duty for cleaning up the mess of last year's books that were returned before school started. Misty and I did inventory while Megan stayed at the register, organizing a new shipment of notebooks and other supplies that we'd gotten in today. The air-conditioning had finally been fixed, and even though it was a week late, I blessed it.

"It's night and day compared to last week in here, isn't it?" Misty asked. Since the air had been turned on, Misty wore her hair down for the first time since I met her. She looked pretty, a little tired and worn down, but pretty. While we shelved, Misty talked about her two daughters, Nora and Sabrina, who were a year apart in elementary school. Today they were with their grandma, who babysat them while Misty worked. Their father was never brought up, and I didn't mention it.

Since business ran slow, Misty let us play music in the store. We kept it to Top Forty radio, and Megan and I even busted out some of our fabulous dance moves as we stocked. No matter what Zoe says, I am a great dancer. Megan and I got to talking and I figured out that she was from the next town over. She still lived at home and commuted the twenty minutes every day. She said she was an English major. I asked if she'd taken a class with the supreme asshole Finn Harrisburg before.

"Well, yeah." She smiled. "He's *the* professor here. I've heard they've offered him jobs everywhere around the country, but he never takes them. It's fascinating more than anything else."

"He's kind of an ass," I said.

"A hot ass," she replied. When I scrunched up my face, she elaborated. "Like in a George Clooney way, you know? He must have been hot in his day."

"Megan, he's probably like thirty-five. . . . George Clooney is in his fifties," I said.

"Are you kidding?"

I laughed. "Not kidding. But really, did you learn anything from him? I mean, Monday he seemed so set in his ways that he wouldn't even take anyone's opinions without making fun of them."

"Did you say you hated poetry?"

"Um, yes?" I said.

"Rookie mistake. He always banks on that being the first

85

thing someone complains about. He spends pretty much the entire semester attempting to convince everyone that poetry is the best thing to happen to the English language after that. He especially uses the poetry complainer as the example," she said, wincing a bit.

"Great," I said.

"Who knows, with my heads-up maybe you can give him a run for his money," she said with a wink. Misty called my name from the back, and I picked up my stack of books to bring with me. She had put the pile of books up to the wall and had grabbed her purse, car keys in hand.

"I have to head out," Misty said. "But Porter should be here any minute to help. He's closing up, so you can leave around six, Danielle. You're free to go, Megan!"

I nodded, feeling a little lump in my throat. I wasn't sure what Porter's teasing would entail, but I'm sure it would somehow be condescending. I felt myself mentally bracing for one more smartass for the day. Not one second later, Porter busted in through the front door with the Smirk directed at me. Misty patted his arms, giving him quick instructions before leaving. As he sauntered my way I prepared myself with witty comments that I'd been thinking up the whole day. So far I'd landed on nothing great.

"Danielle," he said, picking up a book and placing it on a shelf directly behind my head. He rested his arm on that shelf and faced me, only inches away from my face. That infuriating little smirk still stretched on his face, and I wanted to wipe it off.

"Hello, Porter," I said, turning away.

"I had no idea that I'd be the link to such a fascinating reunion the other night. It really is a small world, isn't it?" Porter asked.

"Small indeed," I said, trying to occupy myself with more books.

"You know, I was going through my journals again last night and came across something especially fascinating," he said.

I stopped and turned to face him completely now.

"I had written that I saw a girl at Moe's staring at Luke, and then I watched that girl and her friend follow him to the party and talk to him. Not such a coincidence, is it, Danielle?"

"It was a complete coincidence," I said, almost too quickly. "Zoe and I go to parties all the time. Don't flatter yourself."

He held up his hands in fake surrender. "All right, all right. How about you prove me wrong. Bring . . . Zoe? by our apartment on Friday and show us how local Denton kids have a fun night."

"Yeah, of course," I said.

"Perfect." He smiled.

———

I came bursting through my front door that night in a nervous (but determined) tornado of energy. I'd promised Porter a good time when I didn't know anything about the party scene in Denton. Did Denton even have a party scene? This wasn't something you could simply google. I contemplated texting Zoe, but I remembered that she was working the night shift at Freeman's Market. Without any other options, I knocked on the bedroom door of my much-cooler younger brother.

"I'm busy," he yelled from inside. I jiggled the door handle and opened the door to find him playing a game on his phone. "Well that was rude."

"I need your help," I said. "I'm desperate."

"Dani, it's like nine thirty. I need my beauty rest," he said.

I yanked at his blanket to urge him out of bed. "Come on, Grandpa. Aren't fourteen-year-olds supposed to stay up until ungodly hours of the night anyway?"

"This fourteen-year-old likes to get in healthy REM cycles," he said.

"Please, can you just come to my room for a second? I need advice," I said. He groaned and followed me to my room. He curled up into a sleepy ball on my bed while I paced around the room, different outfits flung carelessly across the floor. I picked up one of the crop tops that Zoe and I bought as a joke for each other and held it up. "What does this shirt say to you?"

"I have daddy issues?"

"That bad?" I asked.

"Danielle, what's going on?" he asked.

"You are considered cool at school, right? You have popular friends who go to parties?"

"Can you answer something without another question, please?"

I threw my hands in the air. "I agreed to show some guys who are new to town the Denton party scene."

"You?" he asked. I smacked his foot as he laughed for a few seconds at the thought of me going to any parties.

"Yes, me," I said. "I know you're friends with Kayla Masterson. Doesn't her older sister, Paige, host parties a lot? Would you be able to find out from her if there's one in town on Friday?"

"Yeah, no problem," he said. He yawned in a super-dramatic fashion and stretched his gangly limbs over my bed. "Now, I need to fall asleep in twelve minutes to hit my peak cycle. If you'll excuse me."

"Thanks, loser," I said.

"Welcome, loser," he yelled back.

———

Noah's in with Kayla Masterson proved successful. There was a party planned for tomorrow night, and I made sure that Porter, Luke, and Zoe were all available to attend the shindig. The only roadblock between me and the party was my parents, who had not forgotten about my grounding.

We sat at family dinner, a mandatory Thursday night event where we actually all ate at the same time and not in front of the TV. Thursday happened to be the one night open in Noah's acting schedule, and I'd asked Misty for these nights off no matter how much I wanted to avoid sitting down for dinner with my mom after our fight.

Mom made homemade bacon mac and cheese and my mouth watered as it sat in front of me. My hunger almost trumped the nervous feeling developing in my stomach as my body realized I would have to ask about going out tomorrow night.

"So," I started, breathing in deep. "Did I tell you guys who I ran into at school this week?"

I'd set Noah up before to act as the curious little brother throughout dinner even though he already knew about all my plans.

"No, you haven't!" Noah said.

I glared, telepathically warning him to tone down the enthusiasm. "Luke Upton is back and is a student at DCC. On a full-ride football scholarship."

"I had no idea," Mom said. "I'll have to call Carrie and ask all about it."

"He might be a good influence on you, Danielle," Dad said. "I've been e-mailing with Craig, and apparently Luke could have gone to any big school if it wasn't for his injury. He kept a four-point-oh through it all."

"It's funny you mention that," I said, ignoring how much it stung that my dad thought I needed better influences in my life. "He actually asked if I'd be willing to show him around town tomorrow night. But I know I'm grounded, so I can totally tell him no."

"Don't be silly," Mom said. "He's like family. It would be rude to turn him down."

"Just make sure you're home before midnight. You're still grounded," Dad said.

Luke Upton was officially the sexiest Get Out of Parent Jail Free card.

The two hours before our night on the town were split into varying degrees of panic. The first: frantic hysteria. While attempting to find the perfect outfit that fell in between "daddy issues" and "Amish woman," my floor became throwing grounds for every item in my closet. I performed this activity as if I were cracked out on two energy drinks. I jumped from the sound of my own floorboards creaking underfoot. The next phase was deep desperation, which I felt because my perfect outfit was never achieved. During this period, I texted Zoe twenty-seven times canceling tonight. I also shooed away my dear little brother, who had food with him. If that doesn't scream desperation I don't know what else does. The third was guilt. I had already gone to all the trouble of picking out the outfit, and so had Zoe, and probably the boys—I owed it to them to keep my promise. And finally, happiness in the form of a text message from Luke Upton.

LUKE: Can't wait to see you tonight.

Zoe pulled into my driveway at nine thirty on the dot. I pulled on my black shorts as I walked out to the car and tucked a piece of my newly straightened hair behind my ear. I ducked into the passenger seat and looked over at Zoe, whose mouth was hanging open.

"Oh my God, did you finally use the flatiron I bought you for your birthday?" she asked.

"One and the same," I replied.

"Dude, you look hot," she said. "I don't know what you were so worried about earlier."

"This took two hours of physical and mental preparation to achieve. Some would have called it impossible; I like to call it a comeback," I said. "Sorry about texting you so many times. Sometimes that's the only way to relieve my stress."

"That's what best friends are for—repeat texting during emotional crises. No questions asked," she said. Zoe pulled out of the driveway and down the street, leaving my house behind. My palms felt like I'd doused them in slippery lotion that my skin couldn't absorb. I wiped the sweat onto my legs, which made me realize that I hadn't shaved them for at least three days. How was I supposed to be sexy with a small forest growing on my legs? Their place would only be a five-minute drive away, and I struggled to cling on to the little sanity I had left. As if Zoe sensed me reaching my mental breaking point, she turned the radio on full blast. Without speaking, we both jammed out, major head banging involved, until we pulled up in front of the apartment complex.

"This is it, kid," she said.

"Give me two seconds, and I'll be ready," I said. I breathed in, looking back down at my phone. The text from Luke still flashed on the front of my screen, and it filled me with the courage to step out of the car.

It somehow looked much bigger than I remembered the complex looking. I knew a majority of the DCC kids who wanted their own form of independence from their parents lived here, but I'd never actually been inside. Zoe pushed the buzzer outside the door, and a very smug Porter answered on the other end.

"Come on up, ladies," he said. I internally barfed.

The front doors clicked unlocked, and we made our way inside the apartment complex. The apartment seemed aged, like it had been built when Denton had been established. It had the faint smell of weed pressed into the walls and carpets, just another reminder that college students occupied it most of the time. Their apartment was on the second floor, so we went up some narrow and rickety stairs to apartment 2B.

I knocked once before the door was flung open. Porter stood in the doorframe, motioning for us to come inside. "Come in, come in. You must be Zoe, nice to meet you." He held out his hand, and I could tell that she was instantly charmed. He was just mysterious enough to intrigue Zoe and hopefully keep her occupied during my failure of a party night.

"And you must be Porter." She smiled. "Danielle has told me so much about you."

"Has she?" he asked, raising his eyebrows.

"Not that much," I rebutted, giving her the evil eye.

"Luke's still getting pretty; he should be out in a few minutes," Porter said. "Can I get you ladies a drink while we wait?"

My palms did that sweating thing again. Thankfully, Zoe could keep it calm under pressure. "What're you having?" she asked.

"We're having beer, but if you girls want something else—"

"Beer's great, thanks," I butted in.

"Last time you were at a party you weren't much of a beer

fan," Luke said, coming out of the bathroom. My insides flopped, and I wasn't quite sure what my facial expression was. Probably an overly giddy smile that I would regret later.

"She was designated driver last time," Zoe said, coming up to him. "I'm Zoe."

"The best friend," Luke said, taking her hand. "Great to finally meet you."

He came over to me, and I felt that same intense fluttering that I felt during our date. He leaned over and kissed my cheek and whispered that I looked great. I could have died right there and been happy. Zoe was grinning so hard that I thought she might cry. He rested his hand on my lower back and took a sip from the can he'd already been drinking from. Porter handed a beer to Zoe and raised his eyebrows in a silent question to me. I nodded, and he handed it my way. I stared down at the unopened beer can and suddenly felt like a baby in high heels. It's not like I had never drunk before—Zoe and I had some pretty wild nights of alcoholic experimentation when her mom was gone for a weekend—but I never had socially before.

Porter nudged my arm. "This is the only one I'll drink tonight. I'll stay nice and sober so the rest of you can have a little fun."

"Cool, thank you," I said.

He leaned in closer. "You don't have to drink if you don't want to, though. That's totally okay."

In a surge of relief, I popped the tab of the can and shook my head. "Let's have some fun."

Porter smiled. "I expect the sober buddy role to be reversed the next time, just so you know."

"Dude," Luke said.

"It's okay. This is our thing, right, Danielle?" Porter asked.

I felt Luke's hand grip ever so slightly on my back, and I wondered if that bothered him. "I guess so. But I have no problem giving you a hard time, Kohl, don't forget that."

Luke laughed, and his hand found a more relaxed position on my back again. Zoe still had a giant smile on her face. "This is *so* fun," she said.

"Hey, Porter, why don't you give Zoe the grand tour? I have something to show Danielle," Luke said.

"Yeah, sure," Porter said, turning to Zoe. "This right here is our very expensive and cracked laminate flooring that was put in here about fifty years ago. And here is our ancient stove . . ."

I giggled to myself as Luke led me to his bedroom. It was pretty plain, only one poster for a TV show I'd never heard of hung on the walls. He crouched down and looked under his bed, which I assumed he had made for the first time since he'd lived here. If I remembered one thing from the old Upton house, it was that Luke's room always looked like a robber had ransacked everything. He pulled out a shoe box and set it on his bed, quickly sitting down. He patted a spot next to him, and I joined him.

"I found this at our old storage space that we left here. We didn't have room to bring everything back with us, so we always thought we'd come up and get it once we moved. It was Olivia's," he said.

"Oh my God, that was our time capsule. I thought your dad buried that thing!" I exclaimed.

"I guess Olivia left it in there so it'd be easier to find," he said. "You don't have to open it now; I just thought you would want to have it."

I reached inside and peeled out a half-licked candy bracelet that stuck to the side of the box. I didn't know whether to be grossed out or impressed that it stayed intact for so many years. A handmade frame containing a picture of *High School Musical*–era Zac Efron came out next, complete with two shiny lip gloss kiss marks on his cheeks. I pulled out a cracked CD with the title "Best Friends Forever" scribbled on it next, followed by the illustrious wedding planning book. I held it close to my chest, knowing full well that if I opened it now I might cry.

I didn't know what to say; the emotions and memories of my childhood came back quickly. I closed my eyes, remembering the day that Liv and I had said good-bye and she promised to keep this forever. When I opened my eyes again, Luke's face was inches away from mine. We breathed shakily before he leaned forward to meet his lips to mine.

It started out light, our lips meeting twice before he wrapped his arms around my waist, pulling me closer. The book tumbled out of my lap as I scooted closer to him. It felt so familiar, so safe to be with him after all these years. I felt like destiny or fate had known when we were younger that our paths would cross again and that something so sweet would be able to form later in life. I pulled away, and we both had goofy smiles on our faces. "How about we go put Zoe and Porter out of their misery?"

"Sounds like a plan," he said, grabbing my hand and pulling me off the bed. I kept my fingers laced in his as we left the room. When we came out, Zoe and Porter were on their hands and knees, looking under their futon. "What're you two doing?"

"Just showing her where we sometimes throw our dirty clothes," Porter said. Zoe was still laughing and a part of me wondered why Porter was being so nice and charming with her while he'd been snarky to me since day one.

"You never told me he was so funny," Zoe said, patting Porter on the arm.

"Who knew," I said, shrugging. "Are you two ready to go?"

They both got up, and Zoe and I left our drinks on their counter. We went down a different stairwell than we had come in and found Porter's Jeep in the back parking lot. Porter and Zoe scooted into the front seat, and Luke helped me into the back. Once inside, he pulled me close, putting his arm around the back of my seat. Obviously I was in heaven.

"So where are we going?" Porter asked.

"One-ninety Birch Street," I said. "Paige Masterson's house. She went to high school with Zoe and me."

"Sounds good to me," he said, turning up the radio. It had reached the point in the night when the radio played club remixes instead of the normal top forty, and I felt myself dancing to the songs that I'd recognized from work earlier. Luke tapped his fingers along to the beat, occasionally brushing my shoulder. I knew that it was killing Zoe not to peek back at us, but I secretly applauded her for playing it so cool tonight. She really was my saving grace in this entire situation.

The house looked less trashed than the first party we'd been to. Maybe that was the difference of girls owning the house. Where Cody's party had cans and kids streaming out of it, Paige's house was clean; the only sign of a party was the occasional silhouette of a body passing in front of the curtain. Porter had to park a little way down the street, and Luke helped me out of the car. I suddenly wished that I'd decided against heels. Heels are hard enough sober.

We walked in to find different groups of kids in the front two rooms—one group sitting around and talking, and the other side dancing. Paige Masterson popped her head out of the sitting group and waved at us. "Zoe! Danielle! How nice of you two to come! Kayla mentioned that you were asking—"

"It's great to see you too," I interjected, cutting her off from admitting that my little brother had hooked us up with the party details.

"So how are you guys?" she asked.

"We're great, it's been too long," Zoe said.

Paige eyed Luke and Porter and held out her hand. "I'm Paige."

They both exchanged pleasantries, and then Paige turned back to me. "Drinks are in the kitchen. Just give Mike five bucks—your choice of keg or juice."

"Thanks," I said. I took Luke's hand again, and he led me into the kitchen. Luke and Porter both went up to Mike and handed him ten dollars in exchange for drinks. Porter brought his to an eager Zoe and Luke handed me the one he bought. "Are you sure?"

"Yeah, I'll just drink beer," he said.

"Let's go dance!" Zoe said, tipping back her cup. Oh boy. Porter nodded and walked with her into the dancing half of the house where people were mostly just swaying. When the music picked up some jumping occurred, and Zoe grabbed Porter around the neck and danced with him.

"Are you much of a dancer?" Luke asked.

"Not so much." I laughed.

"Me either," he said. "So this should be interesting."

He tipped back his beer, and I followed suit before he dragged me out to the dance floor. Zoe laughed as we joined her and Porter, and I just shook my head. We bobbed to the music, and I threw back whatever was in the cup. My dance moves started out incredibly awkward with my hand in his, sort of swinging it. Then he grabbed my waist and pulled me closer. Sure, I wasn't much of a dancer, but I could get used to this.

Time started to pass in a blur between dancing and more drinks. Sometimes the only thing I could see was Luke's face, so I tried to focus on that to keep the room from spinning. Luke and I wove through the crowd of people that had suddenly appeared, and I struggled to keep ahold of his hand. It felt like the crowd pulsed around me, and the small size of the house started to really dawn on me. My breathing became shallow, and I could feel myself starting to hyperventilate. I stopped dancing, and Luke bent down to talk in my ear.

"You all right?" he asked.

I shook my head. "I think I need some air."

We made our way out the back sliding doors and any thoughts of claustrophobia disappeared. I breathed a sigh of relief.

"You feeling okay?" he asked.

"Fine," I said, still trying to keep him from spinning. I leaned up against the house, and he trailed his finger down my arm, making me shiver.

"We can go and sit down if you want," he said.

I nodded, and he led me back into the house. Another blast of music erupted as we walked in, and a tall guy almost ran into Luke and me. "Man, I need you for beer pong! You're the best player here!"

"Can't tonight, man," he said. "Danielle, this is Max—he's on the team with me."

"Nice to meet you," I think I said. The combination of the loud music and the biggest amount of alcohol I'd ever consumed made my words sound fuzzy.

"Go ahead and play," Porter said, coming up beside me. "I'll get her some water and sit her down."

I turned to Porter. "Where's Zoe?"

He pointed toward the sea of dancers at my little drunken Zoe, who enjoyed dancing with random boys. "She's fine, I'm watching her. Go play, man."

Luke turned to me. "You sure?"

"Yeah, don't let them down," I managed to say. He leaned down and pecked a quick kiss on my lips before bouncing off with the beer pong guy. Porter led me through the people, keeping a light touch on the small of my back. We made our way to the couches where people sat and talked, next to a guy who had passed out. I managed to sink down next to the passed-out guy, and Porter leaned forward.

"I'll be right back. Don't move," he said.

"Wait," I said, grabbing his wrist. "Why are you being nice to me? I thought you didn't like me, but you're being nice now."

He smiled. "I like you fine, Drunky. Please don't move."

I sank back into the couch and crossed my arms. I didn't feel that drunk. Granted, sober me probably would have never said anything to Porter about being mean so blatantly, but it still kind of bothered me that Luke left. It's not like Zoe and Porter splitting up—they weren't on a date.

Porter reappeared in the room with a large glass of water in hand. He moved the passed-out guy's legs a little to the left and crashed down into the sofa extremely close to me. I scooted over a bit as he handed me the cup. "Thanks," I said.

"It'll all be repaid in due time," he said. I rolled my eyes. That was the Porter I knew. He reached into his back pocket and pulled out a small notebook. "I thought this would be a perfect opportunity to play a little game."

"Pin the tail on the dumbass?" I asked.

"Her humor is still intact, ladies and gentlemen!" he yelled. People looked over at us, and I covered my face, laughing. "We're going to play a little game of I Spy."

"I spy with my drunken eye a boy who has had too much to drink," I said, pointing at the guy next to us.

"That's everywhere, Dan, be a little more creative," he said. "How about we add on to that observation? See the girls across the room? One of them is holding a permanent marker. The other girl has obviously been crying, so my guess is that's her boyfriend who had too much to drink and her plans for a fun night out are ruined. Now they're thinking about what to draw on his face."

"Whoa," I said. I watched him write bits and pieces of it down in a notebook and looked back up at him. "What are these for?"

"Documenting the college experience," he said. "I'm attempting to solve clichéd riddles of new adulthood."

I giggled. "You're using some pretty big words to describe stalking."

"I prefer the term *observing*," he said. "Besides, I'm showing you so you can help. You're gaining the true freshman experience. Can you describe how your first night of partying is going?"

I scoffed. "This isn't my first drinking party."

"The fact that you call it a drinking party kind of proves my point," he said.

I curled my legs underneath me. "Well, there's a lot you don't know about me."

He shrugged. "I'm sure."

"But you act like you know everything all the time. It's really annoying," I said.

"Are you always this honest?" He laughed.

I shrugged. "Only time will tell."

A very newly drunken Luke came stumbling into the room and crouched down by Porter and me. He wobbled, almost falling on his butt, but Porter grabbed him by the arm to keep him upright. "We won! They wanted me to play again, but I wanted to come see you."

Porter stood up, helping Luke into his spot. "I'll go find Zoe," he said. He left before I could tell him thank you again.

Luke pulled my legs onto his lap and kissed me, making the room spin again but in a good way. "I had to ask if you would be my girlfriend before I forgot to do it."

"Oh!" I said, a little thrown off.

"Please say yes," he said, pouting before kissing my neck.

"I mean, yeah. Sure?" I said. In a drunken pact, Luke Upton, the man of my eleven-year-old dreams, became my boyfriend. Not necessarily the romantic gesture I'd pictured so vividly for many years, but cute nonetheless.

"So, as your boyfriend, am I allowed to go crush another team in beer pong?" he asked.

"Go for it," I said, giving him an encouraging pat on the back. He popped up from the couch and pointed at me and touched his chest dramatically like a baseball player who just hit a home run before leaving. The party slid around me in a blur of people and music. The lull of the constant noise made me sway in my spot until my body inched farther down the couch, my head hitting the armrest.

I was shaken awake roughly, and the sound of the music that had lulled me to sleep now blasted in my head. I covered my ears and groaned, trying to roll over and fall back asleep forever.

"Come on, time to go home," someone said.

"Zoe?" I asked, reaching out to grab her hand.

"Zoe's already in the car ready to go," the voice said. "This is Porter. No, Danielle, you can't fall back asleep."

"Five more minutes," I said. I nestled into the corner of the couch for a few more blissful seconds before my body was lifted off the couch.

"Zoe, you're *strong*," I said.

"Again, very much not Zoe," the voice said again. "Can you at least wrap your arms around my neck? This whole dead-weight thing is not going to end well for either of us."

"Fine," I said. Zoe's neck muscles had grown significantly since I last touched them. I would have to ask which Zumba classes she'd been taking. We made a slow trip to the car, stopping a few times to hoist me up. Someone opened the car door and helped me buckle up in the backseat. My head rested on the window, and I was finally able to fall back asleep.

"Hey, Danielle. Dan, wake up," the voice said again. "You're home. Where are your keys?"

"In my bag," I said, or at least I thought I had said.

"I don't understand sleepy English. Did you say in your bag?" the voice asked.

I nodded, and the person grabbed for my bag, fishing around for my keys. The person placed them in my hand before patting the side of my face.

"You're really not going to wake up, are you?" the voice asked.

My lack of response must have answered the person's question. The person helped me to the front door and let us inside.

"Can you crash on the couch? Or can you make it up to your room?" the voice asked.

"I'm fine," I said, wrapping the person in a bear hug. "Thank you."

I felt a small pat on the top of my head before they left the hug. "Lock this door behind me."

I saluted the person. I crawled onto the couch and silently prayed to any god who would listen that I remembered to set my alarm for seven a.m. before Mom's clients would be over.

<u>FUTURE</u>:

an expected or projected state.

MY ALARM BLARED PROMPTLY AT SEVEN A.M., and I opened my eyes, disoriented for a moment by being on the floor in front of the couch. My back ached from sleeping on the floor all night, and my head pounded. The only thing that kept me from falling back asleep on the floor was the smell of freshly brewed coffee coming from the kitchen. But if coffee was brewing that could only mean—

"Good morning, Danielle," Mom said, standing over me with her cup of joe.

"Morning," I said, lifting myself from the ground. "I fell asleep at Luke's. I think he must have just been able to get me this far into the house before giving up."

"You are quite the heavy sleeper," she said.

I stood up, straightening out my wrinkled clothes. "I'll just head upstairs before your clients get here."

"I actually have a few minutes before they get here and wanted to talk to you about something," she said. My heart dropped.

"I was talking to Nancy over at the Ohio State admission board and told her about your making up the literature class. She said that if you show evidence from your professor that you will pass halfway through the semester, you could send in an early application to go through an express approval process since you were already accepted once. Do you think that's something you could work out with your professor?" she asked.

"I can try," I said. "We're definitely not chummy yet, but I can try."

"You need to try like this is the defining choice of your future. If you don't pass this class, you'll be a full year behind everyone your age. Employers will look at those small details and ask you why you're a year behind. It's best for you to come out ahead now," she said.

"I'll keep that in mind," I said. I suddenly felt like I was going to vomit, and I wasn't sure if it was from the alcohol or the idea of figuring out my future.

———

With my mom's advice in the back of my mind, I went into my lit class the next week with every intention of becoming more of a teacher's pet to Professor Harrisburg. I was running a little late this morning, so I rolled in right as he stood up from his desk. On the board Mr. Harrisburg had a quote written from Henry David Thoreau—a nineteenth-century writer I could actually understand.

"'I learned this, at least, by my experiment: that if one advances confidently in the direction of his dreams, and endeavors to live the life which he has imagined, he will meet with a success unexpected in common hours,'" Mr. Harrisburg quoted. "Each of the big nineteenth-century American authors, Thoreau, Whitman, and Emerson, had different ideas on what it meant to live life. Today I'm giving you the assignment for the semester. As we read through these nineteenth-century American authors, I want you to find someone who resonates with you on a personal level. Use one of their quotes as a springboard for a thesis on what life means to you as an American in the twenty-first century. It will surprise you how much these pieces are still applicable after so many years."

Everyone did a small groan, myself included. Maybe he hoped that the poetry and literature he forced upon us were going to move us in some way that we'd be compelled to write about it. Shouldn't finding a deeper connection to literature come in a more organic way? Forcing it upon us all seemed a little ineffective.

"Danielle, you seem to be mulling this over quite a bit," he said.

I was a little taken aback that he remembered my name. "Just thinking about which writer I could compare my life to," I said.

"You have the whole semester to think on it," he said. "Don't get locked in on anything until we've had a chance to talk about each of the pieces we're studying."

The class went on with a bigger discussion about Hawthorne, following up on what we'd talked about last week. No matter how hard I tried to pay attention, my mind was preoccupied with ideas of what I felt the meaning of life could be. I didn't even know what I wanted to do with my life, let alone be able to choose a writer whose perspective I identified most with. When the clock reached the final second of class, I started to pack up my things to bolt out the door before I tailspinned into a nervous wreck. I was about to leave when Professor Harrisburg called my name.

"Danielle," he said. I tensed up in the doorframe before turning back to his desk. "I don't want you to get too preoccupied with the final assignment. I cross my heart, the ideas will come as you read this semester. You seem like a smart kid, but I can tell when the wheels of doubt are turning. Don't psych yourself out just yet."

"I'll try not to," I said. "Thanks, really."

"No problem," he said. As if he felt awkward in giving sincere advice, he quickly turned to pack up his things, and I took that as my cue to leave.

Visions of failing this class clouded my thoughts. I couldn't repeat what happened last year. Even with Professor Harrisburg's encouragement, the feeling of dread still floated through my body. On the way to my calculus class, I passed an overflowing bulletin board with competing colorful posters screaming out at me. I looked over the cluttered announcements for concerts coming to Cleveland or student music recitals and saw a small ad for an internship with Green Transitions. They were looking for a student interested in environmental policy looking for some experience. My mind immediately went back to my job shadow with the conservationist and how passionate I had felt about the work she was doing. I pulled out my phone and took a picture of the flyer so I could set up an interview later.

A little fire formed in my gut in a way one never had before. I set a reminder on my phone to call in the morning before heading off to work. After a quick Google search of Green Transitions, I learned that it was an environmental planning and policy office that contracted itself out for different, big government projects in the Midwest. Ameera Chopra, the woman looking for an intern, was an environmental policy analyst who worked primarily on improving local laws. She was involved recently in community development and was really pushing for Cincinnati to use green rooftops. This prompted another search that explained how Chicago was the largest city with the most living rooftops, which helped cut down heating costs for buildings while saving the environment. How neat is that?

Comparatively, work seemed like a drag, and I could barely sit still as I manned the register. Misty and I commandeered the customer service until she left for the night, which only meant one thing: Porter would be coming in. Now, I wasn't sure how to gauge my relationship with Porter since the party night. Was he banking on me forgetting our little conversation at Paige Masterson's? Or were we friends now? We sat in an uncomfortable limbo that I felt entirely awkward in. My stomach felt like it dropped into my butt as the door chimed and Porter walked in, clad in a ridiculously unseasonal leather jacket. Someone must have boosted his ego while he wore it once, and now he wore it even when it was hot out.

"Did we get a new shipment in?" he asked.

Not the conversation I had expected, but fair enough. Maybe he liked to push things under the rug too? "Uh, no. Not today."

"Just a second," he said, heading to the back room.

I honestly scratched my head in confusion. So we weren't on good terms after I'd drunkenly outed him as unpleasant? Did this have to do with Luke? Had he come to his senses? Porter came out with a box that Misty put in the back room before she left. I went to tell him that, but he reopened it before I could say anything.

"What're you doing?" I asked.

"I thought I ordered these," he said under his breath. He pulled out more of his favorite tiny notebooks that I hadn't seen one person purchase the whole time I worked at the store. No wonder Misty put them in the back—they weren't supposed to be delivered in the first place.

"Why do you like those so much?" I asked.

He held up one of the tiny books to me and shook it. "I

have them everywhere. Imagine, I come up with an idea while I'm showering. I have one in the bathroom. I happen to be wearing my tight pair of jeans—there is a notebook in each pair."

"That seems highly inefficient," I said. "How are you supposed to compile your ideas if they're scattered all over the place?"

"That's the point," he said. "I won't compile them until the year is out. It'll be my decision from there in which order I record them, which parts I include, and which parts I throw into a bonfire."

"But wouldn't you want to keep it all? That's a lot of work," I said.

"Some stuff you want to be able to throw away once it's happened," he said. He grabbed a few more of the little black notebooks and stuck them in his back pocket. Resealing the box, Porter placed it in the back room without saying anything else. Was our interaction at the party a portion that he'd want to throw away? Maybe he already had. That's why our conversation stayed in the normal routine. He threw out his observations and previous trust because he realized what a bad idea it was.

He came to the front of the store, already writing in his notebook. Another little fire grew in me and the words burst out of my mouth before my brain had the time to stop it from moving. "Are you throwing out everything from that party? Because I thought we were on good terms now but you won't acknowledge it, and I'm pretty sure you're writing about me now. Don't bother if you're just going to throw it all out. God, I'm so naïve for being nice to you. I don't know why I even tried. Well, I do because of Luke but whatever. I don't need to explain myself to you of all people."

He laughed, looking up from the book. "Are you finished?"

I gripped my hands into fists. "I could go on if you'd like."

"Dan, I'm not trying to upset you," he said.

"Don't call me Dan," I huffed.

"Fine, *Danielle*," he said. "I'm not ignoring what happened; actually I'm trying to do the opposite. Luke says I'm the worst when it comes to having friends. I talk to you like I do to him because I don't have to impress him with being fake. I can be honest without coming out and asking you to be my new best friend, can't I?"

"I guess so," I said, feeling increasingly embarrassed. "Sorry I freaked out."

"No, don't apologize," he said. "It was quite entertaining."

"Hey, just because we're being friendly doesn't mean you can make fun of me for overreacting," I said. I rested my chin in my hands and watched out the window. There were no cars in sight. The bookstore really did make its money in the first week of school. I wondered why Misty even had two of us working at a time when it was so dead.

"Did you have a good day of classes?" I asked.

"Define good," he said.

"Did most people avoid public mental breakdowns?" I asked.

"Then I would say good," he said. He looked back at the notebook and started jotting something down.

"What made you start writing in those?" I asked. I thought that maybe he wouldn't answer, thinking that he was probably too good to answer my silly question.

"It actually started while I was taking this class in high school. We were reading Shakespeare, and my teacher talked about something that people during his era used to do. It was called commonplacing. They would write down lines from literature for inspiration later. But for me, instead of commonplacing from books, I commonplace from life," he said.

As much as I wanted to write him off as a pretentious douche, this fascinated me more than anything. What had he written down just then? What had I sparked for him to commonplace? Sensing my confusion, he smiled and flipped the page toward me. It read "good = avoiding a mental breakdown."

"I narrowly avoided one today in my lit class trying to come up with a final paper idea," I said. "My professor gave us the most open-ended assignment to find a nineteenth-century American author whose quotes resonate with you on a modern level and use it as a springboard for a mini manifesto."

His eyes lit up. "That sounds like a dream."

"Not for those of us who need a really structured system for writing papers," I said.

Porter pulled out one of his notebooks from the back pocket of his jeans. "It's just a matter of finding out who your nineteenth-century author alter ego is. I could put it in quiz form for you if you'd like."

I rolled my eyes at him. Only he would find joy out of creating a quiz out of my main reason for stress—the one thing standing between me and getting into Ohio State. He wrote furiously in his notebook, his eyebrows furrowing as he thought. It was the most focused I'd ever seen him. Just imagine what he could get done if he focused on everything with that much intensity.

"Okay. So you'll need to answer the following questions very seriously. I'm expecting a full level of dedication on this," he said.

"Fully dedicated over here," I said.

"Great. So, you're stranded on an island and can bring one thing. Is it A: your favorite book, B: matches, C: an ax, or D: nothing, you are nature's master," he asked.

"Do I have to take into consideration my actual skill level with these tools?" I asked.

"Yes," he said. "You're really on this island by yourself. What do you bring?"

"I guess B, matches," I said.

"Okay. One person of your choosing arrives on the island by some miracle of teleportation. Are they A: your mom, B: your best friend, C: your significant other, or D: no one, you don't want to bring someone else into this misery with you," he said.

"I wouldn't want to bring anyone into that misery with me," I said. "Plus, I'd probably get sick of whoever shows up anyway."

"Something to tell Luke later," he said, the Smirk creeping onto his face. I kicked him in the shin.

"You can choose to live anywhere in the world. Is it A: on the beach, B: near the woods, C: in the city, or D: Denton."

"Most definitely not D," I said. "Probably B. I'd feel really at peace with the world and whatnot."

He nodded. "You can only watch one genre of movie for the rest of your life. What do you choose? A: drama, B: action/ thriller, C: rom com, or D: documentary."

"C," I said. He raised his eyebrows. "What? I have a sappy side that only a good rom com can satisfy. Next question. Stop giving me that look."

"You order your dream pizza. What is the key ingredient that you love? A: pepperoni, B: mushrooms, C: pineapple, or D: sausage."

"What does this have to do with a nineteenth-century American author?" I asked.

"It's crucial. Most of their great fights were over the perfect pizza topping," he said.

I scowled at him. "Fine. A. A classic choice."

"You can go on an all-expenses-paid trip to one of these four places. Which do you choose? A: Italy, B: Australia, C: Japan, D: France?" he asked.

"I love Paris. My grandparents lived there for a hot second, and it was absolutely incredible. I dream about going back there all the time," I said. "Again, this seems a little irrelevant considering I'm finding an *American* author."

"I'm almost done," he said, waving his hand at me. "If you had to choose one animal to be your pet, which would it be? A: a hamster, B: a fish, C: a cat, or D: a dog."

"For right now I would probably barely keep a fish alive, let alone a dog or cat. But eventually I want to have a dog. Can I answer B and a contingent D?" I asked.

"Noted," he said. "Let me calculate your results. This might take a second."

"No problem," I said, giggling. His concentrating face was back in full force, and I wondered how much of it was just for show. There was no way that these questions could relate directly to an author, but he was treating it all like a life-or-death situation. Which made me laugh even more.

"The results are in," he said, holding his notebook dramatically like a talk show host. "My foolproof, Oprah-approved, Find Your Nineteenth-Century Author Alter Ego quiz has placed you with . . . Henry David Thoreau. Mostly just for your answer about living out in the woods and the matches. He was more of an observer of nature than one who felt like he needed to conquer it. Also, your loner answer was very Thoreau. The other questions I was just curious about."

"You're kidding," I said. "Porter!"

"I really do think you'll like him—he's my favorite out of the group," he said. "Don't get too stressed out about it. You have all semester, right?"

"I'm not the best at staying stress-free," I said.

Porter looked around the store and then at the time on his

phone. "I have something that you might need in the back. Follow me."

Weary, I followed his energy to the back of the store. He was actually skipping. He motioned for me to join him at the fridge and I peeked in.

"It's called Essprestout. It's the glorious combination of coffee taste and alcohol. I know you're not a big alcohol person. I bought this yesterday and thought you might want to try it," he said.

"Coffee beer? That doesn't sound that great," I said.

"It's actually life changing. If you don't want to try it, I guess I will have to drink it all by myself . . . ," he said.

Wrestling with my curiosity (and, let's be honest, boredom), I grabbed one from him with a small smirk. "I won't like it."

"To each their own," he said. He watched with bated breath as I took my first sip of the Essprestout. To my delighted surprise, the taste didn't make me want to instinctively spit it out. What sort of magic was this? An alcoholic beverage that I actually liked?

I smiled bigger at him. "I'm impressed. But I'm also driving home, so one sip might have to do it for tonight."

"I respect that," he said, grabbing it from my hands and taking a big sip. "See, sometimes trying new things pays off."

"You got lucky." I smiled. "Coffee happens to be my weakness."

He pulled out his notebooks and flipped to one of the first pages. There was a page with tally marks that read "Times this week Danielle brings a coffee to work" and there were five tally marks.

"I know," he said. "I've noticed."

＝＝＝

That weekend was the first DCC football game against our rivals at Columbus Tech. Zoe and I had purchased DCC T-shirts with my discount from the bookstore, and she crafted cute color-coordinated headbands for us to wear. My parents were still so in shock that I was going to watch a football game that they agreed to let me go. Again, Luke was turning out to be the best angry-parent deterrent.

We found seats in the bleachers, which were surprisingly full. I didn't even know people came to these games, and I'd lived here most of my life. Zoe laid out a blanket for both of us to sit on, and I frowned at her.

"What? I'm not burning my ass on the hot bleachers. You pick: sweat a little from the blanket or have red marks on your butt for the rest of the day."

I sat on the blanket and waited around for a bit, watching people come into the stadium. I looked down at my phone a couple of times, waiting to see if Luke would text me back. I'd let him know that I was in the crowd and wished him good luck, but I assumed he was busy getting ready for the game.

"I'm going to go get popcorn," Zoe announced after five minutes of waiting.

"Kettle corn if you can, please," I said.

"Obviously," she replied.

Sports was neither Zoe's nor my thing, so I knew we would need a lot of food to help us through. I think the last time I watched a football game was the Super Bowl, which I normally just watch for the commercials anyway.

I heard someone clomping down the bleachers behind me and assumed it was Zoe coming back with the popcorn.

"That was quick," I said. When I looked up, Porter smiled down, wearing a DCC shirt and showing a surprising amount of school spirit.

"Luke wasn't sure you would make it," Porter said, sitting down on my other side.

"I told him I'd come to support him, so I'm here," I said, firmly looking at the field.

"I never said *I* doubted you." He laughed. "Want something to eat?"

"I think Zoe's coming back with something," I said. "She's going to be happy you're here."

He raised an eyebrow. "Oh really?"

"Don't flatter yourself," I teased. "I just mean she'll have some more entertainment. I think she hates me for making her come with."

"You could have just come with me," he said.

"I didn't know *you* liked football," I said.

He laughed. "My brother played while we were growing up, so I've been to my fair share of games. I've picked up a thing or two."

"Hey, Porter!" Zoe said, coming back to her seat. "Danielle, you didn't tell me we'd be having guests. I would have brought a bigger blanket."

"It's no problem, my pants are a bit longer than yours," he said.

"As they should be," I said. "No one wants to see your skinny legs exposed."

"Ouch, Dan," he said.

The players started to run out from behind the bleachers, and Zoe smacked my arm to pay attention. "Look, there's Luke!"

We watched the game, mostly being told by Porter exactly what was happening. After the first quarter we switched the seating arrangement so he could sit in between us and give us the play-by-play. It all made more sense with his explanations (barely) and made the game significantly less painful to sit through.

When the game was finished, we waited around for Luke to come back out. Zoe and Porter talked about some band they were both into as I stalked my phone, waiting for Luke to text me back. We had waited for fifteen minutes before he finally ran out to meet us.

"Thank you so much for coming," he said, giving me a quick kiss.

"Of course!" I said. "It was so fun to watch you."

"Don't worry, I explained to them what was going on," Porter said.

Luke laughed. "Thanks, man."

He turned to me and held my shoulders. "So, there is supposed to be this after-game pizza thing for the team. I know we had planned on going out after the game but—"

"Go," I said. "It's the first game of the season. You have to."

"Are you sure?" he asked.

"Of course!" I said.

He kissed me on the cheek. "Thank you!" he said. He waved at Porter and Zoe, and we were left again in the wake of Luke.

<u>FIRE</u>:

```
to become inflamed with passion;
     to become excited.
```

THE WEEK MOVED BY AT A SLUGGISH PACE AS I WAITED TO HEAR BACK FROM GREEN TRANSITIONS ABOUT THE INTERNSHIP POSITION. I'd e-mailed about it the night after I found the flyer, but I had no clue how long they'd been advertising the position. Finally, on that Friday afternoon, I received an e-mail from Ameera Chopra, the environmental policy analyst I'd be assisting, asking me to come for an interview the next Monday. Since this internship would be nowhere in the realm of a communications position and I was already on thin ice with my mom, I told my family that Luke and I were taking a trip to Cleveland for the day (you know, in case they check the miles on the car or something).

I made the thirty-minute drive after I got out of class for the day with the empowering sounds of Beyoncé blasting. If

I could channel my inner Sasha Fierce for this interview, I would land the position easily. But alas, no matter how much Beyoncé I listened to, the churning in my stomach would not stop. My dad always says that if it doesn't make you nervous, you don't want it enough, and I really hoped that I could apply that logic now.

Cleveland looked bigger than I remembered. My GPS told me a backward route to the office, and I ended up more lost than I would have been without it. I eventually pulled up to a tall building with tiny solar panels sticking out of windows on the fourth floor. This had to be the right place.

I pushed the elevator button to floor four and waited as the rickety old thing shot me up. When the doors opened I collapsed out, convinced that my death was surely going to be by elevator today. A sign indicated that Green Transitions was down the hallway, and I followed it. My nerves started to get the best of me, and my classic armpit sweat started. I stared outside the door, judging when I should go inside. A lady sat at the reception desk but no one else seemed to be inside the room. Had I found the right place?

"Danielle?" someone asked from behind me.

I yelped as I turned around, coming face to face with the person whose entire biography I'd googled just days before. Ameera looked more intense in person than in the photos, which only prompted more armpit sweat. She held out her hand to me, and I took it quickly.

"Ameera Chopra," she said. "Please, follow me."

Without a question I became Ameera Chopra's lapdog. I

followed her into the office and smiled briefly at the reception-ist, who waved almost sympathetically at me. What had I gotten myself into?

"This is the office. It's nothing fancy, but we are the force of much of the environmentally friendly implementation in this state. Our team consists of ten people currently—most with an assistant or intern. Do you feel comfortable working in a collaboration space with other interns and assistants?" she asked.

"Yes. Yeah, sure," I said.

"Good," she said, leading me to the door with her name plas-tered outside.

The office was perfectly neat and had furniture made out of what looked like recycled metal with green cushions placed on top of them. Plants lined the large window behind her desk, and I could just barely see the solar panels sticking out over the edge that I'd seen walking in. Her computer sat on a sleek desk with no photos gracing the top of it. She pointed to a small area in the corner equipped with a laptop and high piles of paper stacked all around it.

"We're trying to go completely electronic," she said. "We just have to put all our back files into the system. That would be the main function of this position—I just don't have time to complete this myself. Do you feel comfortable working with database programs?"

"I don't have any experience with them, but I'm a quick learner," I said.

"Good," she said. She motioned for me to sit on the chair

across from hers, and on my way down an entire stack of papers went flying across the room.

"Oh my gosh," I said, scrambling to pick them up.

She held up her hand. "Just leave them—I'll reorganize them later."

My face radiated embarrassed heat, and I wanted to melt into the chair until I disappeared. She pulled out a tablet and started reading her prepared questions. I watched her mouth move, but everything sounded like a whooshing inside my ears. She paused and tilted her head in my direction, obviously waiting for the answer to a question I had no idea she'd asked.

"I'm sorry, can you please repeat the question?" I asked.

"I asked how you found out about this position," she said.

"Oh, right," I said. "I found a flyer at Denton Community College and was extremely intrigued. I am interested in helping out the environment, but I've never known how to go about really making a difference. Seeing this posting seemed like a sign from the universe."

"So you have no experience with an environmental planning office?" she asked.

I flushed again. "I don't. But I have a lot of experience with office work from my mom's in-home business. I also run a considerable amount of inventory at the Denton Bookstore, where I've worked for a few weeks."

"What do you hope to get out of this position?" she asked.

"A lot of it is that experience you asked me about earlier. I want to be able to have a solid internship so I can find a great job doing what I love," I said.

"And what makes you passionate about environmental policy?" she asked.

"It's something I've been thinking about a lot lately, actually. I job shadowed a conservationist when I was young and thought that her job was the coolest thing in the world. Being able to work to preserve the world around you? It sounded like a dream to me. I'm trying to tap into that feeling again, and seeing this flyer really sparked that in me," I said.

"So why Denton Community College?" she asked.

In this moment, I could insert my standard "I didn't know what I wanted to do yet," but for some reason I still can't wrap my head around, I decided to tell Ameera the truth.

"I failed a class I had no business taking in high school and then didn't get into the school I'd been set to go to. I'm making up the class at DCC to get back on track, save some money, and prove to my parents that I'm more than my mistake."

I exhaled, and we both stared at each other for a few seconds. I had no idea how this would shake out. I went to add something else before she stood up.

"That about wraps up my questions," she said abruptly. She stretched out her hand. "Sheila will be in contact with you next week about our decision. Again, thank you so much for making the trip."

"Thank you," I said, my stomach sinking. I should have never told her the truth about DCC. I should have stuck to my standard saying and kept things simple.

The whole ride home I replayed the interview, from papers falling to revealing my failure, and cringed. There were so many moments that could have been so different, and I felt so ashamed by how it all unfolded. If I never heard from Sheila I wouldn't even blame them.

In an effort to cheer myself up after the horrible events of the day, I decided to make a pit stop at Luke's place. I pulled up outside his apartment complex and prayed that no one would come by and scrape the car on the small street. I hadn't texted him most of the day since I had been quite busy, and I just wanted to forget about everything that happened and watch a funny movie or something.

I buzzed his intercom and got no reply. I tried again for the next few minutes and kicked myself for not seeing if he was home before I stopped by unannounced. I started to walk back to the car when I heard someone shout my name.

"Danielle!" Porter yelled. He had his keys in hand and was waving to me.

"Oh hey," I said. "Luke must not be home. I can just call him later."

"He should be back soon," he said. "I just got done with work. Want to come up?"

I looked down at my phone that still had no text from Luke and sighed. "Yeah, sure."

I followed him up the small staircase and into their apartment. The first thing that turned on was a motion-sensor, light-up monkey lamp that made me laugh.

"Do you know where he's at? I haven't heard from him all day," I said, taking off my shoes.

"I think he had some training today? And maybe the team

was going out afterward?" he said. "There's a game this week-end."

"Oh, duh," I said. It was still an adjustment to consider the football games as a regular part of my schedule now.

"You'll never guess who came in the store today," Porter said, grabbing a beer from the fridge. "You want one?"

"Nah," I said. "And who?"

"The passed-out drunk guy from that party, girlfriend and all," he said.

"You're kidding!" I said. "Was there any permanent marker on his face still?"

"Unfortunately no Ghosts of Sharpies Past to be seen," he said.

I laughed and looked longingly down at his beer. He scooted it toward me, and I took a sip. He reached behind him and got another out for himself.

"So what did you write about him this time?" I asked.

"I believe the words 'whipped' and 'delusional' were the adjectives I used," he said.

"Man, I'm so mad that I missed it," I said.

"You always miss the most interesting days at work. Or maybe I just don't have anyone to laugh with on the days that you aren't there, so the days you are there seem more inter-esting."

"Great point," I said. "Megan is a good dance partner, but she's hardly mean enough to be my real friend and observe people like you and I do."

"I'm a great dancer," he said.

"That's debatable," I said. I took another swig of my beer and pushed the chair out and stood up. "Show me."

He pulled out his cell phone and put on some obnoxious techno dance music and started pulling off ridiculous dance moves. I opted for my standard jumping-in-one-place move, with the occasional hand movement. The music got quieter as it built up to the bass drop, and he crouched down, motioning for me to join. As the music swelled we grew taller and taller until the music finally dropped and we both jumped around like the floor was on fire. He grabbed my hands, and we both swayed as we jumped. He spun me around, and I screamed as I almost flew out of his grasp. He pulled me in again, this time keeping a better grip on me as we moved.

The song changed to a rap song with the f-word tacked tastefully in between sentences, and I pulled away, laughing and trying to pose in my most gangster stance.

"I didn't know you were so hood," I said.

"I don't like to brag," he said. He took a long swig from his beer before jumping into the intricate rap part of the song, nailing every single word. I was in tears laughing so hard, doubled over and resting on the edge of the couch.

In the middle of my laughing, the lock on the front door was wiggled open and Luke walked in. Porter turned off his music, and Luke came up to my side.

"Hey, I didn't know you were coming over," he said.

"Sorry, I was on my way home and thought I'd stop by," I said.

"No, no, I'm glad you came," he reassured me, kissing me deeply. I pulled away and patted his chest.

"I'll just go hang out in my room," Porter said. "See you at work tomorrow, Danielle."

"Thanks for the beer," I said. Porter nodded before ducking away.

Luke dropped his gym bag near the couch and grabbed a sports drink from the fridge. He held up my beer and squinted at me. "Since when do you like beer?"

"Porter brought that kind to work the other night, and I actually liked it. It's some magical hybrid of coffee and beer. Who even thought of that, you know? Like who was sitting at home and was like, 'Hey, I'd really like to wake up with a nice refreshing cup o' beer.' So unexpectedly delicious," I rattled on.

"Sounds . . . interesting," he said, taking a giant swig from his sports drink.

"So, how was your training?" I asked.

"Pretty brutal today," he said. "But I think Coach is getting us to be more of a team, you know? I'm excited to see what the game is like this weekend. I think we're really ready."

In an effort to again get in my parents' good graces, a marvelous idea popped into my head. What better way to keep them from asking questions about my trip to Cleveland than having Luke over for dinner the next night?

"Tomorrow night, after the game, do you want to come over for dinner? My parents are dying to see you, and I can totally convince my mom to make your favorite lasagna," I said.

His face contorted a bit, and he pulled away from me. "You know that there's always a team dinner after the game. I won't be able to."

"I mean, you've been to the last two," I said. "Can't you miss one?"

"They're really important for team building and boosting morale. It's important that I go to them. You understand, right?" he asked.

"Sure," I said. "Yes, of course."

"Another time for sure," he said. He pressed a kiss to my lips, sealing that promise to them.

=====

As my dad had promised, part of my punishment for my OSU lying scandal was to drive Noah around when needed. On the day of my interview with Ameera, Noah had gotten a call from his agent saying that he made an audition for a movie called *Peace, Love, and Corn Dogs* that was filming in a different Cleveland suburb. My mom excitedly brought him to all the rounds of auditions, and we found out today that he was cast as the little brother of the lead girl. For his first day of a table read of the film, I was in charge of taking him and waiting around while it lasted so I could bring him home afterward.

I dropped Noah off at a house location that *Peace, Love, and Corn Dogs* would be using and decided to drive around the little town. I found a coffee shop that served the best Americano that has ever graced my taste buds and nestled back into a comfy couch. I brought my anthology for my lit class to get some good reading done, and perhaps see what all Porter's hype about Thoreau was really about. As I started to get sucked into the idea of secluding myself in the woods and writing about it with Mr. Thoreau, my phone began buzzing.

LUKE: Are your parents available for a dinner on Thursday? I feel bad about not being able to make it after the game.

ME: I don't see why not! Let's plan on it.

LUKE: Good. I feel like I barely see you.

I huffed a little, holding back from typing something about maybe if his football schedule wasn't so busy, but I didn't want to be that girl. Plus, at this point, I was equally busy with my job at the bookstore and being Noah's personal chauffeur.

ME: We'll be better about it. I promise.

When I'd told Zoe about Luke asking me to be his girlfriend, she'd mocked how quickly it had happened. "Hasn't he ever heard of hanging out? Seeing if you really have more in common than a shared fence in your old backyards?" I'd replied that she needed to be willing to go out on a romantic limb with me—a limb that we hadn't climbed out on very often in the past. The most romantic thing we'd experienced was when Cale Roberts was sending Zoe love letters in ninth grade. He moved to God knows where in California and left her to cyber-stalk him on Facebook, dreaming of what might have been.

Luke and I didn't need to spend the time getting to know each other. We already knew all the important things. Plus, not that much has changed since we were kids. This was destiny. I wouldn't let Zoe's doubts get into my head.

I tapped my fingers on the table, waiting for him to reply, but he never did. I hefted the anthology back into my lap when my phone buzzed again. Excitedly expecting Luke to have called, I picked up without looking.

"Hey there," I said.

"Is this Danielle?" a female voice asked on the other end.

"Oh! Yes, it is," I said.

"Hi, Danielle, this is Ameera Chopra from Green Transitions."

I almost dropped my phone on the floor. "Hello! Hi. How are you?" I asked.

"I'm great, thank you." I swear, she almost laughed on the other end of the line. "I just wanted to call and officially offer you the position as my intern at Green Transitions if you are still interested."

"Really?" I asked. I managed to stop myself from asking the "Why?" that bubbled up inside me.

"Yes, really," she said. "I admired your honesty and passion for environmental policy. You have to be passionate to go into this line of work, especially when you will constantly have people against you for one reason or another. I see that fight in you, and I want to be the one to help cultivate it, if you'll let me."

"I would be absolutely honored," I said.

"Good," she said. "Can you come in Monday afternoon?"

"I'll make it work," I replied. "See you then."

"Looking forward to it," she responded. "Talk to you soon, Danielle."

We hung up, and I stood up and did a happy dance in the middle of a strange coffee shop. I couldn't contain my excitement, plus the caffeine was really starting to roll through me. I hopped onto my computer to check my work schedule and saw that I worked on Monday afternoon, so I sent a quick text to Porter.

> **ME:** Do you think you could cover my shift on Monday afternoon? I could take a different one of yours in return.
>
> **PORTER:** Hot date?
>
> **ME:** Better. New internship.
>
> **PORTER:** Where at?
>
> **ME:** An environmental policy office in Cleveland. I know, random. I'll tell you about it when I see you next.
>
> **PORTER:** And that will be . . . ?

ME: According to the work schedule, Wednesday.

PORTER: Stop by the bookstore later? I have some new observations that need to be shared.

ME: Stuck at Noah's movie set for the day. Another story for another day. I'll see you Wednesday.

PORTER: Sounds good.

<u>FAMILY</u>:

any group of persons closely
related by blood, such as
parents, children, uncles,
aunts, and cousins.

**THE LAST TIME MY FAMILY HOSTED GUESTS FOR A DINNER
PARTY WAS DURING MY BATTLE ROYALE WITH CLAIRE.** To
say that the thought of another dinner made me nervous was
an understatement. The only thing keeping my anxiety from
paralyzing me was the fact that Luke knew my family. They
were just as excited to see him as I was, and this dinner would
be a breeze in comparison. Mom and I were still not on great
terms, but we were at least speaking again. I hoped that Luke
would help bridge the gap in our relationship and give us something to talk to each other about.

I went downstairs to see what I could cook for the night,

and my dad was sitting at the table reading. He put down his book and looked up at me.

"So, Luke Upton is coming over for dinner?" he asked.

"Correct," I said. I'd always dodged the topic of boys with my dad. We had a mutual agreement that the less we shared, the less awkward it would be in the long run.

"So, are you two . . . official?" he asked.

"Yes, Dad," I said. "Please don't act weird about it at dinner. He's the same kid you knew way back when."

"He's an eighteen-year-old boy dating my only daughter; he's not the same kid," he said.

"Oh, Peter, calm down," Mom said, coming up behind him and rubbing his shoulders. "We know he's a bright kid. Nothing to worry about."

I cringed slightly. She used to say things like "Danielle is a smart girl. We can trust her." I wondered how long it would take for me to gain her trust back.

"He likes lasagna, right, Danielle?" Mom asked.

"He's the world's least-picky eater. I'm pretty sure he'd eat anything you set in front of him," I said.

"It's good to know some things haven't changed," she said. A tiny smile reached her lips, and it made my hopes soar even more. "Danielle, you're in charge of garlic bread and salad. You think you can get the bread ready without burning the house down?"

"I will try my best," I said.

Dad volunteered to pick Noah up from Cleveland for the afternoon so I could stay and help Mom get ready for the dinner. She was surprisingly chatty, asking me about work and school in ways that she hadn't for weeks.

"This Misty just lets you kids run the store at night?" she asked.

"She trusts us," I said. "Besides, there aren't too many customers at night. There is never more than two of us in the store at a time."

"Do you like the people you share shifts with?" she asked.

I spread garlic on some discounted loaves of bread Zoe sent home with Mom. "I do. I usually either share a shift with a girl named Megan who's a year older than I am, or Porter. He's Luke's roommate, actually."

"What an interesting coincidence," Mom said. "Is he cute?"

The loaf of bread leapt from my hands and landed garlic-side-down on the floor. "Porter? I mean, probably to certain people he's considered attractive."

"Did you really just put that bread back on the tray?" she asked.

I shrugged. "It only hit the ground for a few seconds! It's totally eatable."

"You truly have a gift for clumsiness," she said.

The garlic bread made it into the oven (and still looked delicious and not like it had been dropped on the floor, by the way), and we set the table for dinner. Noah and Dad came home and kept peeking in the kitchen, trying to steal bites of the garlic bread. I kept checking my phone for word from Luke about when he might be over, but I didn't have any texts as it reached the time he was supposed to arrive.

"This is not cool, Dan. You know how hungry I am after a day on set," Noah whined.

"Eat a crouton and suck it up," I said. He stuck his tongue out at me, and I threw a crouton at his head. He managed to catch it in his mouth, and he lifted both of his arms and yelled, "Goal!"

The doorbell rang, and I sprang up, trying to beat my surprisingly fast mom to the door. She was steps behind me when I opened the door to find Luke, colorful flowers in hand and all. He looked especially attractive in a light-blue button-up that matched his eyes and made him dangerously cute.

"Hi," I said.

"Hi," he said back, showing a little smile that played tricks with his dimples. It had been so long since I'd seen him that I had somehow forgotten how adorable he was. His almost-white blond hair had been trimmed on the sides and he had a fresh, clean-shaven face that made him look more like the little boy who stole my heart so many years ago.

"Luke, it's wonderful to see you again," Mom said from behind me. I moved to the side to let him in the door. In standard Mom fashion, she opened her arms for a hug. When he pulled away, he held out the flowers to her.

"Thank you for inviting me to dinner, Mrs. Cavanaugh. These are for you," he said.

I could have sworn Mom blushed. "Aren't you sweet. Thank you. We are glad to have you."

Mom took the flowers to the kitchen to find a vase, and Luke and I followed slowly.

"Trying to earn bonus points with my parents?" I asked.

He winked. "It never hurts to be on their good side, right?"

"I think you've just made it to the top of my mom's favorite person list," I said.

We were herded into the kitchen and hastily asked to pick out our ideal piece of lasagna. Noah looked longingly from the table as Luke chose the coveted middle piece. I managed to grab all my food without any spilling, and I noted just how delicious the garlic bread that had a small stint on the floor looked.

Luke and I sat down on one side of the table, across from where my mom and dad sat. Noah sent another glare after realizing he was hard-core fifth wheeling this dinner. He mouthed a small "you owe me," and I mouthed back "tough luck."

"So, Luke, we've all been wondering about why you decided to come back to DCC," Mom said.

"I don't know how much Danielle has told you, but I got an amazing scholarship to play here," he said. "I tore my ACL in my senior year and I barely played, which really hurt my chances of going anywhere big. But at least for this year, DCC will be a good place to be."

"This year?" I asked.

He turned to face me, making a confused face. "Well, yeah. I'll transfer somewhere bigger once schools see that I've healed and what I've accomplished here. It might even happen at the end of this semester, if I'm lucky."

"Oh," I said. He'd never mentioned this before. "Yeah, that makes sense."

Mom rested her chin in her hand, like she was concentrating extra hard on something. "And your parents? Are they coming up to visit anytime soon?" she asked.

"Actually they're going to come watch the game tomorrow. You all are welcome to come if you're available," he said.

"That sounds like so much fun!" she exclaimed. "Dan, wouldn't that be fun?"

"I work tomorrow night during the game," I said. "But I can totally meet up with you all after! Don't let me hold you guys back."

He sent me a little sideways glance. "I won't be able to do anything after since the team goes out to dinner after the games. Maybe we'll have to do it another time. They will come to other games, I'm sure."

"Danielle, you could trade shifts with Megan or Porter, couldn't you?" Mom asked.

"I can try. It's sort of late notice," I said. The mood in the room was edging dangerously close to another battle royale dinner, and I hoped that someone would turn it in a new direction.

Luke shifted in his seat, taking a quick bite of lasagna. "Danielle was telling me about your movie role, Noah. That's so cool."

"Thanks," Noah said. "It's been a really cool experience."

Luke nodded, and we sat in silence for a few beats. "I also heard from a little bird that congratulations were in order."

The blood ran cold in my veins.

Luke continued, "Porter told me that Danielle got a new internship in Cleveland."

My mom's head snapped my way. In my effort not to jinx the good thing that the internship had been so far, I hadn't exactly told everyone in my life about it. To be fair, the only reason Porter knew about it was because I needed to trade a shift with him.

"This is news to me," Mom said. The air deflated from my lungs as I tried to grasp for the right words to say.

"I was going to tell all of you, but I didn't want to jinx it," I said. "I just found out that I start next Monday. I swear, I was going to tell you after I went for the first time and figured out that it wasn't some computer error that I was accepted."

Mom set down her fork with a loud clank on the nice dinner plates, and she wiped her mouth methodically with her napkin. "Who is the internship with?"

"Ameera Chopra at Green Transitions," I said. My hands shook as I waited for her to reply.

"And what will you do there?" she asked.

"Ameera's an environmental policy analyst. I will be helping her specifically," I said. I felt like I was back at my interview with Ameera, trying to prove myself worthy once again. This time, the stakes were higher.

"Environmental policy?" she asked. "Do you even enjoy that type of work?"

"I do," I said. "I'm actually kind of passionate about it."

"You've never expressed interest in it before," she said. I looked over at my dad, who was frozen in mid-chew on a bite of lasagna.

I urged him to jump in to my defense, but when Mom was in interrogation mode, everyone knew to steer clear.

"I mean, yeah I have," I said. "Don't you remember when I job shadowed a conservationist in ninth grade and loved it? And I took AP Environmental Science in high school? It's not some big secret."

Her mouth formed a tight line, and she folded her napkin. The scraping of her chair on the linoleum sent shivers down my spine, and my stomach sank as she stood up from the table.

"Luke, I apologize. I'm not feeling very well," she said. She placed her napkin on her chair and walked slowly up the stairs. Tears stung the corner of my eyes, and I felt like I might vomit all over the table.

"Dani, she'll come around," Dad said, trying to reach out to touch my hand. I wiped a straggling tear from my cheek and stood up, leaving out the front door. My breaths came out in staggered huffs, and I felt like I might faint. I sat down on my front lawn, putting my head in between my legs to try to keep from passing out. Footsteps crunched on the ground next to me, and I felt someone's hand on my back.

I peeked under my arm to see Luke, who sat silently and patted my back in a way that he meant to be comforting. I felt like I was being suffocated. We stayed out on the front lawn for God knows how long before he finally spoke.

"Do you want to go back inside?" he asked.

"Not really," I said, wiping under my nose. "But I should. It's getting late. You have school and a game tomorrow."

"True," he said. "Do you want to go somewhere? You could stay at my place for the night. Just to get away."

"You're very sweet, but I think leaving with you would make her a thousand times angrier. I better just go back," I said.

He hopped up and reached his hands out to help me up. He patted my head as if I were a little kid he was telling to chin up. "It'll be all right, Dani. You and your mom fight all the time and work it out. It always works out."

"You're right," I said. No matter how many times different important people in my life told me this, I still couldn't believe it. Mom and I had been walking a tenuous line of peace for weeks, and now I felt like I'd severed the line permanently. I should have told her. I should have done so many things differently with her.

<u>FIRSTS</u>:

being before all others with
respect to time, order, rank,
importance, etc.

**ONCE AGAIN, I'D SWIFTLY AVOIDED MY MOM FOR THE
WEEKEND.** I only left my room when I knew she was with a
client, and I'd become an expert in eating dinner elsewhere. And
by elsewhere I mean either at Zoe's house or at the bookstore.
Today was my first day of the Green Transitions internship,
and all the nervous energy I'd felt before my interview was
back and multiplied by a hundred. I weaved in between cars
on the highway with an extra-jerky nature and was a bit too
brake happy the whole way there.

When I finally pulled into the Green Transitions office, I
took a deep breath. Zoe, being the superhuman best friend
that she is, texted me exactly five minutes before my shift was
supposed to start.

ZOE: You're going to kill it. Go save the environment, you badass boss lady, you!

I sent back a mixture of happy and scared emojis before stepping out of my car. I took the same rickety elevator that scared the daylights out of me last time I was here and vowed to find a flight of stairs to use for the rest of my time at Green Transitions. Sheila was at the front desk when I walked in, and she directed me to go on back to Ameera's office. I knocked on her door and waited for her to open it.

"Danielle," she said as she opened the door. "Come in."

I walked into her office, which looked the same as the last time I saw it, except for a small desk that now sat in the corner of the room. A computer was set up for me and everything.

"This is where you'll be working," she said. "Right next to your desk is a filing cabinet that holds the data you'll be inputting. I'll have Sheila come by in a bit to show you how to use our server. If you want to get started by getting onto your computer and getting acquainted with all the files on there, I will let Sheila know you're ready for your instructions."

"Okay, sounds great," I said, taking in the giant filing cabinet next to my desk. I looked it up and down and then back at her.

"I have a meeting to run to, but I will be back in an hour or so with more instructions," she said. She picked up her laptop and a cup of coffee before exiting in a flurry. I stood in the middle of the room, unsure what I really should be doing at this point, and then headed toward the computer. I sat down on the chair and was just about to turn it on when the door opened back up.

"Oh, Danielle?" she said.

"Yes?" I asked, turning around.

"Welcome to Green Transitions."

———

It was finally Wednesday, which meant it was my shift with Porter. And it happened to be my turn to be really annoying with the notebooks. I was bored one night when I was closing up alone, and I decided to write down things that I saw and thought about in the day. I took it with me to class, back home, and even out to dinner with Zoe. I would write little messages like, "There's a man with very bad body odor sitting behind me. I hope he's not going on a date, otherwise it is going to end badly for both of them."

"Are you using some of the notebooks that I've been ordering behind Misty's back?" Porter asked.

"I actually have." I smiled. "It's a little therapeutic."

Porter smirked. "I feel like someone told you it might be."

"Yeah, yeah," I replied, flipping the "Open" sign to "Closed."

"Did Misty leave a lot for us to do tonight?" he asked.

I groaned. Wednesdays were always restocking days. She'd asked us to stay behind and organize a shipment that came in this morning. It was in preparation for next semester already, and I couldn't believe how fast the time was going.

"I'm sure," I replied, already heading toward the back of the store. There were five big boxes stacked up in the back room with a sheet of paper that said "Organize Me" on top. I grunted as I tried to drag them outside the room. Textbooks will now and forever be my greatest enemies. Porter laughed a little as he pulled a full box out without a problem.

"I brought something for us to eat. It's in the fridge if you're hungry," he said when we went back into the room to pull out another box.

"Please tell me it's pizza," I whispered.

"It's your lucky night," he said.

He started taking the books out of the boxes and setting them in alphabetical piles around him. I did the same with another box, and we'd eventually combine them when we finished that box. We were a pretty good team. When Misty worked with us she always gave little hints and suggestions that were . . . less than helpful. But with Porter we worked quietly and efficiently, getting the job done faster than normal.

"Question," I said, finally breaking our working silence. "So, you're from Valley View, right? How come we've never met before?"

"I only moved to Valley View in my senior year," he said. He continued to stack up books, and I wanted so badly for him to elaborate. It looked like I would have to pull some teeth to get this story out.

"Why did you move here in your senior year?" I asked.

He shrugged. "I moved in with my dad. Will you pass me the *Intro to Psych* books? I need them over here."

"Sure," I said, pushing the box his way. He continued to work in silence, but I was too curious to let this go.

"Did you like living with your dad?" I asked.

"It wasn't ideal. But I survived," he said.

I opened my mouth to ask another question, but he beat me to the punch.

"I'm going to grab some pizza; do you want a slice?" he asked. I nodded and continued working.

He brought the box out to me with two plates, and I gladly took a piece. My mouth watered at the sight of Moe's pepperoni pizza in all of its garlic-crust glory. We both took a break, sitting on the ground and using the piles of textbooks as tables. My phone started buzzing in my pocket, and I saw that my dad had called me three times. Apparently since I'd forgotten that I was working late, I hadn't told him that I was, in fact, alive and not dead in a ditch.

"Whoops, forgot to tell my dad that I'm working late," I said.

"Do you still have a curfew?" he said.

"Nah, he just likes to know that I'm not off being murdered or whatever," I said. I sent him a quick text telling him I was closing up.

He smiled and looked down in a very Porter way. In these little glimpses you could understand why girls in might find him maybe, possibly attractive. He liked to act all tough and smart and cool, but really he was just a nice kid with eyelashes that were too long for his own good.

"What about your mom?" I asked. "How does she feel about you going to school up here?"

He shoved more pizza in his mouth and took a long time to chew and swallow before responding. "She's fine with it, I guess. One less person to intrude on her time at home."

I frowned a little, and he backtracked.

"I'm just being dramatic, she's like me. She likes being alone," he said.

"No one really likes being alone," I said.

The click that I'd become so accustomed to of the lights turning off happened above us. We sat in the dark for a few seconds before I got up and waved my arms around until they turned back on. Porter didn't speak as he took another slice from the pizza box. Darn those lights. I'd been on such a roll.

"And your dad—"

"Do you want another piece?" he interrupted me.

I nodded and reached for the slice in his hand, a stray pepperoni dropping onto my leg. He picked it up from my leg and ate it, licking the grease from his thumb. He smirked, and I felt my face getting hot.

"We should probably finish up soon. I told Luke I'd call him in a half an hour," I said.

"Yeah, okay," he said, wiping his hands on his pants before standing up. He offered his hand for me to stand up, but I pushed up on my own. In my urge to be independent I put my weight on the stack of books that I had been piling up and they slipped out from under me, sending the alphabetized pile into a tizzy. I cursed and started to reorganize them as Porter finished the rest of the other piles.

We worked quickly and closed up before anything else could spill.

FOREBODING:

a strong inner notion of future misfortune.

THE NEXT FEW WEEKS PASSED BY IN A BLURRY FRENZY.
Between spending shifts at the bookstore, driving Noah to his movie set, and working twice a week at Green Transitions, I'd become a productivity tornado. My communication with the outside world came only by way of text message, but even I realized that I'd become almost unreachable in the past few weeks. The fact that my best friend and boyfriend hadn't disowned me was some sort of miracle.

What used to be an intimidating stack of backlogged papers at Green Transitions had finally started to dwindle down. I met all the other interns, who were working either with policy makers or engineers in the office, and I was becoming more familiar with the environmental lingo that they all used without a second thought. And even though Ameera was a woman of few words, we'd managed to bond a little over our mutual love of coffee and Shonda Rhimes's smash hit *How to Get Away with Murder*.

That morning I'd made the drive into Cleveland early and picked up two coffees at Ameera's favorite place, The Morning Brew (we ordered the yin and yang of coffees—her coffee black, mine with so much cream it was white). I was already going through my e-mails for the morning when she stormed in.

"Have you seen this?" Ameera asked, holding out her phone to me.

I glanced down at the screen to see a blaring headline. "Denton Named Least Green City in the State." I scrolled down a bit to see where other cities ranked and let out a little sigh.

"I hadn't seen it," I said, handing the phone back to her. "But that's pretty bad."

"An understatement," she said. "We're going to need to do some damage control. You're from Denton. I would love it if you could speak at an upcoming city council meeting about what it means for you, as a lifelong resident of Denton, to be living in the least environmentally conscious city in Ohio. I think they'd be more responsive to you than they would be to me."

"You want me to talk in front of a bunch of people? On purpose?" I asked.

"You'll be a natural, Danielle. Plus, I bet you know someone on the council. That could sway some of their decision," she said.

She did have a point. The city council included one of my old teachers and an overly friendly neighbor. Even with that small amount of clout, I wasn't sure if I could form coherent sentences in front of a group of people. I barely passed speech class in high school because my words would stick in my throat every time I attempted to give a speech.

"You're putting a lot of faith in a C-plus-average Speech and Language student," I said.

She shook her head. "We've already established you're more than your grades. The city council meeting is at the end of the month. Bring me a mock-up of your speech the next time you're in."

———

The remainder of the week I attempted to channel my inner Porter Kohl. I tried to find inspiration for my speech every-where I went, but I wasn't coming up with very much. I never understood how people could sit down and let their little muse take over. My muse required a lot of coaxing and brib-ing to even scribble out a coherent paragraph.

On that Wednesday night, Porter and I had a surprising number of customers at the bookstore. Some of the students complained that their professor had assigned some last-minute books before midterms, and we were caught off guard by being busy again. The clock ticked to eight, and Porter turned the sign to Closed. I sat in the back corner next to the main book-shelf and added more to my speech after a stroke of inspira-tion hit out of nowhere. I was so engrossed in writing my ideas that I didn't realize Porter was standing above me. He snatched the notebook out of my hands and, to my horror, began reading my city council speech.

"Hello, everyone. How about that last speech? [Insert funnier joke here.] My name is Danielle Cavanaugh, and I am here on behalf of Green Transitions Environmental Policy offices in Cleveland," he read dramatically.

I stood up and tried to grab it out of his hands, jumping to try to reach it. Why did he have to be so tall! He stood on his tiptoes so he could continue reading it while I fought for the notebook.

"I saw an article last week that made me pretty upset. It said that Denton was the least green city in Ohio. As a lifelong resident and environmental advocate for this city, I knew I had to find a way to make a difference," he continued.

"Seriously! It's not done. Give it back!" I yelled, now attempting to pull him down via piggyback. He started to lean forward and I saw the ground quickly approaching. I clung on to his shoulders and waist and let out a scream as we changed altitude.

"I thought about tying myself to the biggest tree in Florence Park to make a statement. I thought about going door to door to remind people of the joys of recycling. But the thing that I ultimately knew would make the most impact would be to speak with the policy makers of this city that I love so much. You all," he continued.

He abruptly stood up straight again, and I slid off his back. He handed the notebook back to me, and I huffed as the blood rushed from my head to the rest of my body. I tucked the notebook into my pocket and crossed my arms.

"You're incredibly annoying," I said.

"And you're a good writer," he said back. My stomach flopped. No one had ever said that to me before. I'd always been told that I could work harder, finesse this or that, but when I was writing about something that I cared about, it came out in a better form. "When is your speech?"

"Like I'm telling you," I said. "I can barely speak in front of strangers, let alone people I actually know."

"Can't you just picture everyone in their underwear?" he asked.

"I would prefer not to picture you in your underwear," I said.

"Ouch!" he said. He picked up a book that had been misplaced on the shelf behind me and rearranged it, resting his hand right above my head. I held my breath for a few moments as I realized just how close we were. "For the record, I've been told that I look rather refined in my underwear."

"Can we stop talking about underwear?" I said, slinking out from under his arm. I looked at an invisible watch around my wrist. "Look at the time. I have to head home. I'll see you next week."

"Aw, come on, don't leave!" he yelled after me as I walked away. "You don't have to be embarrassed about picturing me in my underwear."

"Good-*bye*, Porter," I called over my shoulder and out

the door. I could hear him snickering as I closed the door behind me.

I stomped out to the Jankmobile and shook my head, ridding myself of all visions of Porter Kohl sitting at the city council meeting in his underwear. I turned up the music full blast to clear my head and to inspire the muse to shift its focus back to environmental policy and off half-naked Porter.

<u>FAME:</u>

a public estimation
or reputation.

NOAH WAS ALMOST FINISHED WITH SHOOTING *PEACE, LOVE, AND CORN DOGS,* **AND THEY WERE GEARING UP TO FILM A HUGE CARNIVAL SCENE WHERE THEY NEEDED EXTRAS OF EVERY AGE.** I was told to recruit some of my friends to join me on set as extras for the day, and the lucky folks who decided to come were Zoe, Luke, and Porter. We got up incredibly early and carpooled in the Jeep to make it to Cleveland for a seven a.m. call time. I thanked each of them eternally, and Porter reminded me a million times that he was only in it for the craft services, which prompted a million eye rolls from me.

When we made it onto the set, Noah flitted into the actors' tent and hugged all his friends, including the director. It was an independent film, but apparently this guy was a pretty big deal for almost-Hollywood. Luke, Zoe, Porter, and I immediately found the craft services (which were admittedly pretty incredible). They had tiny grilled cheeses. How much better can life get? We stayed there for a long time, trying all the different jelly-filled donuts on the table along with engulfing an entire bowl of rock candies. If they didn't stop us soon we would have to be rolled onto the set.

"They aren't going to make us do anything too embarrassing, do you think?" I asked Zoe.

"That's why it's called *acting*, darling. Today we are ac-*tors*," Zoe drawled.

"Do the boys agree? I think they're still just really impressed by all the free food," I said.

"Who cares about the boys; this is our moment to be on screen together. We've finally made it. I hope I get to eat a corn dog in the background. That would be epic," she said.

Porter came up next to me, holding a deep-fried Oreo in one hand and a mini grilled cheese in the other. He held out the Oreo to me. "You have to try this. It's life changing."

The cookie, which had no business being deep fried, melted in my mouth, and I let out an audible groan. It truly was a life-changing experience.

"Did you just *moan* after eating an Oreo?" Porter asked.

I smacked him on the chest. "Shut up. It was delicious."

"You!" A lady yelled at us, and we all jumped, thinking we were getting scolded for eating too much. "Short girl, gangly boy, come with me."

Porter swallowed his mouthful of grilled cheese, and we

shrugged at each other. I looked back at Zoe, whose eyes were huge, and Luke gave us an overenthusiastic thumbs-up. Oh boy.

The casting director, who introduced herself quickly as Meredith, pulled us into a room where at least ten people sat around various screens looking at the shots they'd just taken around the carnival scene. She pointed to Porter and me flippantly.

"How about them?" she asked.

Everyone looked up from their screens simultaneously, staring at us for a few seconds before nodding as a group. Meredith clapped her hands and led us back out the doors without another word. Porter and I exchanged glances of confusion before being delivered into the heart of the carnival. There were set designers repositioning carnival booths around the open lot, and the carousel they'd brought in came to life as we walked out. "Check the gate!" we heard someone yell. It was all pretty magical.

"Okay. So the line for Marcy and Ian is 'Ugh, isn't that just cringe-worthy?' as they pass you two. How do you feel about kissing on screen?" she said.

My heart dropped, and we quickly shut her down. "Oh no, we can't possibly—" I started.

"I mean, we aren't like—" he said.

"*Romantic*," I finished.

Meredith cocked her head. "You get paid more to be a featured extra. It's for twenty minutes max, and you get the better food. Still have a problem?"

He looked at me for a while, gauging my response. "Danielle, we don't have to. This is . . . a little bit more than we signed up for, right?"

"Well . . . it's to help out Noah's movie. . . . And we are ac-*tors* for the day, are we not?" I asked.

He bit his lip and looked around as if waiting for Luke to come around the corner. "I mean, if you're okay with it one hundred and ten percent—"

"Let's make a decision, people, we have a lot more to shoot today," she said.

I looked down at the ground for a few seconds and breathed to calm myself. "We'll do it."

They had us set up on a bench near the entrance of the carnival, and I had a giant plushy pink teddy bear sitting next to me. Apparently that bear warranted whatever kiss I was supposed to give Porter. My typical hand sweat was coming back, and I felt like I might throw up. Should I have said no? Should I have asked for Luke to replace him? They picked us because of our look, right? Because we made the most sense cinematically to kiss in the back of the shot? I had no time to debate because the director came up and shook our hands and introduced himself before starting. I told him that I was Noah's sister, and his face lit up.

"He's so talented," he said. "I can't wait to work more with him. I can't believe this is his first film. You've got to get him out to LA."

I took the enormous compliment for my brother and smiled. The director described that we'd be cued to do different things to get the best reaction out of Marcy and Ian. He said that we should keep it simple first and we'd go from there. My sweat rate continued to go through the roof, and I was starting to feel dizzy thinking about doing this. Where was Luke? Would he see this and get angry? Or was he still mesmerized by the craft services?

"All right, Danielle, Porter, we're about to start," he said. "And . . . action."

I stared at Porter's chest for what felt like forever. I couldn't look him in the eyes now that we were faced with having to really actually kiss. He bent down to meet my eyes and stopped just inches from my face.

"We really don't have to do this," he whispered.

"Cut!" the director yelled. He walked toward us, and I could feel my face heating up. My legs were bouncing up and down uncontrollably, and Porter leaned his closer to mine so they were touching, a small form of comfort.

"When I say action, you guys should just go for it. I'll let you know if we need less. For now, more is more," the director said.

I nodded and looked back at Porter. He looked even more conflicted, and his eyes were searching mine, looking for any doubt that I might still have.

"I'm okay," I said. "Let's do this for real."

"You sure?" he asked.

"Action!"

I reached out for his thigh, and Porter raised his eyebrows. I started to lean in toward him, and he matched my movement.

My whole body was shaking in anticipation, and I couldn't tell anymore if it was scared or excited. We stopped short, feeling the electricity in our breath. I closed my eyes and let my body out of its misery by giving in. It was a light touch at first before he kissed me deeper. I instinctively scooted closer to him. I wasn't sure how long it had been before he pulled away, looking at me curiously.

"Hey," he whispered just to me. I leaned in again, pressing my lips against his harder. I felt his fingers trail up my neck and lock behind my head. My nerve endings were on fire, and my hands started to move involuntarily. They found his knees naturally, and he shifted when I touched him.

"Cut!" the director yelled, pulling us back into reality. We separated but didn't break eye contact. Every part of me wanted to reach back to him, but I crossed my arms and legs as we listened to the director talk. "That was very good. I don't know what more we should try. Could I have you drape your legs across his lap? Good. Yes, like that. Now I want you to tuck his hair behind his ear and laugh. You can tell jokes for all I care. This is a little subtler if the editors want to keep it PG."

How PG-13 had we been? My legs were in his lap; I felt his thumb start stroking my calf, and my whole body shivered. I took my hand from the back of the bench and ran it through his hair. His little smirk was making me smile too, and I honestly didn't know what was coming over me.

"You know what I keep thinking about?" he said.

"What?"

He leaned in a little, and my stomach flopped thinking

we'd kiss again. He stopped to whisper in my ear. "That we'll get the best donuts *ever* in the special extras tent."

I laughed out loud and could feel his laughter in his stomach against my legs. He gripped me tighter around the waist, and I let my legs rest more comfortably against his torso.

"Cut!"

The director took time to talk to Marcy and Ian for a while, and I took a piece of Porter's shirt and twisted it in my fingers. He stared at me while I did this until I looked back up at him.

"What?" I asked.

"Nothing," he smiled. The director had us doing variations of the same thing, never kissing again. Even though we never kissed, every part of my body that touched him lit up. It was almost more incredible when we weren't quite touching and we could feel that same electricity moving between us.

Suddenly, Porter shifted so my legs fell off his lap, and I followed his gaze. Luke and Zoe appeared around the corner, Zoe giving me a thumbs-up and Luke waving. They hadn't seen the kiss, then. My stomach twisted into a giant knot, and I could barely look at Porter anymore. We finished out the takes with minimal touching, but my body still tingled, wanting desperately to reach back out to him. This was a problem. A major problem.

I spent the rest of the shoot as far away from Porter as possible. I watched Zoe shoot a scene where she was a featured roller coaster rider. The fact that she didn't throw up after riding the

Cyclone fifteen times really impressed me. Each time Porter came into a tent where I was, I'd duck out. I knew we were acting, that we'd mutually agreed that it was for the movie, but I know if Luke or Zoe had seen that they would have asked questions.

We stuck around until Noah's scene was done for the day and piled into Porter's Jeep. I ended up being squished in between Zoe and Noah in the back, and I played absentmindedly with my nails while Noah, Zoe, and Luke talked about their scenes. After everyone was done gabbing about their fun time, Porter turned the radio on and everyone either jammed out silently or sang along.

Porter kept looking back at me in the rearview mirror, and I avoided him each time he tried to make eye contact. A few times he actually turned his head, but I pretended to be so deep in a conversation with Zoe that I couldn't possibly respond.

About a half hour away from home, Noah declared that he needed to go to the bathroom. Porter pulled off to a gas station to fill up while Noah used the bathroom. Luke offered to fill the car, and Zoe went inside to grab an iced coffee. Porter turned around after everyone left, and I had no choice but to look at him.

"Are you okay?" he asked.

"I'm fine. Are you okay?" I asked.

"Fine," he said. "Things aren't . . . weird with us now, are they?" he asked. His eyes searched mine again, and I thought it should be illegal for someone to look at another person that they weren't romantically interested in that way.

"No. It was acting; everything is fine," I said.

He nodded and turned back around. "Good. Glad we're on the same page."

"Good," I repeated.

<u>FASTER</u>:

acting, functioning,
or moving quickly.

**IN AN EFFORT TO AVOID PORTER AT ALL COSTS, I'D
SPENT THE PAST WEEK PLANNING ELABORATE DATES
WITH LUKE AND ASKING FOR MORE HOURS AT GREEN
TRANSITIONS THAN THE BOOKSTORE.** We'd worked one
shift together since the movie set, and we barely spoke two
words to each other. We should have never agreed to film that
scene together. It ruined our friendship that we'd worked so
hard to build.

As part of the week of dates, Luke planned a nice dinner for
us at the fanciest restaurant in town. Zoe, my personal designer,
came over to get me ready in a ridiculous black dress and
intricate updo. I mean, I didn't look awful, but it definitely
wasn't my style.

The headlights of Luke's car shined through the front window, and my stomach burst with butterflies. Even though we had become familiar over the past two months, every time he came over I still got nervous. He rang the doorbell, and I wondered if he knew I was patiently waiting on the other side of the door for him that whole time. I breathed, trying to compose myself before swinging it open.

"Hey," I said. He smiled instantly, and that only made those butterflies flutter even harder. He looked dapper in his black dress pants and the red tie I'd helped him pick out earlier in the week.

"Hi," he said. We stood there for a few moments before I got the sense back into me to invite him inside.

"Luke, don't you look handsome!" Zoe said, passing by on the way outside. She was so good at keeping it cool in most moments. This was not one of those moments.

"Hey, Zo," he said. She wiggled past us and unlocked her car.

"You two have a blast! I'm tempted to embarrass you more and take pictures!" she said.

"Bye, Zoe!" I said, urging her to leave.

"Fun killer!" she yelled back. She blew me a kiss as she pulled away, and Luke and I both laughed. We hopped into his car and headed off to Denton's finest cuisine.

Le Bistro came into view, and I clasped my hands. The last time I'd graced Le Bistro was after my graduation. So much had changed since then, not just me going to Ohio State but personally. It's funny how things change so much in just a few months. He actually opened my door for me, which only added about a thousand more points to our cheese level for the night. It felt like we'd known each other forever, which we kind of had, and I felt safe with him. He even agreed to go to my cousin's wedding with me, which was a huge leap into serious boyfriend territory.

We sat at a secluded table away from the other customers. I had seen at least ten of my parents' friends as we walked in and, for the first time since they knew me, I wasn't completely embarrassed when I saw them. I had something to show off that was pretty great, if I did say so myself.

"Olivia says hi," he said as we looked over the menu.

"That's great! I've missed talking to her," I said. I had wondered what Olivia thought about all of this. I knew she remembered my giant crush from when we were kids, but now that it was actually coming to fruition she had to be freaking out a little bit.

"She misses you too," he said. He clasped his hands into fists and took a giant sip of water. "That's actually something I wanted to talk to you about."

My stomach dropped. "You aren't moving back, are you?"

"Oh God no," he said. I breathed again. "Actually the opposite. Our family has a little reunion at the end of the month where we all go out to my uncle's place in Indiana. He has a huge ranch that we stay at. I was wondering if you'd like to come with me this year?"

"Of course!" I said. He smiled, relieved, and took another sip of water.

"You don't have to if you don't want, it's just a nice way for you to meet everyone and see Olivia and the family again," he said.

"Yes, I would love to come," I replied.

"Really?" he asked. "You don't have to say that just to be nice; if you really don't want to go that's fine."

I grabbed his wrist across the table. "Stop. I really want to go. I've already told you how much I've missed your family."

"You're the best," he said.

"I try." I smiled. The waitress came up to the table, and we both ordered Diet Cokes like the little kids that we were at heart. After she left behind the bread basket, Luke selected a giant breadstick and took a bite.

"Porter and Emilie are coming too," he said. "It should be a fun time."

"Emilie?" I asked.

"Yeah, Porter's sort-of girlfriend. She's been hanging around our place more lately, and she overheard me talking about it and invited herself along," he said.

"I've never heard him talk about her," I said. "Or anyone, for that matter."

"Don't feel bad, he doesn't really tell anyone anything," he said. "He'd rather write everything in his little notebook, you know?"

I nodded. "Yes, I do."

"Speaking of Porter, I think he's gone for the weekend. He said something about his brother going to Chicago for the weekend and meeting up with him," he said.

"Oh?" I said, my heart racing. Sure, Luke and I had been getting to know each other better over the last few months, but we'd never broached the whole sex topic before. Luke didn't like to talk about his past, and I was vastly unexperienced in mine.

"We could go back to my place after dinner?" he asked.

"Yeah, sure," I said. My heart beat in my ears, and I felt this dread in the pit of my stomach. Luke and I were in college, and we had been dating for a few months, but most of our time together involved in-between moments fitted around his football training schedule. He was attractive, *very* much so, but I wasn't entirely sure if I was ready for this step.

The car ride back to his apartment was rather quiet. I waited for him to ask me what was wrong, but he never did. Every part of my body sparked with nervous energy, and I sat on my hands to keep them from visibly shaking. This was exciting, right? I was going to finally have sex—the true college experience. The thing that so many people my age were able to do so casually. It was no big deal.

I followed Luke up to his apartment, my hand in his. Could he feel how sweaty it was? Or how fast my heart raced? Was his racing too?

"Do you want a drink?" he asked.

"No, I'm fine," I replied quickly. His face turned down a bit. Would a drink make me feel better? More relaxed?

"You do look so beautiful tonight," he said, taking out the bobby pins that held my hair in Zoe's updo. He set them down on the kitchen counter behind him without taking his eyes off me. I took in a shaking breath, and he brought my hand to his mouth. Slowly, he kissed up my arm. I sucked in a breath as he reached my neck, which gave him motivation to reach my mouth. I stood still as his mouth moved against me, his arms starting to envelop me. The same nervous energy sparked at higher volumes.

"Who would have thought after all these years that I would end up with Dani Cavanaugh?" He smiled. He meant it in a nice way, but it felt like a slam. Like he didn't fantasize about it and wish for it the same way I did. Like it was some strange fate that brought us together and not a mutual attraction that has lasted all these years.

"I thought it," I whispered. I said it so quietly that I'm sure he didn't hear me.

He took my face into his hands and kissed me deeper again before pulling away. Our foreheads rested together before he took my hand and led me to his bedroom. The pounding of my heart spread throughout the rest of my body. He sat next to me on the bed, still holding on to my hand.

"I've been thinking about this moment for a long time," he said.

"Me too," I said, looking down. He brought my eyes back to his eye level and stared at me for a long time.

"Do you want this?" he asked.

He was what I'd always wanted. I nodded.

<u>FESTIVITIES</u>:

the enjoyment or merrymaking
typical of a celebration.

AMEERA MADE ME WORK LATE, EVEN ON THE DAY BEFORE I LEFT FOR THE UPTON FAMILY VACATION BRIGHT AND EARLY THE NEXT MORNING. We'd been tweaking and perfecting my speech as the day of the city council meeting grew closer. I felt more confident each time she took a fine-toothed comb through my words, and I had been practicing saying it aloud in front of my bathroom mirror every night. I was determined to make a damned good speech to call all of Denton to environmental action.

"Great job today, Danielle," she said. "You can leave now."

"Good night," I told her as I packed up. I practically sprinted out the door and made my way to the car. I'd promised Luke that I would help him pack tonight before we left. If the other drivers on the interstate couldn't tell that I was antsy just by how quickly I dodged in and out of them, they could tell by the three times that I honked on that ride back, which is a rare occurrence for me. Gearing up to meet Luke's extended family was more nerve-racking than what I originally thought it would be.

I screeched into Luke's parking lot and rang the bell to his apartment five times before he unlocked the door. Annoyed, I knocked on the door, waiting to give him the wrath of the girlfriend who had to wait outside for over ten minutes.

Instead of Luke opening the door, a tiny blond thing came up and tackled me into a hug. We swayed back and forth for a few seconds and I was honestly convinced that Emilie was the one giving me a bear hug. I tried to shrug her off me before the little blond thing spoke.

"Dani, I've missed you so much!" I pulled her away to find Olivia Upton staring back at me. I think I screamed the girliest scream known to humankind in that moment, and we both jumped up and down.

"Luke, you ass! Why didn't you tell me she was coming?" I said.

"I wanted to see this reaction." He smiled. "And I wasn't disappointed."

She grabbed my face and smiled. "How did you get so freaking gorgeous?"

"I'm the one who should be asking you that!" I said. It was honestly a blast from the past. Olivia looked exactly the same, only where her baby fat used to be was a strong bone structure and makeup under her eyes. She still populated the

0.1 percentile on size—almost like she stopped growing after sixth grade.

"Oh stop," she said.

"What on earth are you doing here?" I asked. "I thought you were meeting us in Indiana?"

"My parents decided they wanted to stop and check in on Lukey," she said. "And while they stay at a hotel Luke has been kind enough to offer me his couch. You can stay over if you want—we could have a catch-up sleepover for old time's sake?"

"I'd love that," I said, turning to Luke. "But isn't Emilie here? Where will she stay?"

"I'm assuming Porter's bed?" Luke said.

I flushed. Duh. "Oh, that works out then. Where are they?"

"He's probably taking her to Moe's. Valley View doesn't have diners like Moe's," he said.

I frowned again. The only time I'd ever heard the name Emilie mentioned was in passing the first night Luke figured out who I was. Porter was taking Emilie to a date at Moe's. Hearing Luke mention that she was from his hometown made the whole Emilie thing seem more significant somehow—like she could actually become a part of the Denton equation. Or take a certain part out of it.

"They should be back soon," Luke said. "And I don't actually need your help with packing. That was my pretense so Liv could have her grand entrance."

Olivia took my arm and led me to the couch. "Now it's your turn to leave, Lukey. We have some much-needed gossip time, and you're not invited."

"All right, all right, I can tell when I'm not wanted," he said, holding his hands up. He picked up a shirt that had been flung into the hallway on the way back to his room, slamming the door in a dramatic fashion. Olivia and I both laughed.

"Luke hasn't told me much of the story yet. How did you two meet up again? I can't believe how amazing it is that you two are finally together." She beamed.

"At a party, one that I didn't really want to go to in the first place." I laughed. "I was out in the kitchen, and Luke came and talked to me, all the while not knowing who I was."

"Typical Luke, can't see what's right in front of his face," she said.

"It's cute now that I look back on it. I actually work with Porter, and Luke came to the bookstore one night and finally put the pieces together. We had our first little date that night, and the rest is history," I said.

"That's so romantic," she said. "Luke is so lucky to have seen you again! I bet you make Denton worth it to him."

"What do you mean?" I asked.

She wrapped her arms around her legs and paused for a moment. "Well, he really didn't want to come back here in the first place. He wanted to take a year off to heal and then try to get in other places. My parents offered to pay for his school, among other things, to come here."

"I thought he got a full ride?" I asked.

"A full ride from the Bank of Mom and Dad," Olivia said. "They pretty much bribed him to come here so he didn't goof off around the world with his ex-girlfriend. The 'rents were not a fan of her or his big idea."

I was about to ask more when the lock on the door fiddled open and in walked Porter and a girl I assumed was Emilie. They each had a Cup o' Moe's to-go in their hands and smiles on their faces. Emilie had long dark hair that went past her shoulders. She wore Porter's Remembrants' T-shirt, and a little part of my stomach lurched.

"Sorry to interrupt your catching up," Porter said. "Emilie, this is Danielle, Luke's girlfriend."

"Oh no, you're fine!" I said, walking up to Emilie. "It's nice to meet you."

"You too." She smiled. "These three have told me so much about you."

I couldn't exactly return the compliment because I had virtually heard nothing about Emilie in return. Instead I just nodded awkwardly and waited for Porter or Olivia to break the silence.

"Well, Luke is in his room getting all packed up. You guys can join Dani and me if you want?" Olivia said.

"Uh . . ." Emilie turned to Porter, patting his chest. "I think we better get you all packed up, don't you?"

I hadn't realized that my arms were crossed until Porter raised his eyebrows at me. I quickly let them go to my sides and put a smile on my face. Emilie smiled at me as they passed, Porter putting his hand on her lower back as he led her to his room.

My suitcase for the trip felt like it contained a dead body. I never really understood the whole "packing light" concept. Luke came out and grabbed my suitcase, managing to shove it into the trunk with everyone else's bags. He definitely couldn't see out the back and that was a bit scary. I hoped that Luke would drive the majority of the way because Porter was a terrible driver. I'd volunteer myself before allowing him to go behind the wheel.

"Here, do you want to sit up front?" Porter asked, stepping out of the passenger side.

"Nah, you boys can have boy talk up front, I'll sit back with the girls," I said. I swear Emilie scowled. If she was going to be all passive-aggressive the whole trip I'd definitely have to have a little chat with her.

All I have to say is thank God for the radio. If it weren't for the top forty chart blaring, the Jeep's awkward silence level would have reached its max. I was also glad that Olivia volunteered to sit in the middle—I think riding next to Emilie would have provoked me to accidentally jab my elbow into her side on many occasions.

We stopped about two hours in at a rest stop, and when we came back from the bathroom, Emilie had pulled Porter into the backseat with her, her arms wrapped around his neck. They laughed and *rubbed noses*, and I thought I would barf.

"They're pretty gross, right?" Olivia said, coming up behind me.

"It's just so . . . not Porter," I said. "I've never seen him like this."

"Trust me, it won't last long," Olivia said. "He may be trying to prove a point more than anything else."

"A point for what?" I asked.

Olivia just giggled and hopped into the backseat by the lovebirds. I sank into the passenger seat and was followed by Luke carrying a giant soda. He handed it to me, and I took a sip gladly. He turned the car on, and I punched the radio off, looking out the window.

"You all right?" Luke asked, grabbing my hand.

"Yeah, I just have a headache," I said.

The Jeep bumped along in the silence and, if I remembered anything about Olivia, I knew that the silence killed her. It was only a matter of time before she piped up and broke the tension.

"So, Porter, how did you meet Emilie? Besides the obvious living in the same town part of it," Olivia said. Actually I didn't mind her attempt to make things less awkward. It was a question that I had as well.

"Porter and I had a few classes together at Valley View. He was too scared to ask me out, but we hung out so much that everyone just assumed we were dating by default." She laughed.

"Hey, that's not true. I made it very clear that I was interested," he said.

"Yeah right!" she said. "I wouldn't have known if I hadn't read your little journal one day while we were hanging out."

"I think I made it clear in other ways," he said.

"I guess so," she replied, hooking her index finger under his chin and pulling him in for a kiss. I looked back in the rearview mirror to see any reaction from Porter. Emilie had admitted to looking at his notebooks, the most secret and sacred things that Porter had, without batting an eye. He continued to look at her like she was the missing piece to his happiness puzzle. I looked back out the window.

We were already more than halfway there, so close to the ranch yet so far away. I turned the radio back on after twenty minutes of silence and could feel myself starting to fall asleep. Car rides always made me sleepy, even since I was a kid. I drifted off, my cheek pressed against the car window.

"Babe." I was shaken awake by Luke.

"Are we here?" I asked, wiping the drool from the corner of my mouth. I looked out the window and saw that we were surrounded by massive trees. The cabin was at the end of a trail and just visible out of the corner of my eye.

"Yes." He smiled. "How in the hell did you sleep through everyone getting their stuff out of the car? I was sure you'd wake up."

"Mom always says that a bulldozer could go through our front door and I'd still sleep. One of my many talents," I said.

"Speaking of moms," Luke started.

My door flew open, and I was embraced in an almost identical Olivia hug. But this time the perpetrator was Mrs. Carrie Upton. "Dani girl! How are you?"

"Carrie, oh my God, hi," I said, wrapping my arms around

my second mother's neck. She physically *lifted me* out of the car and planted me in front of her.

"You look great, honey. You feeling okay?" she asked.

"I'm feeling wonderful," I said.

"I know Luke had a hard time waking you up." She laughed. "That's the Dani I know." She led Luke and me up the trail and toward the cabin. As we went up the dirt walkway I could see other cabins not far off. We were right on the edge of Indiana meeting up with Lake Michigan. It had been a while since I'd seen one of the Great Lakes, and Luke promised that some boating would be included in the family vacation.

Mr. Upton opened the door to greet us and gave the same, apparently hereditary, hug that the rest of the family had. We exchanged more pleasantries as we shuffled into the cabin that was already stuffed to the brim with people. The family sat around the kitchen table and into the living room, all staring at us as we walked inside. I vaguely recognized some of them from Olivia's childhood birthday parties, including Uncle Henry, who owned the beautiful cabin. Luke described Henry as the "ultimate bachelor" who would rather spend time on the lake than try to find a companion.

"Well, you all made it in one piece," Henry said, standing at the front of the kitchen. "I managed to clear out some sleeping space for my wonderful siblings, but the kids can either sleep in the living room together or in tents outside."

"Are we the kids?" I whispered to Luke.

"Most definitely," he whispered back.

"Olivia, are you still up to helping me cook?" he asked.

She smiled. "I promise not to start any fires this year." All of the family laughed, and I'm sure I missed some inside joke.

"On a more serious note, I did want to thank you all for making it for the weekend. I know this is what Dad would have wanted," Henry said. I'd almost forgotten about Luke's grandpa. He passed away about six months ago. That's another reason that it was important for their family to make it, this year especially.

Everyone nodded, and he raised an invisible glass. "To our . . . eccentric family traditions." A group laugh erupted, and everyone raised their invisible glasses to match. I raised mine, looking over at Luke as I did. This weekend wouldn't be bad at all.

FORMAL:

done or carried out in
accordance with established
or prescribed rules.

**THE UPTONS AND COMPANY CHANGED INTO SWEATSHIRTS
AND JEANS ONCE THE SUN WENT DOWN.** We sat around the
nicely contained fire pit in the various lawn chairs the Upton
family had managed to pull together. Luke and Olivia's cousin
Sammy, who I remembered playing with as a kid, came up
and gave me a hug. She was at least four years older than
Olivia—I remember her bratty teenage years when she made
it very evident that Liv and I were babies that she could no
longer associate with. She had managed to pull me aside from
the family, cornering me in the kitchen for the first interrogation of the trip.

"So, Danielle, how have you been?" she asked. Honestly, if

I had a quarter for every person who asked how my life had been since the Uptons left . . .

"Oh, fine," I said. "How about you, Sammy?"

She smiled. Obviously this was her tactic all along. "I'm just wonderful. My husband, Ritchie, over there? He's perfect. I couldn't have asked for anyone better in my life."

"I'm happy for you," I said.

She touched my shoulder. "Not as happy as I am for you and Luke. I'm so glad he found a nice girl. He really pissed his parents off with the last girl he brought here. What was her name? Cameron? Callie? Something like that. But you don't want to talk about her."

"Talk about who?" Porter asked, coming up behind us. For the first time I felt thankful for Porter's ability to interrupt conversations.

"Oh, no one," Sammy said. She took this moment to ditch, leaving Porter and me standing by ourselves. He watched Sammy leave, and we both shrugged at each other.

"I think she just wanted to tell me about her new perfect husband and now that she has, she left."

"I see," he said, picking at his nails. Since our movie day, we'd barely talked. I still didn't know where we stood, but the fact that he'd brought Emilie along made me think that we were allowed to be cool again. Friends, even. He tugged at his leather jacket that had come a bit more in season now and started fidgeting with the zippers on his pockets.

"Emilie seems nice," I said.

"She is," he said.

"How come you never told me about her?" I asked.

"It never came up," he said.

"That's some crucial information to tell a friend," I said, folding my arms.

"If I didn't know any better, I'd say you're sounding a little jealous, Cavanaugh."

"Jealous? You're ridiculous," I said.

"You would have met her if you came over more," he said, shrugging.

"Sorry I'm busy actually doing things with my life," I said.

His eyes crinkled a bit, deflated by my words, which I hadn't meant to sound so cruel. Nothing came out right around him anymore. "That's not what I meant," I said.

"No, no, I think it is," he said, walking away. I watched him leave, and my heart sank. I royally blew it.

Luke came up behind me, hugging my waist. "We're setting up a fire. Come sit with me?" he asked.

I nodded and followed the rest of the family out to the fire pit. Luke already had a spot on the ground with a giant blanket. Olivia sat on one side, and she patted the middle for me to take a seat. Luke seemed especially cuddly in the firelight, and I nuzzled into his sweatshirt, trying to erase the thoughts of a hurt Porter and the Cameron/Callie that Luke brought here last year—the one that Luke's parents would bribe him with money to stay away from.

The Uptons passed around graham crackers, marshmallows, and chocolate bars so we could make s'mores. Olivia managed to drop at least three marshmallows into the fire. Finally I took her stick away from her and fried her marshmallow to the perfect darkness. You know it's bad when I'm the one who has to take over a food-related task. We laughed as the chocolate dripped onto the blanket and all over the front of her sweatshirt.

Uncle Henry quickly became the showcase of the bonfire, pulling out his guitar. Sammy sang along with him, and I had to admit it, she was actually really talented. Her perfect husband, Ritchie, sat on his phone near the house claiming to have too much business to attend to back home. At one point, and I'm not kidding, Olivia went over and took the phone out of his hands and led him back to the fire to hear his wife sing. She was the sweetest person I knew, but when it came to people being rude, she took it upon herself to make it right. I saw Sammy smile at me from across the way and I winked, curled up in a blanket with Luke. Even Emilie stayed pleasantly quiet the whole time.

As the adults grew tired they began to trickle into the house. Eventually the only people left were the cousins who sat around the fire, no longer inhibited by the presence of the parents. Luke's cousin Matt reintroduced himself to me, and I instantly remembered him joining forces with Luke on the toad front. Olivia and I hid from them for the entire week when Matt and his twin brother, Ryan, would come into town.

"You're in for a treat tomorrow, Danielle," Matt said. "Have you ever played a competitive sport with this guy?"

I turned to look up at Luke. "I don't believe I have."

"Family touch football is like war. I hope you have some skills." Matt laughed.

"Matt's making me sound a lot scarier than I actually am," Luke said.

"What about you, Emilie, you a good player?" Matt asked across the way.

She scoffed. "Oh definitely. The challenge will be getting Porter here to play."

Porter shrugged. "What can I say? I was born with an athletic deficiency. I wouldn't want to hurt anyone by my tripping and falling."

"You can't be that bad, man," Ryan said.

Emilie pecked his cheek. "It's okay, baby, you can cheer me on."

"I'll most likely join Porter," I said. "I wouldn't want to bring anyone's team down."

Emilie frowned. "I'm sure you're fine, Danielle."

Everyone looked around at each other in silence before Ryan chimed in. "So . . . anyone want to play Never Have I Ever? High stakes. Losers skinny-dip in the lake."

"It's cold, Ry!" Olivia said. "If I lose you all better shut your damn eyes."

"You won't lose, Liv, you're the most innocent one here out of all of us," Matt said.

"It's been a while since we last played; you don't know as much about my life as you think you do," Olivia said, puffing out her chest.

"Well then, it will make things more interesting, won't it?" Ryan asked. He clapped his hands. "Let's get started!"

"Okay, I'll go first," Emilie volunteered. "Never have I ever . . . been out of the country."

Ryan and Matt groaned. "Too tame!" one said. "So boring!" said the other. I sheepishly put one finger down and realized I was the only one who did.

Matt chimed in. "Never have I ever barfed at a family dinner," he said.

"That's targeting!" Ryan replied, trying to defend himself from having to put his finger down for an obvious family inside joke.

"I've got one," Olivia said proudly. "Never have I ever failed a class."

"That's cheap, Liv," Matt said, pushing her over. He put a finger down, and I debated owning up to it or keeping my secret failure just that. I put my finger down slowly, hoping no one actually saw. Of course, no such luck was mine.

"Dan? You've failed a class?" Porter asked.

I cringed. "Yeah . . . that's actually the reason I'm at DCC."

"Aw, Dani, I didn't mean to make you feel bad!" Olivia said. "I just knew that Matt had failed a class, and I wanted to get him out sooner."

"Rude," Matt said under his breath.

"No, it's really fine," I said. "I've kind of had to own it in the last few months."

Porter kept looking at me like I'd killed his pet fish. I curled up my legs and rested my chin on my knees, trying to block his gaze.

"Okay, I have one," Ryan said. "Never have I ever lived in Denton, Ohio."

"That's really cheap!" Olivia said, pushing him back. All the Denton residents of past and present put a finger down.

"That's the game, cuz," he said. Olivia stuck her tongue out at him.

Emilie piped up again. "Never have I ever kissed a girl," she said. The guys groaned as they put a finger down, and I saw Olivia put a shaking finger down.

"Liv! How naughty!" Ryan exclaimed.

"I told you you didn't know everything about me," she said. She tried to say it playfully, but somehow it held more weight. I made eye contact with her for a few seconds longer, trying to make her realize she could talk to me about it if she wanted to.

"Never have I ever blacked out drunk," Luke said.

"Finally! A good one!" Ryan said. Both Ryan and Matt put a finger down along with Emilie. I kept mine up.

"Wait, Dan, you need to put your finger down," Porter said from across the fire.

"What? No way!" I said.

"Yes way. That house party? Do you remember me basically carrying you to your house afterward?" he asked.

"Zoe took me home that night," I said, feeling my entire body heating up in anger.

"I might have been very drunk, but I do remember Porter saying he'd get you home that night," Luke chimed in. He wrapped his arm around my shoulders and kissed the top of my head. "It happens to the best of us, babe."

My hand shook as I put my fourth finger down. What had I done that night? What had I said thinking that he was Zoe? The thought was mortifying. Who knew what my unfiltered brain would have admitted to.

Emilie shifted to sit on her knees, leaning toward the fire. "Never have I ever cheated on anyone," she said.

My eyes slid immediately to Porter, and we both looked away as soon as we made eye contact. We hadn't cheated. We'd kissed for a movie, an acting role, which was no big deal. Even though I could justify it in my head, my stomach filled with a pool of guilt. I looked around the circle of us and no one put their fingers down. Either we all were lying for the sake of each other's feelings, or everyone but me was a decent human.

"I'm tired; I think I'm going to go to sleep," Emilie said, standing up from the group. She looked from me to Porter and then stormed off toward the cabin. Porter hopped up quickly to follow her and all I could do was sit back and watch them leave.

"So much for our game," Ryan said. "Who wants to hear some ghost stories?"

We sat around listening to some especially scary stories about wolf children that came and dragged innocent campers out of their tents at night for another hour. I was too distracted to be scared, waiting to see if Porter or Emilie came back. Neither of them did before we decided to go to sleep in the tents Uncle Henry had set up for us.

Luke and I climbed into the tent that was meant for Luke, Porter, Emilie, and me to share. Since they were apparently still inside the cabin, we claimed the left side of the tent. I slunk out of my sweater and shivered before climbing into the sleeping bag. Luke wiggled in beside me and he wrapped his arms around me from behind. I turned around to face him, the words from Olivia still ringing in my head.

"Why did you really come to Denton?" I asked him. "I know you didn't get a scholarship."

He started to protest before coming to the realization. "Liv told you."

"I don't know why you'd lie about that," I said. "I wouldn't care if you got a scholarship or not."

"It's kind of embarrassing to admit that your parents bribed you to go somewhere," he said.

I laughed a little. "You know you're talking to the girl whose parents didn't give her any other option of where to go to school for her whole life, don't you?"

"They would have given you the choice if you had expressed interest in somewhere else. My parents just wanted to keep their hooks in me for as long as possible. To fill that dream that my dad was never able to fulfill. I wanted to take this year off and explore," he said.

"With your ex?" I asked. I regretted being so nosy the moment it came out.

"Yeah, with my ex," he said. He ran his hand up and down

my arm. "She is my ex for a reason. I haven't talked to her in weeks."

"Weeks?" I squeaked out.

"Months," he assured me.

"I'm not accusing you of anything," I said. My back now faced him. I rested my head in the crook of my elbow and waited for him to talk again.

He didn't. We both pretended to fall asleep.

In what felt like an hour later, the tent was slowly zipped open. I opened one eye to watch Porter and Emilie climb in. Porter looked over at us, and I quickly shut my eyes but kept my ears open like the horrible eavesdropper that I am.

"Are things any better with your dad?" Emilie whispered.

"They sent him home, but they think he could end up back in the hospital soon," he said. "Can we not talk about it?"

"Yeah, sure," she said. My eye popped back open again, and I watched her reach to touch his face. He leaned into her touch, closing his eyes. After a few seconds, he turned his head and kissed her palm. My body burned, and I turned over, feeling like I'd intruded on something completely personal. They were both quiet for a moment, maybe gauging if I would wake up, before they got into their sleeping bags.

━━━

Upton family touch football was not a joking matter. They banged on our tents early in the morning, making me practically rip my sleeping bag from jumping so high. Randi, Matt and Ryan's mom, unzipped our tent and peeked her head inside.

"Breakfast is up," she said. "You'd better hurry before all the bacon is gone."

Luke groaned as the light hit his face, and he rolled over, covering his eyes. The cold air slapped my face, and I joined him under the sleeping bag, trying to find any last warmth. I thought Luke had fallen back asleep until I felt his hand slip around my waist. We stayed in the warm cocoon of the sleeping bag until Matt ran in, ripping the bag off us.

"Mom told you to get up already, kids," Matt said. "T-minus thirty minutes until UTFL. Get up, you wussies."

"What's UTFL?" I groaned.

"Upton Touch Football League! Come on, Danielle, I expect more out of you," Ryan said, barging in behind his brother.

"All right, we're coming," Porter said, taking the bravest move yet—unzipping his sleeping bag. Emilie curled her legs up to her chest while the cold air hit her body and a small shiver went through her. I heard her moan a small "why" under her breath, eyes still closed. We rolled out, racing into the house to avoid the cold. Inside we quickly packed on as many layers of clothes as we could and chugged coffee to warm and wake ourselves. All the "kids" were exiled to the floor; only Sammy and her husband were allowed to sit with the rest of the adults. I watched her look back at us while we laughed. It seemed like she wanted nothing more than to join in with us, but Ritchie kept her anchored to the adult table.

Competition must have been laced in the bacon grease with all the trash talk over breakfast. Luke was the number one culprit, spouting on and on about how he would personally deliver Matt's death via touch football. It was as hilarious as it was histrionic. Even Olivia, the supposed sweetheart, jabbed at her cousins. The pressure only made me more nervous. I was definitely sitting this one out.

"All right, everyone, it's time!" Uncle Henry yelled from the front door. "Keeping up with tradition, I will be a captain along with my baby brother, Craig."

Luke and Olivia's dad stepped forward and waved, a loud whistle erupting out of Randi behind us. Craig locked eyes with Luke and waved him up next to him, resulting in boos and comments like "That's not fair!" from the rest of the family. The rest of the teams were picked, and I drifted to the back of the pack, resisting all their attempts to get me to play. A few others sat out, including Sammy and Porter. I sat contentedly in the middle, keeping my focus on Luke, the obvious family superstar and source of jealousy for the opposing team.

Porter came up next to me, sitting with his small notepad out. We didn't talk, but I had so much I wanted to say. I wanted to ask what Emilie had meant about his dad. I wanted to make sure that he was okay. I wanted to ask if he knew anything about Luke's ex. All questions that seemed über inappropriate in the moment. I tried to distract myself by making a flower crown out of the dandelions around me or cheering on the team, but I couldn't get over Porter sitting right in my peripherals and not speaking to me.

I felt a tap on my shoulder and turned to face him. One of his notebooks was laid open on the ground, and I read his little scribbled note.

We need to talk.

My stomach flipped, and I felt blood rush to my ears. I managed to mouth back the word "later" and turned away from him. It took everything in my power to ignore him for the duration of the game. What did he want to talk about? His fight with Emilie? Did he no longer want to be my friend? Did he think we should tell her and Luke about the movie kiss? No good conversation ever started with "we need to talk."

Luke's team won and only took a little bit of grief from everyone else. Olivia seemed the most torn up about it, really believing that she could outwit her brother a couple of times. She pouted next to me, resting her head on Porter's shoulder.

"I really thought I had him this year," she said.

"You can't beat the master," Luke said, coming up behind us. He sat down, kissed my cheek, and put his arm around me. I ducked out of his embrace, still not in the mood to be loving after our conversation last night. He frowned my way and opened his mouth to talk until Emilie came up and plopped onto Porter's lap. She held out her hand for a high five from Luke.

"We make a pretty good team, don't we, Skywalker?" she said, laughing at her own joke. Emilie and Luke talked through the play-by-play of the game, highlighting some of their best acts of teamwork while I zoned out.

Liv saved me from awkwardly sitting through another half hour of listening and we pulled off to the side of the yard, sitting down on a set of lawn chairs some of the parents brought out earlier. We had a good view of the boys and Emilie, who made a point of laughing loudly and constantly touching Porter and Luke as she talked.

"Can I be honest with you for a second?" Olivia asked.

"Of course," I said, turning toward her. She had a little smile on her face and closed her hands, fiddling with her fingers. I remembered back to her confession during Never Have I Ever— the thing the boys deemed "naughty" that might mean that much more to her.

"I have learned so much this past year about being who I want to be, which goes along with being with who I want to be with. Being in a relationship to please the people around you isn't a good foundation of a relationship," she said.

I frowned. "What do you mean?"

"I love Luke so much, obviously, because he is my brother, but I like Porter. I think he's a good guy," she said.

I continued to frown.

"You and Porter," she said, staring at Emilie.

I started to protest, but she held up her hand. "There's just something in how he looks at you. You have to realize it, right?"

And in a single sentence, all my fears were confirmed.

<u>FEAST:</u>

an elaborate meal for
many people that celebrates
an occasion.

OLIVIA AND I DIDN'T TALK FOR THE REST OF THE DAY, AND I FELT A LITTLE GUILTY ABOUT THAT. It wasn't her fault for speaking her mind, but my mind could not wrap itself around what she meant. She politely kept her distance, and no one really noticed. We spent the majority of the afternoon helping Carrie and the rest of the family make a big dinner for our last night, with enough turkey and stuffing to feed fifty people. I kept my duties minimal, Luke politely warning everyone of my lack of cooking skills. Porter and Emilie had gone on a walk around the lake, and I was thankful not to have his presence in the room. I would just overanalyze all of Olivia's ridiculous claims if he were here. And no one had time for that nonsense.

If there was one thing that kept me a little bit sane during the day, it was Sammy and me gabbing constantly. She acted more like I remembered when she wasn't bragging about her great life, and it was nice talking to someone who really had no preconceived notions about me other than my apparent lack of fashion sense in the sixth grade. We talked about movies and books and even frivolous things like our favorite celebrity couples, but it was nice. She could be normal without her new perfect life taking over her personality.

Dinner called for fancier attire, and we all changed into dresses and nice pants. I thanked Zoe internally for making me pack a dress just in case. She saved my ass on so many occasions that I really wondered what I would do without her. There was a knock on the door of the room I was changing in, and I jumped as someone cracked it open.

"Dani, can I come in?" Carrie Upton asked.

"Yes, of course!" I said, relieved to hear her voice.

She looked me over and smiled. "Don't you look beautiful."

"Oh, thanks," I said.

She sat down on my bed, patting the spot next to her. I sat down dreading some sort of confrontation. Had Olivia talked to her?

"Gosh, remember when you and Liv would raid my closet and makeup drawer and pretend you were fashion designers?" she asked.

"Yeah." I smiled. "We wanted to be grown up so badly. You don't realize it until you're finally considered an adult how scary it actually is."

She put her hand in mine and rubbed it. "You and Liv were

such good friends, you always knew the right thing to say and how to cheer her up—having you at our house was one of my many joys when we lived in Denton."

"That's so sweet," I said, feeling the guilt creeping into my chest again.

"You are going to give that same treatment to my son now, and you have no idea how happy it makes me to see him in a relationship with such a good girl—a girl that we love too," she said.

I felt tears start to prick my eyes as she pulled me into a hug. Carrie was the same woman who healed my scrapes, took me to see my first play, and loved me like a second daughter for so many years. I felt pressure in a new way, like I could never disappoint them when it came to their son. That if I ever hurt him I would hurt their family. I suddenly felt suffocated, trapped in a situation—that I was some sort of solution to all their problems. But what if I had my own problems to figure out before I could heal theirs?

———

Luke and I made our way to the table with the rest of his family. It felt like all the big moments lately revolved around a family dining table. It was like every time any variation of my friends and family finally sat together the world fell onto our shoulders and reality was too much. Tonight my weight of guilt took over for many reasons—my guilt for being mad at Olivia for speaking her mind, my guilt for avoiding Porter, and the uneasiness I felt about Luke after figuring out the truth about why he came to Denton. And who he left behind. The Uptons laughed and chatted around me, passing out the last of the sides to one another before Uncle Henry called everyone to order.

"As per tradition, we are all going to take a turn saying what we're thankful for this year. Since Thanksgiving is too much of a challenge to get everyone together, we're officially starting it tonight. Who would like to start?"

Craig Upton raised his hand, and Henry patted him on the shoulder. "I would like to say how thankful I am that our family can still join like this once a year and that everyone is happy and healthy. I know Dad would have been the first to make this same speech this year, and I know he is here with us now, trying to steal the best turkey leg." Everyone laughed solemnly, Carrie Upton wiping away a straggling tear. "He always had one sentiment that I have tried to pass on to my kids, and I hope they will too. Family is forever. No matter how far they go, they will always be there to embrace you when you come back."

He looked at Luke in this moment, and I reached my hand into his. He gripped it so tightly that my hand turned purple. Mr. Upton winked at me, and I smiled back, looking up at Luke.

"I'd like to go next," he said, dropping my hand and standing up. "I'd like to say thank you to everyone who showed me the true meaning of family within the past year especially. I could not have made it this far without your help, especially the help of my parents, who always look out for my and Liv's best interests above everything. And to my sister, for giving me a dose of harsh reality when needed.

"I figured out after my injury that I'm pretty damned lucky to have such an amazing support system surrounding me. I couldn't have asked for anything better," he said.

Uncle Henry raised his glass in response. Luke sat back down quickly as if figuring out that he was embarrassed now that he'd said so much. His aunt Randi smiled at me, and I realized that everyone was looking at me now to speak. I tried to open my mouth to say something, but nothing came out. Thankfully Porter picked up on this and spoke up.

"Uh, I'll go next," he said. He didn't stand up, which I was also thankful for. If everyone was expected to stand up to make their speech I would have probably passed out. "First off I want to thank Craig and Carrie again for letting Emilie and me come with—you are a lot more tolerant of us hooligans than I would be."

They both giggled, and Carrie smiled at Porter very similarly to the way she did at me earlier. She always loved having her kids' friends around.

"You've all made me feel like a part of something, a part of a family this year. That's something I haven't had in a long time," he said, looking at me.

All those times that we talked about Mr. Harrisburg's class assignment, how I didn't know what I was living for—he'd been holding out. Living for him was having a family who cared. It broke my heart that I didn't realize that before now, that I'd been too self-centered to even ask more about his family or his past. He nodded at me before looking down at his plate and waiting for someone else to talk.

"I'll go next!" Sammy announced. They went around the table talking again about how lucky they were to have their health, that they were thankful for all the time they got to spend with their family, how much they missed their grandpa. I held Luke's hand under the table while everyone spoke. Every time I slid my eyes to the end of the table I found Porter looking at me. He didn't try to hide it now, and it made me a little mad. He shouldn't look at me that way, it wasn't fair to anyone. I watched as he sipped from his drink more and more as the dinner went on, seeing the telltale signs of drunk Porter starting to form.

It finally reached me again, and I felt just as frozen as I had before but now had no one to save me. Luke squeezed my hand for reassurance. "I guess I wanted to thank the Uptons for letting me come to this. Even though Luke and I have been dating for . . . three months now? I feel like we have been forever. I appreciate everything you've done for me over the years, and I am glad to still be a little part of the Upton family's life."

Luke kissed the side of my head, and everyone started to dig into their meals. Ryan and Matt were the needed comedic relief of the evening, always working off each other to tell hilarious stories about their college experience. They told us about all the pranks they played on people in their dorm, and I was beyond glad that I didn't live within a hundred-mile radius of these two.

We brought our dishes back out to the kitchen, Luke and I helping with the cleanup process. We were all chatting before we heard the door slam and Emilie whiz past the kitchen to the bathroom. I looked at Luke, who started to follow Porter, but I grabbed his arm. "Go check on Em. I'll find him," I said.

I opened the door and instantly regretted not throwing on a coat. I wrapped my arms around my chest and followed the male footsteps out into the woods, hopefully following Porter's path. He must have heard me coming because the crunching of his feet stopped as I caught up.

"What's going on?" I asked. His hands were gripped into tight fists at his side, and his breath was shallow. I'd never seen this side of him either.

"You should probably just leave me out here," he said.

"I'm worried about you," I said.

He laughed. "Since when?"

"Well that's not fair," I said. "Are you drunk?"

"There are a lot of things in life that aren't fair, Danielle," he said. "Now why don't you go back inside and find Luke. It'll make everyone much happier in this situation."

I stepped closer to him. "You can tell me what's wrong."

I watched his eyes dart back and forth, trying to find the words. Candid was never a word that I would assign to Porter Kohl, but maybe the alcohol would finally let some truth spill out of his mouth.

"How come you never told me why you were really at DCC?" he asked.

"It never came up in conversation," I said, quoting him

from earlier. "How come you never told me that you brought me home that night? And why the hell would you bring it up in a game like that? Give me an honest answer, not a bullshit one."

He swayed a bit while he found the right words. "It did come up in conversation. I asked you about DCC, and you didn't tell me. I thought you trusted me enough to be honest with me."

I laughed. "That's a funny sentence coming from you. I don't know anything about you—about your life in Valley View, about your family—nothing!"

"I didn't tell you about my life there because it was awful. I hated it. I hate my dad, I can't take care of my mom anymore, and it's just fucking depressing to chitchat about," he said.

"Porter—" I started.

"I didn't tell you about the house party night because I didn't want to embarrass you. You were . . ."

"Obnoxious? God, I know I had to have said something bad," I said.

He raised his eyebrows. "I was going to say affectionate."

"So obnoxious. Great," I said. "I'm assuming you wrote all about it in your notebook. Do I get to read the 'Danielle's Great Drunken Adventure' chapter?"

"Why are we fighting right now?" he asked.

"Because," I started. "Because you keep looking at me."

"Looking at you?" he asked.

"Yeah," I said, crossing my arms. "Looking at me in ways that friends probably shouldn't look at other friends."

"I think you're interpreting things a little bit wrong," he said. "We are friends. Just friends."

"You know what?" I snatched the flimsy notebook out of his hands, and he tried to smack it out of mine. I ran back so I was just out of reach, and he stumbled hard before giving up. "I think before you can judge people in your little observation notebook you have to take a careful look at yourself first. You walk around like you're high and mighty and a fucking *philosopher* when you don't know anything either," I said.

He ran up and was eye to eye with me, but I still gripped the notebook. I held it up higher, threatening to throw it across the woods.

"Why can't you just admit what's going on so we can get past it?" I asked.

He grabbed my shaking wrist, still holding the notebook, and my breath became shallow. We locked eyes for a few seconds, and I leaned toward him. His breath mixed with mine, and the same electricity that came through on the movie set zipped through me.

"Are you sure you want to get past it?" he asked before snatching the notebook back.

I walked away, back toward the cabin. I hoped I never had to look at Porter Kohl again. I'd do whatever it took to never feel this mad and upset again. I heard his footsteps speeding up and catching mine. He grabbed my arm, and I whipped around.

"Luke isn't right for you," he said. His glossy eyes looked even more wild in that moment.

"Oh, what? And you are?" I asked.

He let go of my arm, and I walked back toward the house. "Isn't this clear enough?" Porter asked.

I shook my head. "I'm not doing this right now. You're very drunk. I know you will regret everything you're saying in the morning."

"But I won't," he said, trying to catch up to me.

"Porter, go to bed. I don't want to talk to you anymore," I said, feeling tears running down my face.

<u>FEVER:</u>

a rise of body temperature
above the normal. A state of
heightened or intense
emotion or activity.

TO SAY THAT NIGHT ENDED POORLY WAS AN UNDERSTATE-MENT. Porter and Emilie refused to talk, and I had no stomach to face to him either. I refused to tell Luke what had happened because it would only upset him. Basically Liv, Luke, and I slept in a tent with the crying Emilie while Porter camped out inside on his own, refusing to speak to any of us. He wouldn't even talk to Luke. We were packing up the rest of our things when Luke pulled me off to the side.

"What did he say to you last night?" Luke asked for the twentieth time.

"I already told you," I said. "He was just drunk and said something rude to Emilie that he didn't mean. He felt bad about it."

He raised his eyebrows. "Are you sure?"

"Yes," I said, feeling my gut twist the way it did when I lied.

"Why won't he talk to you?" Luke asked again. "Seriously, Danielle, if he said something awful to you—"

"I already said no! I don't know what more you want me to say!" I actually yelled. I held my hand over my mouth and felt my face getting hot. "I'm sorry—"

He started to walk away. "We're leaving in twenty minutes. Get your stuff ready." Family events are the worst. I managed to alienate everyone who was ever nice to me in a brief two-day outing.

I gave Olivia the same twenty-minute heads-up, and she smiled at me. I'm glad at least we had patched up our differences. Carrie and Craig Upton had left earlier that morning to catch a plane and left Olivia the car so she could visit one of her friends she'd made over summer camp who lived in Iowa. She was staying an extra day to help Uncle Henry organize things a bit before heading off, so these were the last moments that we'd see each other for a while.

"So this friend . . . ," I said.

"She's more than a friend," she said quietly. "Mom and Dad know, but I'm working on telling the rest. You saw how seriously Ryan and Matt took it the other night."

"They will take it seriously. And they won't care—they love you. You were born into the most loving family I've ever met. You know that, right?" I said.

"I do," she replied. "I can't believe we got to see each other again after all these years. I feel like our lives aren't done being connected."

Liv, always so adamant about destiny and fate. She was the one who convinced me that the cosmos sometimes worked in our favor. I would be lucky to have that influence on my life for the rest of it.

"I feel like that too," I said.

"Text me all the time," she said. "Good, bad, ugly, I want to know every detail."

"I will," I said. We hugged each other for a long time, and I whispered loud enough for only her to hear, "You were right. I will be careful."

She nodded, and Emilie emerged out of the bathroom, giving both of us apologetic looks. It was the first time that I felt bad for Emilie. No matter what flirtatious front she put up, she obviously had her feelings hurt last night. Luke came out of the room down the hall carrying my bag and his, taking them out to the car.

"It'll be fine with him," Olivia said. And then Porter showed up from God knows where, and we all went quiet. He didn't make eye contact with any of us and made his way to the car without a word. This would be a fun five-hour car ride.

Porter was already sitting in the passenger seat when we made it outside, and Emilie and I gladly took the back. Olivia and Uncle Henry waved at us from the front porch as we pulled away from the beautiful cabin. The music was turned on almost immediately, and I didn't mind. Emilie texted someone furiously, and Luke tapped his fingers idly on the steering wheel to the sound of the music. Porter stared outside. I hoped he was hungover to make the ride as miserable as possible for him.

About two hours in, Emilie was the first to announce her need for a bathroom break. Luke pulled into a gas station to fill up, and I followed Emilie inside to get some snacks. I trailed down the candy aisle looking for something wonderfully high in sugar and carbs to distract me. I decided on something with peanut butter and chocolate, because you can't go wrong with that combination. I couldn't have wanted to be left alone more in any moment. So Porter naturally sensed that vibe and came over.

"I'm sorry about last night," he said.

I kept walking down the aisle until I got to the peanuts, picking up a package. "I don't know why you're apologizing to me, you should be talking to Emilie."

"I don't regret what I said to Emilie," he said.

I scoffed and walked faster down the second aisle of Indiana mugs and key chains. He followed behind me. I stopped abruptly, and he smacked into my back. "Please stop following me."

"Please, Danielle," he said. The sincerity was back in his eyes, and I finally listened. "Last night I was drunk. I said things I shouldn't have, things that hurt you, which was never my intention. I also said some things that could hurt Luke . . . I-I'm not sure how to handle that right now—"

"We aren't going to say anything about it," I said. "I told

him you were upset about something you said to Emilie and that's it. That's all that was said. End of that story. Now let's go back in the car and talk to Luke so he doesn't feel angry about something he shouldn't."

He looked like he was going to say something else but just nodded. I bought my various peanut products and headed back into the car, sliding in next to Emilie, who had put her headphones in and bought a neck pillow. I figured she was pretending to be asleep because it was easier than being awake at this point, and I was the first one to really break the silence.

"That was a nice trip, Luke. It was great of Uncle Henry to have all of us over," I said.

Luke looked surprised as he glanced back at me. "I thought so too."

Emilie and I occasionally made eye contact from the back, and her previous looks of understanding had vanished since I started talking to Porter again. I had to shake it off if only to keep a small shred of sanity for the rest of the trip. As we blasted some major rock songs out the windows we could almost act like things were normal again, like there were no confessions in the woods last night. That there was no need for the ulcer of guilt forming in my gut that grew every time Luke smiled at me. Only two more hours. Then I'd be planted in front of the TV watching *American Horror Story* reruns with Zoe. Our communication had been minimal during the trip, but she knew something was up. Her opinion would probably be the most knowledgeable—she was the only one of my friends who actually knew Luke and Porter and had witnessed us in social settings before. She'd probably think it was romantic. I couldn't think that way.

When Luke finally pulled into my driveway I didn't think I'd ever been so happy to see my brother standing in the window waiting for me. He sauntered out trying to act cool, but we were both excited to see each other again.

"Did you guys have fun?" he asked.

I took my bag from Luke and strapped it around my shoulder. "So much fun," I said. "But it's good to be home."

Luke's smile flickered a little before kissing the side of my head. "I'll call you later."

Noah helped me lug my things inside, and I was greeted by my very tired father on the couch. The weekends were his time to take a break, and I worried that he was working too hard lately because of the amount of time it took him to recuperate. Noah sat next to him, and they both laughed as their favorite cartoons played. These were the moments that I was happy to be home for, the times when everyone was at peace even if they were watching mindless cartoons.

═══

Seeing as Zoe and I had met just a few times in the past few months to have a true girls' night, we decided that tonight was the night—no exceptions. We had it all planned, a nice feast out at Moe's, reruns galore, and then we'd pass out on Zoe's couch. I got control of the Jankmobile tonight, and I clunked out of the driveway and to Zoe's.

Her little sister, Alyssa, answered the door and smiled at me. I mean, I'd take a smile over everything she's been giving to Zoe lately. I went down the hall and to her burnt-orange room. Zoe had such bold taste that only worked for her. If anyone else tried to pull off the Zoe Cabot style, it would just look silly.

"I feel like I haven't seen your face in ages," she said, standing up and giving me a hug.

"I'm sorry I've been kind of a shitty friend lately," I said.

"Girl, you've had a lot to handle. Don't be sorry," she said. Zoe put on her jacket and grabbed her purse as we made our way back out to the Jankmobile.

"Okay, so you're going to have to tell me everything about the trip," she said.

"It was pretty fun. Olivia surprised me by being at Luke's the night before we left, and it was amazing being able to catch up with her. It was just like old times," I said.

"Don't get too comfortable with her. I'm still reigning best friend and not looking for any usurpers," she said.

I laughed. "You're always my number one, babe."

The parking lot at Moe's was surprisingly crowded for a Sunday night, but I could see through the window that our favorite booth was still open. Our very favorite waitress, Laurie, promptly brought us a blueberry muffin to split while we waited for our food. I asked Zoe a little bit about how things with her sister were going and if she'd sold any of her new creations online yet. She'd actually made around two hundred dollars just in her custom buttons.

"So, is business still booming since the last time we chatted?" I asked.

"Since the last time I texted you saying that I'm making hella money? Things have only been getting better," she said.

"That's amazing," I replied. "And your family has been cool with all of it?"

"Mom is really supportive. She's been sending me these links to internships in LA and New York that offer scholarships. This summer could really be my shot to do something great," she said.

"You will get accepted somewhere. Anyone would be so lucky to have you intern for them," I said, tapping the tip of my shoe onto hers. Zoe picked off a blueberry and popped it in her mouth, a smile creeping onto her face.

"So, were you able to sneak away with Luke at all?" she asked, wiggling her eyebrows.

"Not really," I said. "His family was around at most times."

"Well that's unfortunate," Zoe said. "Who wants to go camping if you don't get at least a *little* action?"

My mind flashed to Porter grabbing my wrist, his face inches from mine in the woods. I touched my wrist, remembering the feeling.

"I know that look. Where are you zoning out to?" she asked.

I weighed my options in telling her everything. I might receive the wrath of Zoe, or she might be heavily Team Porter. It was a tossup what her response might be. Taking a deep breath, I decided to tell her everything.

"Please don't be mad at me, but I haven't been completely honest," I said.

She sat back in her seat, taking a sip of her Diet Coke and bracing herself for the newest Danielle bombshell.

"You know how Porter and I got pulled away at Noah's movie set? And I said we just walked in the background of a scene together?" I asked.

Zoe nodded profusely, urging me to go on.

"Well, we actually kissed. For the scene! Not just for fun," I said.

She tilted her head, as if she was calculating her response. "Why didn't you say anything if it wasn't a big deal? If it was just acting?"

"It . . . I'm not sure. I haven't been thinking straight since then," I said.

"Do you still want to date Luke?" she asked.

"Of course," I said. "I've wanted to date him since I was eleven years old."

"I don't know, Danielle, but whenever I talk to you it's Porter this and Porter that, and Luke is almost an afterthought. To be honest, I don't even understand why you're still with Luke," she said.

"Luke is a good guy. A great guy. We . . . well, *you know.* We're kind of serious," I said.

"Are you happy with Luke?" she asked.

"Of course," I said.

"Then you have to stop. I don't know what it is about you

being around him, but if you want to be with Luke and be fair to Luke, you have to stop with the Porter thing, *capiche?*"

"Capiche-iest *capiche*," I said. "I'm embarrassed that we even had to talk about this. You know how much I like Luke."

She smiled devilishly. "Yes, I know every detail in *that* department. You're better than *50 Shades of Grey.*"

"Zoe!" I whisper-yelled, turning bright red.

"Oh, don't choose now to be embarrassed, please. You know I have to live vicariously through you, so let's just let it happen."

"You know if someone was listening in they'd probably find that very creepy," I said.

"We've already established that creepy is, in fact, my middle name," she said. This was the Zoe I missed spending time with. This was the part of my life that I would work hard to keep intact, no matter how hectic the rest got.

———

In the span of two weeks I got back into my regular routine—going to class during the day and working at the bookstore at night. I was given more hours by Misty, and so my nights of homework were usually spent at the cash wrap. I was still going over the notes for Ameera's city council presentation. She wanted me to talk on behalf of the program, something I was certainly dreading, but something I knew was necessary.

Porter and I had securely pushed the "are you sure you want to get past it" incident under the rug, barely saying more than a few words to each other. Zoe and I had talked through the Luke/Porter situation at length and she boiled it down to one thing: it's impossible for boys and girls to be friends. She deemed it all a little crush that would fizzle out—but in the meantime I should probably avoid him as much as possible.

Which I had been doing, by the way. Or at least trying to. It was pretty easy to keep things civil at the store, occasionally asking about classes or talking about music, but anytime we had to stay later than normal I scooted out of the store quickly before we could have time to really talk. That was, until the week of Luke's flu epidemic.

I would have never predicted Luke to be a pathetic sick person, but that he was. He lay in his bed all day waiting for Porter to bring him water and washcloths. At one point in the week I got a frantic call from Porter saying he didn't know what to do about Luke anymore—he wasn't getting any better.

"Porter?" I asked as I answered.

"You have to come watch him for a while," he said.

"Oh no, is he getting worse?" I asked.

"He's being impossible and keeps asking for you," he said.

"I'll be over soon," I said. I popped a few vitamins like I had been for the past few days and headed over to their apartment in the Jankmobile.

I knocked on the door and could hear Luke's pitiful sick voice saying "Danielle? Is that you?"

Porter pulled the door open to a bundled-up Luke shivering on their old couch watching cartoons. He had a trash can by his head, a glass of water, Sprite, and a sports drink on the table, saltine crackers in hand with a wet washcloth on his forehead.

"Oh, babe," I said. I knelt down next to him and planted a kiss on his damp forehead. "What have you been able to eat today?"

Porter rested his hands on the back of the couch. "He's eaten some peanut butter toast and those saltines without . . . you know."

I nodded, handing Luke the cup of water for him to sip. "And his temperature?"

"Been staying around a hundred and two," Porter said.

I looked down at the shivering mass of Luke and back up at Porter. "He's going to have to go to the hospital soon if he doesn't shake the fever. It's been, like, three days."

"No," Luke whined.

"Don't you want to feel better, babe?" I asked.

"I do feel—" He sat up abruptly, and I instinctively grabbed the trash can in perfect timing to catch his vomit.

This went on for the rest of the afternoon, Porter leaving around four to go to the bookstore. He was supposed to tell Misty I couldn't come in today. We both agreed that if he still had the fever and was sick by the time he got back that we'd take him to the ER. He had to be getting dehydrated no matter how many glasses of water he drank.

The clock hit ten by the time Porter came home and, after so kindly cleaning out the puke bucket, he helped Luke stumble into the front seat of the Jeep. I prayed that he could keep the puking to a minimum on the ride to the hospital, and as if he heard my silent prayers, he managed to do an ugly dry heave at every turn.

Pulling up to the hospital, I ran inside to grab a wheelchair for him. Porter maneuvered Luke out of the car and into the seat with ease, and I wheeled Luke inside while Porter parked. As we came in, the woman at the front desk got on the phone, saying we needed a doctor immediately.

"Hi," she said. "Do you have his information?"

I handed her his insurance card from his wallet and looked toward the doors, waiting for Porter to come inside.

"Do you have his driver's license?" she asked. I handed her the rest of the info and rubbed my free hand on his back. The doctor came outside in that moment and held out his hand.

"I'm Dr. Haughbon. You look like you're having a bad day, sir," he said.

"He's held a hundred and two fever and been throwing up for three days. It won't get better on its own," I said.

He nodded. "That sounds like the flu that's been going around. Some cases get this extreme if you aren't treated earlier. Here, let's take him back and get him hooked up to some fluids. Are you family?"

"We aren't, but they are on the way," Porter said, coming up behind me.

"Okay, you two stay out here with Nina, and we'll get some more information." Porter nodded and patted Luke on the shoulder.

"It's going to be okay, man. We'll be out here," he said.

Luke gave us a little smile before being wheeled back by Dr. Haughbon. Porter and I were instructed to stay in the waiting area until they were ready to have people visit him. They said this could take anywhere from one to two hours and to make ourselves comfortable. Making yourself comfortable in the hospital had to be the most ridiculous thing I'd ever heard. We sat on the uncomfortable gray chairs and watched bad reality television on the small screens while people fell asleep, sliding down their chairs and starting to snore. The occasional cough would break up the silence, but for the most part, an eerie calm fell over the place. Porter's knees rhythmically bounced up and down, and he kept fidgeting with the blue notebook that happened to live in this pair of jeans. After thoroughly cracking all his knuckles, he looked my way.

"Want to go get something to eat?" he asked.

"Yes, please," I said. I'd take anything over waiting in this room longer than necessary.

It didn't take long to find the area that connected to the rest of the hospital, including the cafeteria. There was a little section that was still open, boasting their delicious coffee for people who needed a pick-me-up. We walked into the small area and got two coffees, retiring to some couches just outside the waiting room. It was more pleasant out here—not so drab. I curled my legs up underneath me and sipped from the scalding coffee cup, coughing as it burned my throat.

"I'm glad I didn't have to do this alone," Porter said.

"You should have called me earlier if he was driving you nuts," I said. "We could have gotten him in here sooner."

He nodded. "I hate hospitals; I was trying to keep it as a last resort."

My eyebrows furrowed.

"I was always in and out of hospitals with my mom growing up. She took care of my brother and me on her own up until last year, when social services caught on to me living alone in our house while she was recovering from another episode. Of course, right when I'm seventeen—a year away from being able to legally take care of myself," he said.

"Oh my God, I had no idea," I said.

He shifted uncomfortably. "I don't talk about it because it's embarrassing—my family is royally effed up and being here, knowing people who didn't know my dad or mom, is refreshing. It's nice not getting those pity looks all the time."

"Porter?" I asked. He looked up and met my eyes, lazily so you could barely see into them underneath his long eyelashes. I was momentarily distracted and seemed to have completely lost my train of thought. I thought back to the night with Emilie in the tent, her mentioning that his dad had been in and out of the hospital lately.

"Uh—" I fumbled. "How does your dad fit into this?"

"He took off when my brother and I were kids. Only moved a few towns over but never bothered to get to know us. He knew that Mom had episodic breaks, that her mind would take importance over our care, but he left anyway. We basically raised ourselves. Then, within the last year, my teacher watched my mom snap in the parking lot of the school and called social services. I either had to move in with my dad or go into foster care for a few months. I thought moving in with him would be the lesser of two evils," he said.

His fingers twitched in his lap, and I took his hand in mine. He did that killer eyelash look at me again, and I felt something cold trickle through my body. I couldn't tell if it was the way he looked at me or if my body was purely dreading the end of the story. But I listened.

"I slept on this tiny air mattress in his living room for the year, and we barely spoke two words to each other. He didn't get me, and I sure as hell didn't understand him. How could someone leave his kids like that? How could he look me in the eye every day and not apologize for everything my brother and I went through? My brother, Phoenix, lives in New York now. He got as far away as possible. I can't bring myself to leave, though. Mom will need me again someday when she's out of the hospital, and without me, she'll have no one."

Tears formed in my eyes, and I felt his hands tremble in mine. I gripped them both tightly and waited for him to go on. If he even had anything else to say. I imagined Porter sitting alone in waiting rooms like this so many nights, how scared he must have been. Porter inhaled a shaky breath, and I could feel the panic building up inside him, the same way it starts to swirl in me. It comes from my toes and bursts out my throat, and I could see it moving through his body like a ripple.

"Hey," I said as he shook. "Hey, look at me. Please."

His lips trembled, and tears dotted the corners of his eyes. "I'm right here. I'm here with you. Those are memories, they aren't happening right now. Tell me. Tell me something good that's happened in the last week."

"I-I finished a notebook yesterday," he said.

"That's good," I said.

"Luke just has the flu," he said. I squeezed his hands tighter. His tears dropped into his lap, and the faintest smile started to form on his lips.

"I'm not alone."

===

Luke's eyes widened in relief when we walked into the room. He had an IV hanging out of his arm to keep him hydrated, and his skin looked like it was starting to go back to its normal color. I took his hand and sat on the edge of his bed.

"How are you feeling?" I asked.

"Better," he said. And he did look so much better. I only wished we'd come sooner so he didn't have to be so miserable for so long. "They want to keep me overnight to make sure I keep something down. You two go home; I won't be any fun here."

I ran my hand through his hair. "No, I'll stay with you."

He looked at Porter. "Please, make her go to bed."

An unspoken thought passed between them, and we waited for a good half an hour to talk to the doctor and make sure everything was set for us to leave. The doctors predicted that they would discharge him sometime after noon tomorrow and that we should be here to pick him up then. Porter agreed to come since I had class during that time. I kissed

Luke good-bye and headed out the same sliding doors I wheeled Luke in so many hours ago.

Porter drove slowly back to my house, most of Denton asleep for hours already. My dad was most likely up in his recliner, waiting for me to get back with the TV on. If it wasn't for that fact I would probably have gone to Zoe's.

"Oh shoot, my car is at your place," I said.

"You're too tired to drive," he replied. "Want me to pick you up in the morning so you can take it to class?"

"You don't have to—"

"What time?" he interjected.

"Is nine okay?" I asked. He nodded. As we drove on I kept going back to the image of Luke sitting in the hospital bed so helpless, or him not being able to keep anything down and apologizing profusely. I shouldn't have left him there by himself. He would have stayed with me. "I should have stayed there with him."

"No, he would have rather had me carry you out than have you stay. He felt bad for the whole day already," he said. I began to protest, but he reached out and touched my knee, which certainly shut me up. "He'll be fine."

I shifted and his hand fell off, leaving a hot trail down my leg. I crossed them and forced myself to look out the window. I was about two minutes away. I could make it two minutes without talking or looking at him, right?

Directing people to my house was always difficult at night since all the streets looked the same in the dark. We finally made it down mine, and I could see the flicker of the TV in the living room. I looked at him, not sure what to say. He rubbed his hands over his eyes, and I quickly opened the door.

"Thanks for the ride," I said.

"See you tomorrow morning," he replied. As he pulled out of the driveway I'd never felt so cold.

I was so tired when I stumbled through the door that I hadn't noticed my mom waiting up for me on the couch. I froze in the doorframe, as I'd swiftly avoided one-on-one contact with her for the past few weeks. The only reason I was allowed to go on that camping trip with Luke's family was because Carrie Upton personally called and asked. If it was up to Mom, she would have kept me in this miserable house with her for as long as possible. I attempted to scoot up the stairs without her acknowledging me, but I had no such luck.

"How is Luke?" she asked.

I turned around slowly, gauging what my response would be. "He's spending the night there to make sure that he keeps everything down. We'll pick him up in the afternoon."

"We?" she asked.

"Me or Porter," I said.

"I see," she said, nodding. I attempted to continue up the stairs, but she stopped me again. "Come here, Danielle. Let's talk."

I walked slowly over to the couch and sat down across from her. We kept a healthy distance between us as I wrapped my legs underneath me, pretzel style.

"Have you worked on getting your transcripts sent in early to Ohio State?" she asked.

I kicked myself internally. I'd been so busy with other things that I'd forgotten to ask Professor Harrisburg about sending my projected grade over sooner than the end of the semester.

"I'll take your lack of answer as a no," she said.

Anger bubbled up inside of me. I didn't know if I was angrier with her for asking about it again or at myself for letting my relationship drama get in the way of my remembering to ask in the first place.

"It's been a long night. Can I please just go to bed?" I asked, no, begged.

"It's not that difficult to ask your professor a simple question, Danielle. Or are you trying to ruin your future? I honestly can't tell at this point," she said.

Her words smacked me in the face and caused tears to start forming in my eyes. "I've been busy with other things going on in my life. A good mom would know that things have been hard lately."

"I didn't ask you to sit here so you could insult me," she said.

"Oh, so you just wanted me to sit here so *you* could insult *me*?" I asked. "Right. Duly noted."

"You've always had such a mouth on you," she said.

"I've learned it from the best," I replied, crossing my arms.

She sat silently for a few moments and rearranged the pillows she was sitting on. I watched the wheels in her mind churning and wondered what she would say back.

"How did we get to this point where you don't tell me things?" she asked. "How did I not know that you wanted to be involved with environmental policy? It's my job to recognize what a kid's full potential is—what they actually want to do with their lives. How could I have missed yours?"

"You've been busy these last few years. Your business is growing, and with Noah's acting, we haven't really had much time for just us," I said.

Her shaking hand pinned back a loose lock of hair that had fallen out of her bun, and I saw tears starting to form in the corners of her eyes.

"You always said that you wanted to go to Ohio State. You were always so great with language—quick witted and easy to communicate with—I thought you wanted to do communications. Or be a teacher. Remember when you wanted to be an elementary school teacher? That wasn't that long ago," she said.

"That was when I was eleven," I said.

"Ohio State was your dream," she said. "And it had the perfect program."

"It wasn't my dream, Mom; it was yours," I said, raising my voice a bit. "You were so preoccupied with this image you thought you had of me that you didn't bother to pay attention to me like one of your clients. Do you know how hurtful that was? How awful it made me feel to have this mom that everyone loved for helping them find the perfect school, for understanding what they really want, and have her not see her own kid like that?"

"I didn't know I'd become such a monster in your eyes," she said, starting to stand up.

"Don't do this," I said. "Don't shut me out. It's not fair to either of us."

Her tears streamed down her face now, and I could see her wrestle with the urge to run up the stairs and slam her door like in every other fight or stand her ground. I sure as hell wasn't leaving. We were in a standoff.

"I wanted things to be different with us," she said. "I wanted a different relationship than my mom and I had. That's why I started working from home—to be closer to you and Noah. But then he was so sick when he was little, and then the business picked up and . . . and . . ."

"Don't blame this on Noah. That's not fair to blame it on him," I said.

"Our problems with each other have been a two-way street, Danielle. I'm not the only bad guy here," she said.

"I've apologized to you so many times I can't even see straight, Mom. I will never be exactly what you want me to be, and, I'll say it again, I'm sorry about that. But you need to accept me for who I am and what I want to do," I said. "And, for the record, I would be more than willing to open up to you if you showed any interest."

She pulled out the same bobby pin she had been messing around with earlier and put it into her mouth with a shaking hand. She smoothed out the part of her hair that fell out of her bun with two hands before putting it back in its place.

"I'm going to go to bed if you have nothing else to say," I said, standing up. I made my way to the foot of the staircase before she spoke up.

"I am sorry," she sobbed. "So, so sorry."

I turned around to find her with her face in her hands, shoulders bobbing up and down. I froze for a few seconds, thrown off by seeing this woman who had always been full of strength and poise broken down into sobs. I'd never seen her cry like this before, much less over something that I'd said. I walked back over to the couch and sat down right next to her, my arms wrapping themselves tightly around her shaking shoulders.

Her arms found my waist, and I nuzzled into the spot where her shoulder and neck met. The spot that I craved every time I'd fallen down and scraped a knee as a kid, the spot that brought comfort when my best friend moved away.

She pulled away, still holding on to my arms. Her eyes searched mine, and she wiped away a tear that started to fall down my face before she wiped away her own. "I'm going to do better. I am going to be a better mom."

"I'm sorry, Mom. For not coming clean about Ohio State, for putting your business in jeopardy, and for not telling you about my internship sooner. I was so scared of how you would react that it was easier for me to pretend it wasn't happening than tell you," I said.

"I'm sorry you felt like you couldn't talk to me," she said. "I'm sorry you still feel that way."

I nodded. "I really am enjoying myself at my internship, and it is shaping the way that I look at the world. I feel so passionate about something, and it's really refreshing. I've never felt this way about anything."

She grabbed my hands. "That's all a parent ever wants. I know this isn't the plan we had, but life makes its own plans. Not everything is prescribed. This is what I tell every student that walks into my office, and I am so devastated that it was never able to resonate with you. That I never validated that you can do whatever you dream."

"But you did," I said, tears already starting to form. "I only ever wanted to be like you. I didn't know what I wanted to do, and you steered me in the best direction you could."

"I let my own pride get in the way of the love and support you needed. I will never be able to forgive myself for that," she said.

"Please forgive yourself. Because I forgive you. And I need my mom back," I said. She wrapped her arms around me, stroking my head as I nestled into the crook of her neck. My safe place.

FORTUNE:

fate; lot; destiny.

THE MORNING CAME MUCH TOO QUICKLY, AND I BARELY HAD THE ENERGY TO EAT A GRANOLA BAR BEFORE POR-TER WAS IN MY DRIVEWAY AGAIN. I sank into the passenger side and slammed the door behind me. He wore the same outfit from last night, as if he'd passed out when he got home and hadn't bothered to change his clothes.

"Rough night?" I asked, barely mustering up a laugh.

He nodded sheepishly and yawned before backing out. I was happy that we didn't talk because I wasn't sure that I could form sentences. It would sure be fun to make it through an English class this morning.

The Jankmobile beckoned to me as we reached the apartment complex, and I vowed to go through a coffee drive-through somewhere on the way to school. I had to get perked up. The city council meeting was tonight, and Ameera was depending on me to make a speech. Since I'd been working for Ameera I'd thought about everything I was doing to stay environmentally sustainable and found myself unplugging all the appliances in the house. My mother was still extremely confused about who was doing it.

When I came into the room, Mr. Harrisburg had written a small note on the board. *Connectivity*, it read. If I had to guess I was sure he would lecture us on the importance of feeling a connection to what we were reading and writing (which was *Moby-Dick*, by the way). We waited for him to emerge from his little desk and spout his wisdom, which hadn't impressed me yet in the way Megan promised it would.

"Connectivity," he said, underlining it. "By definition it is the state of being connected or the ability to connect. Your dictionaries probably also like to tie this to computers, but imagine with me how connectivity can be poetic in this sense. Connectivity is the ability to connect to everything—nature, literature, people—you name it. In the case of *Moby-Dick* we have Ishmael, a narrator who is enraptured by this man who is obsessed with hunting one specific whale in the entire world. When we think about connectivity, we need to think about what draws Ishmael to Ahab's singular quest and comment on how it is an allegory for the things that we ourselves connect with that others don't understand.

"Let's talk about it," Mr. Harrisburg said, clapping.

A girl named Abbie raised her hand. "I almost think that Ishmael wants to see himself in Ahab so much that he overlooks some of his obsessive behavior because he's afraid that whaling was a bad endeavor and will eventually make him lose it too."

"Good point," Harrisburg said. "Like we've established, Ishmael is educated in a way that most of the crew is not, and while he's been trying to justify whaling as a righteous venture with Ahab as the example, he needs to validate that things are okay. Can we talk about their connection more deeply, though?"

"That's true," said a guy named Austin. "But they are removed from each other. Ishmael recognizes some of the craziness and recognizes that Ahab is a different man. One that has lost everything, like his sanity as well as his leg, to Moby-Dick and he's, like, messed up. Ishmael recognizes that but still respects him. I don't think he's afraid of becoming him."

I was staring out the window waiting for the class to be done. I could barely keep my eyes open let alone focus on a discussion that I wasn't terribly interested in.

"Danielle? What do you think?" Harrisburg said.

I internally cringed. "What am I thinking about?"

"Connectivity; it's underlined and everything for your convenience," he said. The class snickered a bit while I tried to gather my thoughts.

"I mean, he's definitely not connected to Ahab in the way that he is to Queequeg. Their connection is, like, a lifelong friendship and deep love. I think we should be talking about their connectivity if anything," I said.

Harrisburg shook his head. "We're talking about the

observer-hero dynamic of Ahab and Ishmael. Why is Ishmael observing the hero of the novel, Ahab, and what does that mean as the deepest level of connection? It's a challenge, it's engaging, and it's timeless. That's why these stories are still popular. There will always be a part of us that enjoys observing the hero but never quite touching their lives. The mystery of it, the allure of it, is distinctly human. That's what I'm trying to get at here. We need to focus on how Melville illustrates this kind of connection and how we replicate that today, whether it be us observing our favorite celebrity or someone who you feel is much braver, smarter, more loving than you are.

"Your assignment for Wednesday is to write about your experience as an observer or a hero. Be creative. And don't forget about the looming final paper of doom. I'm still expecting those to be perfect, since I assigned them at the beginning of the semester," he said.

My classmates all stood up, and I quickly put my things in my bag, ready to head over to Luke and Porter's to check up on Luke. I had almost made it out the door when Mr. Harrisburg stopped me. "Are you able to chat today?" he asked.

I looked out the window again. I *didn't* have to go into work, but I was desperate to see Luke . . . I guess if I didn't stay after today I would be forced to do it another time. "I can," I said.

"Good." He nodded. We waited for everyone to leave before he asked me to pull up a chair next to his desk. I sat with my legs crossed and my sweating hands pushed together. I didn't have much experience with staying with a professor after class, but it was usually to talk about bad news. "I just wanted to kind of clear the air about me singling you out in class. I didn't mean to make you apprehensive, I just want you to think, you know?"

I was shocked. "Oh, don't worry, I'm fine."

"I'm glad. I always have to have one good sport to make me look tougher than I actually am." He winked. "In all honesty, how is your semester project coming along?"

I cringed a little.

"That good?" he asked. "Well, I'm sure you will figure it out. If you want to talk about it, my office is always open."

"Oh, is that it, then?" I asked. I collected my bags to stand.

"And one other thing," he said. "I heard that you'll be talking at the city council meeting tonight. I saw the agenda. I just wanted to say I'll be there too. Don't worry, I'm not contesting anything you'll be saying. I'm there on my own mission."

I raised my eyebrows.

"I'm talking on behalf of the funding for the Pinewoods Nursing Home. You know, the committee figured I'd be the best-spoken," he said.

"I volunteered there in high school," I said.

"It's a wonderful place," he said. "But their funding is being cut, and they're already short on staff."

"That's terrible," I said.

"We'll get it sorted out," he said. I stared at him for a while, probably an awkward while, before he scooted his desk chair out.

"Oh!" I said. "One more thing. Would you be willing to submit my grade minus the final paper to the counseling office this week? I'm trying to get reaccepted into Ohio State, and if they have a good word that I'll pass this class, I'm in."

"Already sent it a while back. Your counselor thought you might need it to keep up with your plan," he said.

"That's incredible. You don't know how much this means to me," I said, relief surging through my body.

"Happy to do it. Good chat, Danielle. Be sure to save me a seat tonight."

———

As if making a speech to the Denton community wasn't hard already, now I had to attempt to impress my English professor with my wordy prowess . . . which should sound ridiculous because it was. On a scale from one to absolute mental breakdown I was at "lying on my floor unable to move."

My vision for the meeting was limited—I should have really gone to one to check it out before. Could nerves be this powerful? Ameera obviously wanted me to speak in Denton because it was my hometown. She said to speak from my experience, and I only hoped that my experience was worthy enough to help persuade the city into more sustainable living.

The seats were only a third of the way full when I walked in, and Ameera was nowhere in sight. I sat by myself in the back of the room looking over my notes and keeping down the vomit that threatened to creep up. This was nerves, at least I hoped, and not the flu that had kept Luke down for a week.

"Thanks for the spot," Mr. Harrisburg said. I jumped as I looked up to meet his eyes. "Sorry, didn't mean to scare you."

"No, no, you aren't the scary part of this," I said. I ran my hands over the top of my jeans to try and keep the sweat off.

"You'll be great," he said. "And if it makes you feel any better, I'll be going before you."

"That helps a little," I said. He reached into his pocket and pulled out a sheet of paper, looking over it in the way I had been a few seconds ago.

"I'd like to call this meeting to order," I heard faintly over the beating of my own heart in my head. I basically tuned out everything until I heard them say, "Please welcome Mr. Finn Harrisburg."

Mr. Harrisburg stood up and winked at me before making his way to the podium. I found it easier to focus on him in this moment than to be glued to the small notecards in my lap. He coughed a little into the microphone before spreading his sheet out in front of him.

"Hello, everyone. As Mr. Jones said, I am Finn Harrisburg, and I'm here to talk on behalf of the Pinewoods Nursing Home. Some of you may be aware that staffing has recently been cut by a quarter while demand for patient care has nearly doubled. Families are forced to take their loved ones farther away from Denton in order to get proper care. The nearest facility is nearly forty miles away. For the Pinewoods patients, Denton is their home. If they're struggling with dementia or memory loss, taking them away from their home can be detrimental.

"My father is one of these patients who is facing the impossible decision of relocating. His progressive Alzheimer's has declined in the past two years, but the one thing that brings back my old dad, the one thing that makes sense to him, is getting to take walks around Park Green just like we used to when I was a kid. I cherish those moments of clarity with him. They are something that no one can truly understand unless you've had a parent go through the same struggle.

"I'm not saying this to make you feel bad for me. I'm here today to bring awareness to a cause that Denton desperately needs to fund. We will be having a luncheon next Tuesday with more information on our plans for a budget if anyone would be interested in attending. Thank you."

Everyone clapped, and I sat in my chair, gobsmacked. His dad was the reason he stayed here, not taking those professor positions elsewhere. I'd been so wrong about him. I watched as Mr. Harrisburg joined me.

"I'm sorry about your dad," I said.

"Me too, kid," he said back.

"Our next speaker is Danielle Cavanaugh from Green Transitions," I heard from the front of the room. Mr. Harrisburg nudged my arm, and I shook out of my scared stupor. I clutched my notecards in my fist and took a deep breath, channeling the inner boss lady that Zoe so frequently referenced. I somehow managed to make it up to the front of the room without tripping over myself. I set my notecards down with shaking hands and adjusted the microphone to reach my mouth. I squinted at the bright lights, trying to make eye contact with Mr. Harrisburg as a form of comfort.

"Hello, everyone. My name is Danielle Cavanaugh, and I am here on behalf of Green Transitions Environmental Policy offices in Cleveland. Three weeks ago an article was published in the *Cleveland Sun Times* declaring Denton the 'least green city in Ohio.' As a lifelong resident and environmental advocate for this city, I knew I had to speak out against this claim and lobby for change," I said.

I looked up from my notes, taking another deep breath. This time, when I looked in the front row, I saw a familiar pair of eyes hidden behind ridiculously long lashes. My heart welled with gratitude for a moment before I read what his shirt said. In permanent marker he'd written "My Underwear." An uncontrollable laugh escaped my mouth.

"Sorry, yes, this is a serious topic," I said, pulling myself back together. "I thought about tying myself to the biggest tree in Florence Park to make a statement. I thought about going door to door to remind people of the joys of recycling. But the thing that I ultimately knew would make the most impact would be to speak with the policy makers of this city that I love so much. You all.

"There are small things that everyone can do every day to make a difference in the world. You could take shorter showers, unplug your appliances when you aren't using them, opt for air-drying your hair. But as a community, there are big changes that can happen to make an even greater impact. Implementing a stricter recycling policy in city buildings would be a great start. From there, the whole city. Opening up a new community garden in Florence Park would not only be beneficial for the environment, but for people like Finn Harrisburg's father it would be a place for everyone to gather and appreciate the beautiful city they live in and love.

"I'm not expecting everything to change overnight. Denton wasn't built in a day. I am here to encourage our city to consider letting Green Transitions perform a full audit of the city's environmental impact and come back with ideas on how to improve. This process takes time and money up front, but the money the city would save on energy usage and other costs will even out in years to come.

"My boss, Ameera Chopra, will be available for questions next week for a second presentation. I believe in this city, and I believe in the impact that each person has on the world. Even if nothing comes of this speech policy-wise, I hope it inspires some to take action and make the changes in their own lives that will help their community thrive. Thank you."

Porter clapped loudly from the front row as I sat back down next to Mr. Harrisburg. Mr. Harrisburg told me that I'd done a great job, and as the third speaker started to talk, I walked out the back door. My blood was still pumping from the residual adrenaline, and little black dots started appearing in the edges of my vision. I sat down on the city hall floor and put my head in between my legs, realizing I was sitting on the Denton city seal.

"Danielle?" I heard.

I lifted my head cautiously, seeing the "My Underwear" T-shirt in my line of vision. I lifted my eyes higher to meet Porter's.

"I told you not to come," I said faintly.

"*Technically* you just refused to tell me the date of your speech," he said. I didn't even have to look at him to know that the Smirk was on his face. "I had to see how it ended after I got my little sneak preview at work."

"And? What's the verdict?" I asked.

"I think my dramatic reading could have been more moving," he said. "But you did all right."

"I can't believe I just did that. I have a bit of a terrible speech-giver reputation around town," I said.

"I think it's safe to say you've changed that reputation," he said.

I finally felt like I was no longer on the verge of fainting, and I was able to sit up and face Porter. His "My Underwear" shirt was rolled up on the sleeves to expose his arms, and my eyes trailed down to his fingers tapping absentmindedly on the floor.

"What are you really doing here?" I asked.

An unspoken tension had lived between us since the moment in the woods and after the hospital. While I'd used every effort to separate us, Porter had foiled every opportunity to be separated.

"Well, I figured you hadn't told anyone else about this and

wanted to make sure you had a familiar face in the audience. That, and you needed someone to remind you that you could picture everyone in their underwear," he said.

I shook my head, which felt like a balloon stuffed with cotton balls. In an effort to stop the sensation, I lay back on the marble floors and let the coolness sink into my clothes.

"I broke up with Emilie," Porter said.

I stared up at the ceiling for a few beats. "Are you sad?"

"Not as much as I thought I'd be," he said. His legs swung around so he could lie down beside me. I counted the tiles on the ceiling to occupy my mind—anything to help me forget that he was lying down just inches away from me.

"I realized she'd become more of a security blanket than anything else. Security blankets have a purpose, but if I am going to fall for someone, really truly fall, I need to be with someone willing to challenge me. To make me see things differently and encourage me to try new things."

I turned my head slowly and met his eyes. My gaze traveled from his eyes to his mouth and quickly back up. If I shifted my weight even marginally we'd be touching, and that realization sent sparks up the right side of my body.

"Danielle—" he started as the city hall doors flung open. The last speech had finished and everyone was leaving. I bolted up to stand and looked down at him, sitting.

"I should go. You should go," I said.

His face dropped along with my heart. What was I doing?

"You're right," he said. He stood up and started to walk away. He turned around to look at me right inside the door as if to show me this was my last chance to stop him. Half of me stayed firmly planted in place while the other half wanted to run to him. The sensible, in-a-relationship half won out as he walked out the door.

The moments of the day flashed before my eyes—me looking up to find him in the audience, the feeling of him being so close to me, his looking into my eyes. Porter was the first person I told about my internship—the first person who I wanted to tell anything just to see his reaction. Everything that I'd tried to push aside between us in the past few months—every look, that *kiss*—why did I keep pretending like nothing was changing inside me?

I couldn't just let him go. I ran out the door to follow him, looking up and down the block for any sign of him. I was too late. He was already gone.

I strolled down the sidewalk and got into the Jankmobile, slowly admitting what I already knew deep down. I was falling in love with Porter. Heck, I was deep in it already. My only reservation all along had been my relationship with Luke, which seemed to be something I constantly had to nurture. I had loved him once, so many years ago, but the love of an eleven-year-old does not make for a fulfilling relationship at eighteen.

To be fair to him, I knew what my dreaded mission for the evening would be. I had to break things off with Luke.

FRUSTRATION:

a feeling of dissatisfaction
often accompanied by anxiety
or depression, resulting
from unfulfilled needs or
unresolved problems.

I WOKE UP TO THE SOUNDS OF CHATTER DOWNSTAIRS, A VERY MALE VOICE FILTERING UP THROUGH THE VENTS. If my suspicions were correct, Luke Upton was in my kitchen. This day just got a whole lot more anxiety-ridden.

I threw on my clothes for class that I'd laid out the night before and did a quick spruce before heading downstairs. He sat at our kitchen counter with two Cup o' Moe's to-go cups, and the gesture squeezed harder at my heart. He was in the middle of a conversation with my mom when they both realized I'd come into the room.

"Isn't this a nice surprise, Danielle?" she asked.

"Very nice," I replied. I walked over and took a sip of my coffee, which had been sweetened just to my liking. Damn it, he was not making this any easier. "Thank you, this is very sweet."

"You're welcome," he said, leaning in to give me a kiss. I turned my head at the last moment so it landed on my cheek, and he searched my eyes.

"Hey, do, uh, do you want to go for a walk?" I asked, my hands shaking. My mom made eye contact with me and her eyes widened, hearing the implication of my question. She politely excused herself as Luke followed me outside.

"This does not look good for me, Cavanaugh," he said.

"I just . . . wanted to talk," I said. He waited for me to elaborate. "What are we doing?"

"I think you're giving me the breakup talk," he said.

"No," I said, blushing. "What are we doing in this relationship? We barely see each other, and when we do it's mostly . . . physical. Do you feel like you're missing something in this relationship?"

"Do you?" he asked.

"Kind of," I admitted shyly.

He put his hands in his pockets and leaned his head back. "I can be more emotional. Let me at least try to be more emotional."

"I don't think it's something we should have to work on— I feel like it's something that's either there or it's not," I said, feeling bolder.

"There's nothing else fueling this conversation? No *one* else?" he asked.

He saw my cringe. I have the worst poker face, especially when it comes to big lies of the heart. He shook his head and walked a few steps away from me.

"Porter?" he asked. When I didn't respond he let out a little laugh. "I told Emilie she was paranoid for thinking you two were hooking up, but I guess I was wrong. How long has he been *emotional* with you for?"

"We haven't done anything, but thanks for the assumption about my character," I said.

"Hey, I'm the one being broken up with. I'm allowed to react a little, okay?" he said.

"I'm sorry," I said. For so many things. Those words hung on the tip of my tongue as my voice was sucked away from me.

"It's probably for the best," he said, finally facing me again. "I'm transferring to the University of Iowa in the spring for training."

"That's—awesome," I said. "Congratulations."

"Thanks," he said. He looked around for a moment before walking toward his car. "I think I'm just going to go home. I'm not good at these things."

"Oh," I said in surprise. "Okay. Luke? I am sorry. I wanted this to work out."

"I know you did," he said. "Sometimes your heart makes a shit show out of what you think you want."

"Was that a roundabout way of saying the heart wants what the heart wants?" I asked.

"I can be emotional, okay?" he said, a small smile on his face. "Bye, Dani."

"Bye, Luke."

I walked back inside after watching him leave, feeling numb. When I pictured a breakup with Luke Upton so many years ago, I thought it would lead to my ultimate devastation. That admitting that we weren't going to end up together with a big fancy wedding and two-point-five eventual children would be the most horrific thought in the universe. I didn't know what it said about me that I felt nothing in this moment. Was I processing? Or was this something I'd processed a while ago when I subconsciously had been giving small parts of myself to someone else?

"Did Luke leave?" Mom asked as I walked into the kitchen.

"We broke up," I said. "So yeah, he bolted the hell out of here."

"What? What happened?" she asked.

"We weren't compatible, Mom. I think we were both staying together because the idea of each other was better than actually being together. Like it was some cheesy Hallmark movie where the boy next door comes home and realizes how cute the little dorky girl next door has been the whole time," I said.

"So you're okay?" she asked.

"I'm still going to binge on cookie dough and reruns of *Gilmore Girls* when I get home tonight, but yes, I'll be okay," I said. I grabbed my backpack and shrugged as I headed back out the door. "I'm going to be late to lit."

"You can take the day off if you want. I don't have any sessions this morning; I could be your binge buddy for the day," she said.

I walked up and kissed her on the cheek. "Thank you for the offer, but skipping this class will not help me pass."

"I like the sound of that," Mom said.

I looked at the clock and cursed, realizing how late I was for class. I hopped into the Jankmobile and felt the same blank feeling I had back at home. I drove along for a few minutes, tapping my fingers absentmindedly before my phone rang. I did the safe-driver thing and put the call on speakerphone.

"Hello?" I asked.

"Danielle, this is Ameera," she said. From her tone I thought she was going to fire me—that she'd somehow seen my speech and was disappointed in how I represented Green Transitions in the meeting.

"Hi, Ameera, how are you?" I asked.

"Great, actually. I just got word from Denton that they have approved the environmental impact audit. You did it, Danielle," she said.

"You're kidding," I replied. "That's amazing!"

"I think you have a bright future ahead of you, Danielle. I wanted to tell you about an opportunity that I'm taking up this semester in case you're interested. I've been asked to be an adjunct professor at Case Western next semester in their Environmental Studies department. I know we've chatted about you transferring either this semester or next year, and I think this department would be a good fit for you. No pressure, but I think it's worth applying if you're serious about staying in this field," she said.

"Thank you for the info," I said. "I will most definitely look into it. Thank you for thinking of me."

"Of course," she said. "I'm proud of all the hard work you've done in the few months I've known you."

"Thank you. That truly means a lot," I said.

"Have a great day. I'll see you Thursday," she said.

She hung up, and my heart filled with warmth. I'd made a difference in my community just by speaking up for what I believed in. Even if Denton decided to ignore any of the ideas that came back from the audit, they still made the step toward changing. That was huge—especially for a city so rooted in its ideals. I had a smile planted on my face for the rest of the ride and made a large note in my phone when I parked at DCC:

LOOK INTO CASE WESTERN ENVIRONMENTAL STUDIES PROGRAM.

When I walked in Mr. Harrisburg winked at me, and I gave him a small wave. Our newfound friendship after the city council meeting was a little strange considering our past, but I could dig it.

"A quick reminder to all my procrastinating folks. Your final paper is due in two weeks when the class meets for the last time," he said. His last sentence was met with a collective groan. "Be happy that I'm reminding you now so your little brains start churning early."

He turned his back to us as we sat in mild states of panic thinking about the paper. He wrote "finishing up *Moby-Dick*" in chicken scratch that I could barely make out.

"So what did we all think?" he asked.

"They all lost their minds and then died," said Brent, a dude of few but well-chosen words.

"I guess, yes, that's technically accurate. But let's look at it from a more . . . literary standpoint. What does it mean that Ishmael was the only one to survive?" Mr. Harrisburg asked.

"I mean, it's obviously an allusion to weak enterprise eventually destroying everyone and everything, correct?" a girl named Elizabeth said.

"Yes, if you're looking at the entire ship as a metaphor for corporation," said Mr. Harrisburg. "Let's talk about Ahab's final good speech to Starbuck. He talks about seeing home in Starbuck's eyes and about how he hasn't left the sea for forty years. Abandoned his wife, a steady life on land—why is he telling Starbuck this in one of their last moments together?"

Elizabeth raised her hand again. "He says he sees home in his eyes. He sees everything he never got to experience that he's now too old and destroyed to do."

"Or he wants his only real human connection to be happy," said Abbie.

"That's more of what I was going for," Mr. Harrisburg said. "Ahab doesn't connect, really, with anyone in the novel except for Starbuck. He tells him to make his own fate, and that is how you find happiness. He's giving him the advice that he would give his son, almost. Does everyone feel that way?"

I felt my throat scratching. "Starbuck has given Ahab everything; I think he's trying to give him something in calling his eyes home. Like telling him that he can be happy when he's moved on . . . but ultimately I guess it doesn't matter. His loyalty is too strong."

Mr. Harrisburg smiled at me. "Not too shabby for a poetry hater."

———

If I had a day to lie in bed and be sad it would have been today. So naturally the universe decided that I should have to work. Plus, it was a Wednesday. My shift with Porter day. What would I say to him? Would I admit that things had changed? Or would we go on like nothing happened? I was mid-freak-out when I walked into the store. To my surprise, Misty sat on a stool perched behind the register.

"I've missed having you in lately," she said.

"Wait, I thought—"

"Porter had to take the day off," she said. "Family emergency."

I gulped. This either had to do with his dad, which I'd overheard him and Emilie talk about, or his mom, which he'd opened up to me about. The scary toss-up made me want to reach out to him even more. To be a source of comfort. "I'm going to drop my dinner off in the back and then I'll get to work."

She shooed me to the back room, and I pulled out my phone. I had to know if there was any way that I could help him.

ME: Are you okay? Can I do anything for you?

I waited five minutes for a reply, fiddling with my phone case and picking at a hangnail in my nervousness. I was about to leave it in my bag and head out to the front when it buzzed.

> **PORTER:** I'm good.
> **ME:** You sure?
> **PORTER:** Don't worry about me. I'm okay.
> **ME:** If you change your mind, you know how to reach me.

I didn't get any more texts for the rest of my shift. His lack of response worried me more than I would like to admit.

———

When I got home the rest of the household was asleep; only the light from the TV and my dad's snoring let me know that they were still home. I made my way into the kitchen and grabbed my leftover milkshake from yesterday, inducing a horrible onset of brain freeze. I sat down at the counter and grabbed my head, trying to remember all the little tricks Noah and I had found over the years to get rid of the numbness in our brains. When it finally subsided, I saw a large envelope on the counter addressed to me. From Ohio State.

> Dear Ms. Cavanaugh,
>
> I wanted to take this moment to for-mally congratulate you on your admit-

tance to Ohio State University for the spring semester. Due to your academic excellence in your English course, your advisor has sent over your projected transcript for the semester, which is in compliance with our policies for the Digital Communications program.

If you choose to accept your admission, please log on to your OSU account. Information for log-in is attached to your orientation packet. Please feel free to call us with any questions regarding your acceptance.

Congratulations, and we welcome you to the Ohio State University family.

Dr. Caroline Bates

Dr. Caroline Bates
Dean of Admissions
Ohio State University

My numbness up to this point diminished, and I crumpled on top of the letter, sobs coming out uncontrollably. This was all I had wanted since this summer, the second chance that I desperately needed, and I couldn't even be excited about it. All my plans for myself had molded, melted, and re-formed so many times that it could make anyone's head spin. Ohio

State was finally in my grasp again, but I couldn't bring myself to accept a position at a school that I didn't feel passionate about.

I stayed up until three a.m. that night, furiously researching environmental studies and political science programs around Ohio and beyond, and made a list of schools that had rolling admissions. In the true fashion of a college psychic's daughter, I created an extensive pros and cons list for each school, a spreadsheet detailing all the requirements for applying, and calculated the odds of admittance to each school. Armed with this knowledge, I scheduled out times during this week to get in applications to my top five schools (and to ask my mom for help, since it's her job to create vacuum-tight applications for eager students). Failure was not an option this time.

=====

That week was rough, to say the least. Between heavy essay revisions with Mom and making multiple trips up to the high school for transcript requests, my life was becoming one living, breathing college app. In an effort to keep my sanity, I distracted myself by helping Zoe with her printmaking. She actually was getting a huge following online, and she'd even gotten e-mails from some local designers who wanted to feature her work. She was too humble to brag about any of this, but as the best friend I felt like I had the right to tell everyone to buy her things because she was wonderful.

The one thing that kept nagging at the back of my mind was Porter. He wasn't replying to my texts anymore, and I increasingly wondered if Luke had talked to him about our breakup. Maybe he decided that we were better off stopping all communication—that we'd both been sending mixed signals that fooled the other into feeling something. No matter how many times I told myself that he was ignoring me on purpose, the other small part of me just worried about him. Something tragic had happened to his family, and no one had heard from him since. What if something happened to him? It was my duty as his friend to check up on him. According to the bookstore schedule, he was scheduled to work tonight. I would just drop by, make sure he was okay, and leave immediately if he wanted me to. No strings attached.

When I pulled up, I could only see Misty's figure from the window. I hopped out of the car and went into the building—maybe Porter was in the back and I just hadn't seen him yet. The bell on the door clinked as I walked in, and Misty jumped.

"What are you doing here tonight, girly?" she asked.

"Uh," I said. "I, um, was wondering if Porter was working?"

She frowned. "Porter went back home this morning. Taking an early leave for break."

I felt my shoulders slump a little—relief or devastation I still didn't know. "Oh."

"Hang on a second," she said, heading into the back room.

When she came out she was holding a stack of papers bound by a thick rubber band. She handed the stack to me. "He left these for you."

I looked down at the pile of small notebook pages to see an envelope on the top with my name scribbled on the front. I unearthed the letter inside.

Danielle,

I'm going home for a little while to take care of my dad. This wasn't meant to make you feel bad, just to let you know that I won't ever throw out your pages.

—Porter

My now-shaking hand pulled apart the other pages that stuck to my palm sweat. I could see my name clearly standing out on each of the pages, part of his daily notes that he wrote to himself. I picked up one toward the middle that had a bit more writing than the others.

She likes to pretend that she's tough, but push one button even marginally and you can see the shift in her eyes. She doesn't take honesty very well, no matter how much she claims to. Sometimes she'll sit and read a book for hours while she's supposed to be working, forgetting to eat until her stomach growls.

Last night we went to a party and I found her curled up on a couch by herself, Luke nowhere in sight. He can really be careless sometimes. I helped her get home, and the whole time she thought I was her best friend, Zoe. She wrapped her arms around my neck, her face resting on my chest. I can't put myself in these situations anymore. I can't be this close to her and avoid feeling something.

She passed the desert island test, saying she wouldn't bring anyone along with her into the misery. Though, if I were playing, I wouldn't mind bringing her along. If nothing else, she'd be able to make a backhanded comment about the weather that would make me laugh. God, she makes me laugh.

Today we went to the movie set. I don't need to bother reminding you what happened—there's no way you'd be able to forget. I should feel guiltier about how much I enjoyed being able to kiss her. Luke is a decent enough guy, but it might be criminal the things I would do just to replay this day over and over.

I think I embarrassed her today. She was writing in one of my notebooks (a fact that still

baffles me since she was so against it in the be-
ginning) and she was writing a speech for her envi-
ronmental policy office. It was great—insightful
and well-written. I'm convinced she can do any-
thing. I wish she realized that.

I showed up at her speech today. It was even
more incredible than when I read it at the store.
I almost admitted everything, almost ruined
everything we had going.

I'm in a bad place with her. A desperate
infatuation with a girl I can't have. She helps me
to forget about home. I can't jeopardize that
comfort with my own feelings.

"Do you need a tissue, sweetheart?" Misty asked, pulling me out of my daze. I wiped under my nose, which was embarrassingly snotty, and shook my head.

"I'm fine," I sniffed. "I think I'm going to head out. I'll see you later, Misty."

She nodded. "He's going through a lot now, sweetheart. Give him a few days to process all his family stuff, and he'll get back to you."

"Thanks, Misty. For everything," I said.

"You're welcome, doll. Get some sleep, and I'll see you tomorrow," she said.

I headed out to my car, gripping the notebooks across my chest. He left these behind because he didn't think I felt the same way. I needed to show him how I felt, how he's made me see things so differently in the past few months. In what might be one of my worst ideas in a long time, I went home, searched the White Pages online, and looked up the Kohls who lived in Valley View.

FRACTURE:

the act of breaking;
state of being broken.

I DIDN'T KNOW WHETHER TO BE THANKFUL OR TERRIFIED THAT IT WAS EXTREMELY EASY TO FIND PORTER'S DAD'S ADDRESS. I drove without a plan. All I knew was I had to tell him that I felt the same way—that his journal entries weren't one-sided. I could tell him the moment things changed. I could tell him that I wished he wouldn't have pulled away at the cabin when he held my wrist. Or that I should have never let him leave city hall without closing the few inches in between us.

Valley View was only thirty minutes away, and before I knew it, my GPS told me I was less than a minute away. As I turned down his street, my pulse raced and I had every urge to turn back. The only thing that kept me moving forward was the thought of Porter taking care of his dad alone. If I could provide him even with a minimal amount of comfort in this time, I had to be here.

The blue dot on the GPS landed over the house across the street from where I was. It was a small ranch, run down by the rough weather. Porter's Jeep was parked in the driveway, which made my stomach jump into my throat and back down again. He was here.

I sat outside, watching for any sign of life inside. It took a few minutes before a figure walked by the window in front of the house. I knew that silhouette anywhere. Porter carried a worn chair and set it directly in front of the window. I swore he saw me as he looked back up, but he turned around and left the room. Another few minutes passed before he came back by the window, this time helping someone into the chair he'd set up. His dad. He held on to his dad as he struggled to walk, and then he sank into the chair with relief. He patted Porter's arm in thanks, and he knelt down to speak to him.

My chest tightened, and I realized what a mistake I'd made in coming. He needed to spend this time with his family. It was insensitive and unthinking of me to come at all. I gripped the wheel until my knuckles turned white and then turned around to search on the floor of my car for one of his notebooks and a pen. By the light of the streetlamp and my phone flashlight, I drafted my own letter back to him.

Porter,

I'm sorry to leave this note for you during this hard time. I know you are

261

healing and processing, and ~~I feel like an asshole~~ far be it from me to interrupt that. I just wanted to tell you that I read your letters. I'm moved by your letters. I'm moved by you. Is that corny? I don't care anymore. Telling you is too important to worry about sounding like a cheeseball.

I've been lying to myself and to you for the past few months. Everything that I've loved so much about this semester, about staying in Denton, was because of you. You encouraged me and supported me in trying new things (even if some of them, like Espresstout, might be a bad influence ☺). You watched me, wanted to learn more about me, and challenged me to see the world in different ways.

You are the first person I want to talk to about my day. And it was that way almost immediately. If I could make you laugh, I felt like I hit the freaking jackpot. I still feel that way.

You wrote about the movie set day and how you would do criminal things to repeat it. Well, I must be a convicted felon at this point, because I replay it in my mind all the time.

~~I broke up with Luke.~~ You probably heard that I am no longer in a relationship with Luke. I don't say that as someone who is looking for someone to ~~get back in the game~~ rebound with. I say that as someone who found it no longer fair to be in a relationship with someone when her heart was slowly belonging to someone else.

You can take this or leave this. I understand that you might need time—not only to process your family situation but to decide what to do with this information. I just knew that I couldn't sleep or function if I didn't tell you how I felt.

I might have made a fool of myself, but hey, my favorite movies are rom coms. I got some faulty advice on grand romantic gestures.

-Danielle

I folded the notebook up and found a sticky note in my purse, writing his name on it. I waited until both figures left the front room to sneak out of my car and onto his front porch. I set the notebook professing my feelings down on his dad's old welcome mat and felt a weight lift off my chest. No matter what he did about it, I could sleep knowing that I told him.

The day after my midnight run to Valley View was the final day of meeting for Lit Theory. I came with my paper in hand. Some might call it sloppy with my thoughts running all over the place, but isn't that the nature of the assignment? It's not supposed to be easy to decide what makes life worth living, especially when you have so many things to live for now.

Mr. Harrisburg sat in his normal spot with a final word on the chalkboard. "Sharing," it said. Oh. God.

"As humiliating as you all may think this day is, I think it's the epitome of everything that your assignment called for. An open and honest discussion on what it means to live and be happy. Now, while I did ask for you to compare your life ideals to a nineteenth-century American author, you don't have to give the class a biography of this author's life. What I'm asking is for you to share the most important section of your paper, the part that you think sums up your life experience the best," he said.

Everyone kept their hands down, naturally, because they all hated the idea of sharing anything remotely personal with the class. Mr. Harrisburg almost pleaded with me when we exchanged glances, and I felt this responsibility in that moment not only to him for putting up with me this semester, but to myself to redeem my initial poetry-hating answer at the beginning of the semester. I'd learned a lot about myself in this semester and a lot about the people around me. I felt like the only thing I could do in this moment was to start reading my closing statement. I nodded at Mr. Harrisburg, and he motioned for me to stand up.

"This semester has been pretty tough for me. For the first time in my life I had a serious boyfriend, an adult job, and the pressure of being successful in college. It was nothing that I had expected six months ago. I was supposed to go to Ohio State but lost it in my own carelessness and refusal to be responsible for my actions. I hated my cousin for having the guts to do everything that I didn't, and I felt unlovable. Coming to DCC would have been the ultimate step back for me as of last year, but now I consider it the biggest personal leap forward that I've ever taken.

"A friend told me that I seemed like a Thoreau kind of gal. After reading a lot of convoluted passages about being one with nature, I started to realize what my friend meant. Thoreau speaks a lot to the value of your dreams, and how regretting a decision, but learning from that decision, is a part of a full life. His most famous and overused quote on everyone's Pinterest inspiration board is 'Not till we are lost, do we begin to understand ourselves.' Being lost, being without the plan I'd armed myself with my entire life, got me out of my comfort zone in ways that challenged me and forced me to grow as a person.

"This semester taught me about how I view people. My predisposed judgments are harsh for everyone around me, including myself. I'd set up these expectations that were impossible to reach in an effort to have what I thought was my dream. But it wasn't until I took a moment to step out of my own selfishness that I realized that my happiness was directly reflected by those around me. I'm happiest when I can make my little brother laugh, or when I kiss my dad good night before I go to bed. The times when I can see my best friend and know that it's us against the world no matter what. I make my own happiness, and for me, my happiness is sharing love and support with those around me."

Mr. Harrisburg winked at me as I sat down, and I felt a calming relief wash over me. I'd said my piece and felt like I left one last meaningful thing hanging on the Denton walls. When it was time to leave Denton, I would be ready to go without any fear. I knew what I wanted, I was happy with my family situation, and the future held nothing but promise. That's all you can ask for, right?

<u>FEELING</u>:

the undifferentiated
background of one's awareness
considered apart from any
identifiable sensation,
perception, or thought.

ZOE'S QUEST TO BE THE BEST FRIEND IN THE WORLD WAS NEVER DIFFICULT. She was my superhero during every major life event, and I was so thankful to be taking her along to Claire's wedding as my extra-beautiful, super-snarky date. She looked gorgeous, her wild hair pinned back into a ballerina bun with a loud floral print shift dress that only Zoe could pull off. I kept things safe with a pink satin dress I'd worn for homecoming one year and high heels I still had no clue how to walk in.

"I don't understand how you're so comfortable being an outfit repeater," she said from my bed. As always, I was the one fussing last minute over my look while Zoe could pull together an outfit with her eyes closed and look like a freaking runway model.

"Not everyone has such great luck thrifting and making their own outfits as you, Zoe Cabot," I said. "I'm wearing my hair differently. Doesn't that count?"

She groaned and rolled off the bed, looking at her phone clock. "We've got to go. Scoot your booty downstairs, girl."

"I'm going, I'm going," I said. I glanced at my phone, seeing if any recent texts had come in. Nothing.

"Still nothing from him?" she asked.

I shook my head quickly. "No. But that's okay! He's dealing with things. I understand that."

No matter how many times I kept telling myself that, I was dying for him to even acknowledge that he saw my letter. It made me wonder whether he even saw it at all. Maybe a neighborhood dog had come by and picked it up, destroying all the evidence of my embarrassing love note. Or maybe he was just ignoring it altogether. That seemed to be the most likely of the scenarios.

"Girls! We're going to be late!" Mom yelled from downstairs. We both bolted down to deflect the wrath of Mom and popped in the car.

Zoe threw on a pair of headphones, listening to her current podcast obsession. I opted to stare out the window and let dramatic and moody thoughts surface about my letter. I had to make peace with the fact that my letter came too late. That he was washing his hands clean of all the drama around our situation. Or maybe I was always the one thing out of reach—

since I had a boyfriend, his roommate, he knew he could never date me, so flirting with me was a feasibly safe thing to do. Then, when I decided to separate from Luke, he didn't find me as alluring.

That had to be it. Why else wouldn't he have texted?

Thankfully, since Marcus and Claire were both from around Denton, we only had to drive to Cleveland proper for the wedding. I passed the time counting different California license plates along the way (racking up a surprising seven). Noah and I also played a really hard-core game of slug bug on every trip, and I could feel a small welt forming on the top of my shoulder in the shape of Noah's fist. Some things never change.

The wedding was in a church as beautiful and extravagant as I would have figured for Claire. Beautiful light pink and white décor draped the old-timey church, stained-glass windows and all. One of Marcus's gorgeous friends escorted Zoe and me to our seats, and she immediately started to analyze the stitching on the drapery in our aisle.

"How much do you think it costs to rent out a place like this?" Zoe whispered.

"Too damn much," I said.

"Oh come on, it's really pretty," Zoe said, leaning into my fresh slug bug bruise.

I winced. "It is really pretty. But it will be your job as my maid of honor to make sure I'm not spending a ridiculous amount of money because things are pretty."

"Marriage on your mind, Dan?" she asked, raising her eyebrows.

"Definitely not," I said. The music started playing, and Marcus walked out to the front of the altar. All the bridal party filed inside, followed by the tiniest flower girl I'd ever seen. After a dramatic shift in music, the crowd stood up and turned to face the door Claire would eventually come in.

When the doors opened, even I gasped. She looked stunning in a mermaid gown with her dark hair curled in flowing tendrils to the middle of her back. She had a genuine smile on her face—a look that I hadn't seen in perhaps my whole life. This was her happy place. Being in a room with undivided attention and no one to compete with was her dream scenario. A few months ago, this realization would have made me angry. But I'd learned that there are better things to spend my energy worrying about than my cousin's actions.

The ceremony went by quickly in almost a blur. I couldn't believe that my cousin, my relative almost my age, was getting married. *Was* married. She walked back down the aisle as Mrs. Marcus Debernardo, and I clapped along with the crowd.

We were directed to a reception hall down the street from the church to start the dancing and dining. Zoe and I made the most of the DJ's open requests, asking for some great NSYNC and Britney Spears classics to sing our hearts out to. We only garnered a few stares. Even my mom was a good sport, sneaking Zoe and me some champagne on the down low. Everything felt perfect, dancing around with my best friend, my mom and Noah joining in when they felt moved by the song. I was in a perfect bubble of happiness.

As we left for the night, I vowed to sleep the rest of the way home. All the champagne had worn off, and I felt sluggish and groggy. Once my head hit the window I was out. I didn't realize we'd made it back to Denton until we hit our cliff of a driveway. Zoe turned to me, grabbing her head.

"Emergency trip to Moe's?" she asked.

"Most definitely," I agreed.

We made a quick transfer into Zoe's car so we could make up for all the champagne with a large pot of coffee and bottomless fries. Moe's sounded better and better as my stomach started to growl. Don't get me wrong, Claire and Marcus had a beautiful dinner for us all, but the wedding portions were too small to feed my humongous appetite. I could already imagine Laurie coming to our table with fresh blueberry muffins as if she could detect us from a mile away. By the time we pulled up I was practically drooling.

Zoe turned to me in the parking lot, grabbing on to my hand. I furrowed my brows and started to open my door.

"This is where I leave you," she said.

"Huh?" I asked.

"I have it on good word that there's a boy waiting for you in there with an exceptionally delicious pepperoni pizza," she said.

"What?" I said breathlessly.

"You're not the only Denton girl who swapped numbers with Porter Kohl at the beginning of the year," she said, shaking her phone. "Get in there."

I wrapped her in a giant bear hug. "You are seriously the most incredible friend in the whole world."

"Don't forget it," she said. "Now seriously, am I going to have to pull you out of this car?"

"I'm going, I'm going," I said.

I suddenly felt entirely silly walking into Moe's in my old homecoming dress as a person who was no longer in high school. A person who was no longer in high school about to meet the boy she'd written a very blatant love letter to only a few days before. My heart dropped as I looked around Moe's, searching for that signature tousled hair or the leather jacket that I'd grown to love.

When I finally saw him I felt like I might explode. Whether it was from nervousness or excitement or a sickly sweet combination of both, I wasn't sure. I started to walk toward his table, and he turned around as he heard the sound of me walking clumsily in my heels. He stood up and met me before I could make my way fully to the table.

"Hi," he said.

"Hi," I said back.

"You look . . . ," he said, gazing down at my childish dress.

"Ridiculous?" I asked.

"Beautiful," he replied. I swayed on my feet for a few seconds, refusing to break eye contact with him.

"I think I need to sit," I said abruptly. "Heels and I are not friends."

"Of course," he said, sliding into the booth across from me.

He reached into his pocket and pulled out the notebook with my sticky note across it, his name written out in my messy scrawl. He set it on the table in between us and scooted it my way. I felt the breath leave from my lungs and waited for him to move, to speak, to do anything.

"Did you stalk me to drop this off, Cavanaugh?" he said, the Smirk creeping up on his face.

I blushed. "Only a little bit."

"It surprised me, I'll give you that much," he said.

"Surprised in a good or bad way?" I asked, feeling my breath coming quicker and quicker.

"A good way," he said. I wanted to reach out and wrap my arms around his neck, to close this horrible distance between us, but I felt like he had more to say. I sat on my hands, keeping myself in check.

Even though I managed to keep my limbs restrained, my mouth had other plans. I felt my anxiety about this whole situation bubbling up into pre–word vomit and had to stand by as it became full-blown word vomit.

"I thought you didn't want to talk to me, or that you didn't find me as alluring now that I was unattached and so the whole ride back I was trying to talk myself out of it. That it was okay that you didn't feel the same way as I did, and that I would move on and be happy next semester, but the longer I thought about it, the more I realized that you were what kept me happy this semester. Not just, you know, *you*, but the way you taught me to look at myself and others. You just—"

"Get you," he said.

"Exactly," I said. As I spoke, my hands had slipped out from under my butt and waved animatedly in the air. One of them rested on the table, and our hands started inching closer to each other's on the table until our fingertips touched. Feeling bold, I placed my hand in his and we both smiled. The same electricity from the movie set flew between our palms, and I almost lost it as his thumb traced along mine.

"One large pepperoni pizza?" our waitress, the ever-lovely Laurie, said.

"Can we actually get that to go?" Porter asked, never breaking eye contact with me.

"Sure thing," she said, with a small laugh.

"You really came all the way to my dad's house to drop off that notebook?" he asked.

"I was going to stay and talk to you, but I saw you with your dad and didn't want to interrupt. Plus, you hadn't been talking to me for a few days up to that point," I said.

"Because I thought you wanted nothing to do with me!" he said. "I basically told you how I felt about you at city hall and when I left, I thought that things were done."

I rubbed my hand up his arm. "I should have never let you go. I should have said something more."

"Here you go," Laurie said, setting the pizza box on the edge of the table.

"Thank you so much, Laurie," I said. Porter reached in his pocket to get his wallet, but she shook her head.

"This one's on me. Have a fun night." She smiled.

My heart filled with gratitude for the love and compassion that the people in this town had been showing me. I mouthed a sincere "thank you" to her as Porter and I walked out hand in hand. He opened the back door of his Jeep and laid the pizza box inside. He came back around to my side of the car and walked up to me, a goofy smile on his face. The smile was the Smirk on steroids.

He stepped forward, taking my face in his hands. "Is it okay if I kiss you now? In a way that's completely romantic and intentional and not with a movie crew watching?"

I nodded profusely. He bent down and kissed me softly, our lips barely touching. I pulled him closer to me, my arms finally wrapping themselves around his neck in the way I'd been daydreaming about doing since the day on the movie set. Since the first day I met him, if I was being honest. He planted sweet kisses down my neck and back up to my lips, where I forced him to stay for a few moments longer. When I pulled away we rested our foreheads together and let our breath mix for a few seconds longer.

"Do you want to go somewhere?" he asked.

I nodded profusely again.

"My place is out, you know, considering the whole Luke thing," he said. We mutually cringed a little.

"And mine is out, considering the whole my-entire-family-lives-there thing," I said.

"To the bookstore?" he asked.

I couldn't help but laugh. "It's kind of perfect, isn't it?" I asked.

We drove to the bookstore, maybe a minute-long jaunt from Moe's. I don't think I will ever get over holding Porter Kohl's hand. When we had to separate to get out of the car, my body felt like it was missing an essential organ. He unlocked the door with his key and I followed him into the bookstore, quickly picking his hand back up in mine. Much better.

"Do you think Misty will care that we're here?" he asked.

"I don't think so," I said. "She's been openly Team Porter and Danielle for a while."

We sat down in our normal spot in the back where the magical restocking occurred. He opened the pizza box, but neither of us reached for a piece. Our hands were still clasped together, and our feet were bouncing off each other's with nervous energy.

"I still can't believe that you showed up to my speech with that 'My Underwear' shirt." I laughed.

"I'm thinking of opening up an Etsy shop where I sell those shirts exclusively," he said.

"I'd buy one," I replied.

"See, the market is already interested." He laughed.

"Thank you for coming to that," I said sincerely. "Especially with all your family stuff going on. You must have known that your dad was really sick that day, and you still showed up."

"I didn't want to miss it," he said. "It was something that would make me happy. You're what makes me happiest."

He looked up at me with those eyelashes that I can't help but think about every time I see him. I reached to grab his face and kissed both cheeks right under each set of beautiful lashes. My kisses trailed down until our lips met again. This time we kissed deeper, without the possibility of someone finding us. His hands fell to my waist, and I repositioned myself so I was lying down. He joined me. I pulled away and traced my fingers across his lips.

"You make me happy too," I said. "So amazingly, ridiculously happy."

I closed my eyes as his hand trailed through my hair. "Have you heard back from Ohio State?" he asked.

"I got in," I said. His face dropped a bit. "But I'm going to wait and apply to a bunch of schools for the fall. Case Western sounds especially nice since I have an in with the coolest professor ever."

"So you'll be here for another semester," he said, more as a statement and less as a question.

"I promise, you'll be sick of me by the end," I said.

"I doubt it," he said, leaving the softest kiss on my lips.

Sure that this was some dream that I could wake up from at any second, I took his face between my hands and deepened the kiss, scooting closer to him but never close enough. He let out a small sigh in my ear that made my heart beat wildly inside my chest, and I reached underneath his shirt, which garnered another gasp.

We both heard a small click from above as the annoying motion-sensor lights we'd grown so accustomed to turned off on us. I started to pull away to do my traditional "bring the lights back" dance, but he pulled me closer to him.

"Leave it," he said.

I couldn't argue with that logic.

ACKNOWLEDGMENTS

I feel like I can't start this out without thanking the two Big Ones in my life, my mom and my dad. They have always been the most ultra-supportive and loving duo, and I am beyond lucky to have the life I've had because of them. And, again, because she's reached the end of reading this book, Danielle's mom is not you, Mom. ☺ Next, to my amazing little sister who is not so little anymore. Abbs, you have read more terrible drafts of maybe-stories than I can even fathom, and you've loved each and every one. I love you for your kind heart and for being my unconditional bestie.

To my wonderful editor, Emily, for picking this story out of the shuffle and believing in it. You have always had the perfect vision for Danielle and company, and I am beyond grateful for all your time and attention to detail while working on this with me.

Since I wrote this book during the terrifying and exhilarating time of college, I feel like I have to give a shout-out to my college family (my Clar Fam). You all were the first ones that I wanted to tell about everything, and y'all were the first to force me out for a celebratory drink. Cheers to the best four years ever.

I can't forget my biological family, the Martins, who taught me what it means to laugh, and the Harringtons, especially Grandma and Papa.

To my wonderful bestie, Stephanie, for always being willing to pimp out my book to anyone she meets. I'm still dying from the day when you came home and told me that your exciting spring break moment that you shared during class was my book deal. ILYSM.

I wouldn't have kept writing if it wasn't for the teachers who encouraged me throughout the years. To Mrs. Joni Livermore, who sparked my love of reading while reading from Junie B. Jones books every day of second grade. To Mrs. Kay Woods, who first told me that I was maybe okay at this writing thing. To Mrs. Diane Hicks, who was my champion all throughout high school. And to Ms. Karen Downing, who pulled me aside after a public reading of one of my pieces and said, "I can see you reading from your book in a Barnes and Noble someday." You each touched my life deeply, and I am so thankful to all of you.

And finally to you, dear reader. You've officially made it through my sappy jumble of words. I hope you had as much fun living in Danielle's head as I have, and I'm wishing you many Porter Kohls to come into your life and shake things up for the better.

FEELING BOOKISH?

Turn the page for some

Swoonworthy EXTRAS

DANIELLE'S JOURNALS

post mutual lovefest.

Porter came over to meet Mom for the first time today. Usually guys will get nervous about meeting their girlfriend's dads, but Mom really gave him a run for his money. She said she's wary of anyone with messy-but-still-good hair.

Accurate statement.

Porter thinks it's hilarious to make his own commentary on my PERSONAL notebooks. If you see any of his illegible scribbles, don't think they're from me.

ANNOYING

Party pooper. My commentary is ~~wonderful~~.

This weekend was an amazing road trip around the Midwest, with many powdered sugar mini donuts consumed. Porter came along to visit each school I'm considering for next year, rating them by the food options available in a walkable distance. I'm glad to have someone looking out for the important things on this trip.

I was more helpful than you're giving me credit for.

I also carried all of the pamphlets during campus tours.

I just found out that Porter's favorite movie is The Princess Bride. THE PRINCESS BRIDE. And he gave me so much crap for loving rom coms!

To be fair, there's _more_ to it than romance.

Whatever. You're a big softy and now everyone knows it.

Mom is officially cutting back on student sessions. By half. She announced at family dinner (a Claire Dinner that actually went smoothly) that she is going to slowly phase out of the business. She deserves it. She works so hard.

This weekend Olivia and her girlfriend, Mel, are coming to visit! It's mostly a trip to meet Luke, but I'm a stop along the way. Porter is still living with Luke. They are on good terms now, but it's safe to say I'm not hanging out there much in my free time.

(At least not in the living room.)

There is no need to be suggestive in my notebooks. ;)

Noah got to see a sneak peek screening of Peace, Love, and Corndogs today. Apparently Porter and I make a "cringeworthy" cameo. For that reason, I feel like I might never watch that scene. Besides, the version I replay in my head is anything but cringeworthy.

I still want to see my face on the big screen.

Of course you do.

Danielle refuses to end this notebook on a mushy note, so I'll do it for her. I am so beyond grateful for every good thing that has come into my life this year. She is the best thing, the thing that makes me happiest. I didn't realize how much I needed someone who challenged and encouraged me to be a better person in my life. Loving every day with you.

You too, Kohl.

A COFFEE DATE

with author Maggie Ann Martin
and her editor, Emily Settle

Getting to Know You

Emily Settle (ES): What was the first romance novel you ever read?

Maggie Ann Martin (MAA): Does *Twilight* count? That's the first book I ever remember truly swooning over.

ES: It totally counts. Who is your favorite fictional couple? Your OTP, if you will.

MAA: This is like picking a favorite child! I am always going to be an Elizabeth and Mr. Darcy fan, but my more modern OTP is Anna and St. Clair from *Anna and the French Kiss*.

ES: Very important question: Are we talking Colin Firth Mr. Darcy or Matthew Macfadyen Mr. Darcy?

MAA: I'm a Colin Firth type of gal. A classic, if you will.

ES: Good choice. Although you can't really go wrong with either. Do you have any hobbies? (And now that you're a Published Author, writing doesn't count as a hobby anymore!)

MAA: Ha! This has been the weirdest question to adjust my answer to lately. Writing was always my go-to. I love live music so I go to as many concerts as I can afford, and I have a soft spot for binge-watching TV shows (I mean, who doesn't at this point?).

ES: That's cool. Do you have any favorite bands/groups/singers that you particularly like to go see live? Or are there any that you really, really want to see live someday?

MAA: I've seen my favorite band, Empires, five times. Whenever they're near me I go see them! I would die to see Years & Years live. They came to Chicago last year and I'm still kicking myself that I couldn't make it.

ES: If you were a superhero, what would your superpower be?

MAA: I go back and forth between whether I'd like to be invisible or read people's minds, but I'm settling on invisibility. Some of the dark and twisty thoughts people think might be too much for me.

The Swoon Reads Experience

ES: Very true. So how did you first learn about Swoon Reads?

MAA: My friend Lydia Albano (Swoon Reads author of *Finding You!*) retweeted or posted something about Swoon Reads accepting manuscripts and I clicked on the link. The rest is history!

ES: What made you decide to post *The Big F*?

MAA: I'd posted my books or parts of books onto other writing websites in the past, but never one with such an amazing opportunity. It felt like a no-brainer, especially since Lydia had been chosen just a few weeks before I uploaded.

ES: What was your experience like on the site before you were chosen?

MAA: I absolutely loved going around and reading other stories on the site. It was a super-positive experience meeting people in this community and I don't think much has changed, minus the Swoon Reads badge on my page now. Everyone was lovely when I joined, and has been lovely ever since.

ES: Once you were chosen, who was the first person you told, and how did you celebrate?

MAA: It's actually kind of crazy—I was in New York visiting my sister, Abbie, at school and my whole family was together. That sort of reunion only happens a few times a year. I got an e-mail one afternoon from my uber-amazing editor (*wink, wink*) at a Buffalo Wild Wings in White Plains, and then set up a call for the next morning. I made my mom, dad, and sister leave our hotel room for the call, and after I was told I'd been selected, I called my family back up to the room and we completely spazzed out. That afternoon we went to Tony's Di Napoli in NYC for celebratory carbs and sangria.

ES: Ha ha, that's awesome. Now I want some of their fettuccine Alfredo!

The Writing Life

ES: When did you realize you wanted to be a writer?

MAA: After I read the Harry Potter books (I was sort of a late bloomer with them, waiting until I was about thirteen to actually read them). Then when I was in eighth grade my teacher, Mrs. Woods, told me that I was a good writer. She was the first person to encourage me to keep writing and I will always be thankful to her for that.

ES: So will we! Do you have any writing rituals?

MAA: I can write anywhere—all I need is a pair of headphones in my ears and the same song on repeat. It has to be the same song over and over, otherwise my brain gets distracted.

ES: I'm jealous of that talent you have there. What song or songs did you usually have on repeat while writing *The Big F*?

MAA: The song "Clean" by The Japanese House became my go-to while editing. The main song that I listened to while writing it was probably "The Deep End" by Hannah Georgas.

ES: I'm definitely going to have to look those up. Where did the idea for this book start?

MAA: I was a freshman in college when I started writing *The Big F* and was feeling a lot of the same emotions as Danielle—I wasn't really sure what I wanted to do with my life and felt this pressure to figure it out. My little sister was starting to look at colleges around that time and she consulted the local "college psychic" in our town for guidance. This made me think, "What if a college psychic's daughter didn't make it into college?" It all kind of snowballed from there.

ES: Yeah, this book definitely reminded me of very similar emotions I also experienced leading up to college! Do you ever get writer's block? How do you get back on track?

MAA: For me, the best cure for writer's block is finding the perfect song. If I can find that one song that I can listen to on repeat and have inspire me, I'll be flying. I definitely have to be in the right mood to write, and once I get myself there with the right song, things start flowing more naturally. I also really liked watching fan videos of Rory and Jess from *Gilmore Girls* for inspiration while writing *The Big F*. They are everything.

ES: What's the best writing advice you've ever heard?
MAA: Just write it down! You can't edit a blank page. Even if the words are jumbled and word-vomit-esque, at least they are words that you can refine later.

THE BIG F
discussion questions

1. What does the title *The Big F* stand for by the end of the book? Is it more than just the original F in the class that started the ball rolling?

2. Danielle hides her college rejection from her family. How do you think you would have handled the situation differently?

3. Danielle and Luke start their relationship on the basis of having grown up together. Have you ever been together with someone where the idea of them became more attractive than the relationship itself? How did you resolve that situation?

4. If you were offered an opportunity to kiss a friend, a very attractive friend whom you might have deep-down feelings for, for a movie role, would you do it? Why or why not?

5. Were you Team Luke or Team Porter, and why?

6. How do you feel about Danielle's relationship with her mother? Do you think her anger with Danielle for keeping the truth a secret was justified?

7. Do you keep a journal like Porter and Danielle do? Everyday observations or personal thoughts only? Why or why not?

8. Danielle finds herself enjoying environmental activism work, which she feels like she has to hide from her family at first. Have you ever liked something that you felt you had to hide?

9. Danielle and her cousin, Claire, have a rocky past. Why do you think Danielle let her off the hook at the end of the book?

10. How do you envision the future for Porter and Danielle? What do you think will happen next fall when she goes to a new school?

One little lie turns
into so much more...

ONE LITTLE LIE TURNS INTO SO MUCH MORE

Just
Friends

TIFFANY PITCOCK

TWO TEENS WHO BUILD A FRIENDSHIP
OUT OF ELABORATE LIES HAVE TO DECIDE
WHETHER OR NOT THEIR LOVE IS TRUE
IN THIS DEBUT CONTEMPORARY ROMANCE.

CHAPTER 1

Jenny

The classroom door swung open.

Every head in the class turned to see a boy with messy blond hair walk in. He gave a nod to his classmates before handing Mrs. Tanner, the slender Oral Communications teacher, a slip of paper.

"Late on the first day, Mister"—she looked closer at the slip in her hand—"Masters?"

"Car trouble, ma'am," he assured her.

She shook her head disapprovingly. "Don't make a habit of this."

"Wouldn't dream of it." He winked before heading to the only open seat in the room.

He collapsed into the seat next to Jenny Wessler. Jenny glanced at him out of the corner of her eye as she chewed the end of her pen. She knew who the boy was, of course. He was the one and only Chance Masters. He'd spent his high school career carving out the most scandalous reputation he could.

"Anyway." Mrs. Tanner called the class to order. "As I was about to say, for your first assignment you will each interview the person next to you, and then perform a dialog together about your summer vacations for the class. Any questions?"

"Um, yeah." Kelsey Molar, a perky blond, raised her hand. "Can we switch partners?" She looked at her partner, Danny Jennings, with disdain while Danny just continued to slumber in his seat.

"No, sorry, Kelsey, but I pick partners in my class. It's the first day of your junior year. It's one of your last chances to meet new classmates," Mrs. Tanner explained. "Could you wake Danny, please?"

Kelsey prodded Danny awake with her pencil, then glanced over at Jenny.

Jenny met her eyes, shrugged, and mouthed, "I wanted to be your partner."

Jenny watched as Kelsey gave a weak smile and turned to start the project. *I better start, too*, she thought as she looked to Chance. He sat slouched in his desk, his blond hair tousled just so and his brown eyes shining wickedly. He flashed what could only be called a smirk and said, "Ready to go, partner?" in a voice that could convince even the most grounded girl to run away with him.

Luckily, Jenny had no time for him. "Look," she began in her no-nonsense voice, "I really, really like having all As, so no playing around. You have to take this seriously. I want to start the semester off right."

"Well, you're no fun. I bet you're the type who excitedly packs her backpack the night before the first day because you just can't wait for school to start." He sat up and produced a notebook. "Let's get this over with, then, Little Miss Really-Likes-Having-As."

"I am not . . ." she hedged, blushing slightly. The truth was, of course, that she was exactly that type of person. She tried to hide her blush by looking over at Margaret Lester, who—with every perfect hair in place—was interviewing the brainless Max Gregs.

"Ah." Chance followed her line of sight. "Margaret Lester. She's not quite the perfect angel everyone seems to think," he said matter-of-factly.

"How would you know?" Jenny turned back to him. "She only moved here at the end of last year."

"Because we went out," he said with a shrug. "We met at a party, and one thing led to another . . ." He trailed off. "You might want to write this down, since the interview is over something we did during the summer."

"I can't get up there and tell the class how you hooked up with Margaret."

"Why not?"

"Seriously?" She looked skeptical. He was a gross pig, just like everyone said.

"Okay, I see your point." He scratched his chin. "Well, I also broke into an abandoned gas station with my cousins, and then we went skinny dipping with some girls they knew, but I'm betting you won't say that, either."

"No." Jenny set down her pen. "Did you do anything school appropriate?"

"Um, let's see." He pretended to look thoughtful for a moment. "Nope."

"Of course not." Jenny was feeling a little uncomfortable with him. She'd heard that he got around, but she didn't expect it to be true. She also couldn't help but think of her own pathetic summer; she'd locked herself in her room and read the entire time.

"Let me guess: You did nothing fun?" He raised one eyebrow.

"I've always wanted to do that," she blurted out.

"What?" He looked taken aback by her bluntness. "Have fun?"

"No, raise one eyebrow," she explained, feeling lame.

He just nodded and went to sketching on a blank page in his notebook. Jenny bit her bottom lip and looked around the room; everyone else was well under way with their interviews. Mrs. Tanner sat at her computer, playing solitaire. Jenny glanced back to Chance as he absentmindedly doodled. "Chance?" she asked.

"Yeah?" He looked up, his eyes surprisingly sweet.

"How many girls have you slept with?" The question sprang from her lips before she could contain it. She quickly looked away from him and blushed. *How could I be so stupid?* she thought. *You can't go around asking people those things!*

He let out an amused chuckle and said, "That's none of your business, Little Miss Really-Likes-Having-As."

"Sorry." She fidgeted with her pen.

"Do you always wear your hair in a ponytail?" he asked. He gestured to the tangled mess of brown hair she had shoved back in an elastic band.

"Yeah, it's a bitch to straighten," she admitted.

His eyes lit up. "Aha, so you're not perfect. Now we're getting somewhere."

"I never said that I was perfect," she mumbled, feeling insecure. "I just try to be."

"Yeah, you do seem like the type who is desperate for approval." He returned to his doodle.

Anger flared as Jenny snapped: "Hey, you don't know anything about me. Don't pretend to."

A lazy smile formed at Chance's lips as he looked up at her through his blond bangs. "Relax, Little Miss Really-Likes-Having-As. I know nothing of your life and I'm okay with that." He flipped to a clean page in his notebook and started writing frantically. "You did give me an idea, though, so maybe you're good for something."

Jenny stared at him in confusion. "What idea? What are you writing? We don't have time—"

"Relax," he said again. "I've got this covered, seriously. When she calls on us, just work off of me and we're golden."

Jenny glanced around the room at all the other partners huddled close together, writing out scripts for their dialogs—and then back to Chance. Was Chance Masters really asking her to trust him? Doubt clouded her mind as she tried to sneak a peek at his chicken scratch.

"You look like you're having an episode," Chance informed her, looking up. He reached out and pushed at the corners of her mouth, forcing them up. "At least look like you enjoy my company. I kind of have a reputation to uphold. Girls love me."

"Oh trust me, I'm aware." She jerked away, trying not to let it show how much his touch affected her. Her heart pounded in her throat as she watched Mrs. Tanner work her way back to the front of the classroom. "Chance, she's going to call time, and we're not ready."

"Yes, we are," he informed her, closing his notebook. "We're ready and we're going to have the best dialog."

"We don't have a script," she reminded him in a frantic whisper.

"Yes, we do." He smirked.

A nervous sweat began to form on her neck and back. "Then would you kindly fill me in?"

"It'll work better this way," he assured her as Mrs. Tanner called the class to order. "Besides, it was your idea."

"What was?" Jenny asked again, frantic.

"Pretending to know you," he whispered back.

Before Jenny could reply, Mrs. Tanner called up the first group: Kelsey and Danny. They had a snooze-worthy discussion about Kelsey's trip to Colorado and Danny's quest to sleep for seventy-five hours straight. All through it, Jenny kept throwing worried glances at Chance, but he seemed as calm and collected as ever. Finally, after five more groups, Mrs. Tanner called on them.

Chance sauntered to the front of the classroom, causing all the girls to pay attention. Jenny meekly followed him, cold sweat drenching her hands. She glanced from Chance to Mrs. Tanner and back again, waiting for this whole thing to blow up in his face. Chance shot her a wicked grin, cleared his throat, and began.

"Well, it was actually pretty fortunate that Jenny was picked as my partner," he told the class. "We spent most of summer break together, since our families are pretty close."

Jenny tried to control her expression, but she was sure the confusion in her eyes gave them away. She didn't know where he was going with this. Mrs. Tanner was nodding approvingly, while the rest of the class looked between Chance and Jenny, trying to figure out how such a friendship was possible.

"You see, Jenny came over the second day of vacation and helped my brother and me decorate for our annual summer cookout, like she does every year." The class nodded, as if this was old information. They were actually buying it.

"Yeah," Jenny jumped in, trying to go with the flow. "I got there at, like, eight in the morning and no one was up. I had to bang on the door for at least ten minutes."

"Well, we like to sleep." Chance grinned, happy that she was playing along.

"You told me to get there at eight," Jenny tossed back, surprised at how easy it was.

"By 'eight' I mean, like, 'twelve.' You should know this already." He turned back to face the class. "Anyway, after barging into our home at an ungodly time, Jenny and I spent the next few hours attempting to put up those tiki-torch lantern things."

"Which is not the easiest task when Chance's brother keeps blowing them out." Jenny sighed, enjoying herself. "We eventually gave up and just went with tiny American flags. It's more traditional anyway."

"After that, we fought over who would light the grill. It's usually me—"

"Actually, we're supposed to take turns," she reminded him.

"I did it the last two years in a row." He crossed his arms, a playful spark in his brown eyes. "Obviously you just don't remember it right."

"Oh please." She tilted her head and smirked. "I got sick two years ago, remember? Your mother accidentally put expired eggs in the cookies and I spent the whole day throwing up. You stole the grill from me my year."

"Whatever, it's my house and my grill." He turned back to the class. "We were fighting over who got to do it, and suddenly—"

"The lighter broke when Chance tried to tug it out of my hands," Jenny finished. "He tends to break a lot of things."

"I broke your Barbie sunglasses when we were seven. Get over it, Wessler."

"You ran them over with your bike, Masters."

"Well, you shouldn't have left them in my driveway," he said, as if that solved everything.

"Anyway, back to the story," Jenny continued, loving the way the class seemed intrigued. She couldn't believe they were actually buying it. "We ended up getting banned from the house while decorating continued."

"We went to Jenny's house instead." Chance took it from her. "We ended up just spending most of our time there, honestly."

"Well, I was kind of trying to cook things for the party." Jenny sighed again. "You just came with me to annoy me and eat my food."

"Not to annoy," Chance corrected. "To relieve you from boredom."

"Either way you word it, a distraction is still a distraction."

Before Jenny could pick the story back up, Mrs. Tanner called time. The class clapped as they had to after every dialogue, and the two made it back to their desks. The rest of the partners went up and spoke, but Jenny didn't pay them any mind. Her thoughts were all on Chance and how easy it was to get up there and play make-believe with him. Hell, she half believed their lie herself.

She looked over to find Chance looking back at her. He smiled his boyish grin and gave a thumbs-up. She returned the gesture and the grin before giving her attention back to the speakers. After everyone was done and Mrs. Tanner congratulated the class for their hard work, the bell rang, signaling lunch.

Kelsey came up as Jenny was shoving her books into her backpack. With a cautious look at Chance, Kelsey whispered, "I didn't know you and Chance knew each other."

"Oh, yeah." Jenny smiled, keeping up the charade. "We used to live next to each other when we were little."

"Now that you mention it, I think I used to see him around once or twice." Kelsey nodded eagerly, her blond curls bouncing around her face. "You must've mentioned him at some point."

From the corner of her eye, Jenny saw Chance looking at them. She smiled and continued packing. "Totally."

"Well, I'm going," Kelsey said, sensing that Jenny didn't want her there. As soon as the bubbly blonde left, Jenny turned to look at Chance. A smirk formed at her lips.

"Well, I apologize for freaking out," she said. The boy leaned against the edge of his desk and smiled, encouraging her to continue. "Obviously, you were able to handle things. I should've just relaxed."

He shook some hair out of his face and laughed. "Thanks, Little Miss Really-Likes-Having-As. Coming from a model student like you, that means something."

"Don't push it, Masters," she threatened, pointing a finger.

He reached out, grabbed her accusing hand, and shook it, smiling what she was beginning to think was his signature smile. "Jenny Wessler, this is clearly the start to a beautiful friendship."

"And that is an overused line." But she smiled back anyway.

Chance slung his backpack over his shoulder before offering her his arm. "Wessler?"

Is this still part of the game? she wondered. After a moment's hesitation, she laced her elbow through his arm, blushing slightly. "I'm going to regret this one day, aren't I?"

"Fat chance," he scoffed. "Apparently, you've had years to get away from me."

A knot twisted in the pit of her stomach, excitement welling up in her. "I guess I haven't learned my lesson yet."

Check out more books chosen for publication by readers like you.

Photo © Larissa Wilming

MAGGIE ANN MARTIN

hails from Des Moines, Iowa, but moonlights as a New Yorker. She has a shiny new BA in English and journalism from the University of Iowa, the most welcoming literary community in the world. When she is not writing, you can find her binge-watching TV shows or passionately fangirling over fictional characters on the Internet. *The Big F* is her debut novel.

MAGGIEANNMARTIN.COM